A PAINKILLER TO DIE FOR

A PAINKILLER TO DIE FOR

DR MARTYN PRITCHARD

The manufacturer's authorised representative in the EU for product safety is Authorised Rep
Compliance Ltd, 71 Lower Baggot Street, Dublin D02 P593 Ireland
(www.arccompliance.com)

Troubador Publishing Ltd
Unit E2 Airfield Business Park,
Harrison Road, Market Harborough,
Leicestershire. LE16 7UL
Tel: 0116 2792299
Email: books@troubador.co.uk
Web: www.troubador.co.uk

ISBN 978 1836283 591

British Library Cataloguing in Publication Data.
A catalogue record for this book is available from the British Library.

Printed and bound in Great Britain by CMP UK
Typeset in 11pt Minion Pro by Troubador Publishing Ltd, Leicester, UK

I would like to thank the patience and understanding of my wife, Deborah, as well as Jessica Pritchard and Dr Isabel Gonzalez Fernandez for their helpful comments on early drafts of the book.

CAMBRIDGE

January 2024

I hope I'm not being embarrassingly naïve here, but my guess is that many people dream of being the inventor of something that would benefit humankind, if not the world itself. A solution to our climate change. A plentiful source of food for all and the end of famines. Free energy. Make your own list. And there must be some of you out there who share my very own dream of being the inventor of a life-saving medicine. But, you see, I'm fully qualified to be allowed to have exactly such a dream, as I'm a scientist, although that doesn't seem to have made any difference, as my dream remains just that. So far. Like all bar a precious few of us, no groundbreaking medicine will ever likely be attributed to me. Not so the case, however, for a certain Dr William Jeavons. The celebrated inventor of a new drug that will surely transform how chronic pain is treated. A once-in-a-generation revolution in medicine. The first truly non-addictive, non-opioid drug to offer real hope of saving all

1

those so many lives blighted by prescription opioid abuse. Jeavons was someone who not only had the dream but also lived it. A dream and a conviction that had driven him ever since the dark, dark days of his childhood. A passion that had kept him at work when he should have been at home and kept him awake when he should have been asleep. The realisation of his dream was no overnight success but one borne through countless setbacks and disappointments. The time had now arrived, however, for him to step back, take time to smell the roses and celebrate his extraordinary success. Or was it?

*

Will felt as if he hadn't slept for more than an hour. Normally, the reason for this would be much more pleasurable: a woman by his side. He was, of course, fully aware of his notoriety and if he was being honest, he rather revelled in it. He was a cad and a bounder, to use an old-fashioned phrase, but he had honour of a sort. Or so he tried to convince himself. The women were always willing to join him in his bed and often at their behest, but he was always open with them that a long-term relationship was out of bounds. He told them it was because his true mistress and the only one he was ever faithful to was his work. As dedicated to his work as he clearly was, he really knew that wasn't entirely true. His hedonistic addiction had much to do with the mental trauma his mother had left him with, even if he didn't like to think about that too often. But maybe there was now a saviour at hand and a cure for his affliction. A woman who had recently come into his life. That different woman. A woman that had beguiled, confused and never failed to surprise him even though they had known each other for almost two years. Would she be the one to become the only one? Was it even possible that there would be an only one?

But not even that different woman had shared his bed that night. There was no one other than himself who Will could blame for his staring at a ceiling slowly coming into vision as the weak sunlight of a winter's morning crept through his curtain-less bedroom window. The reason for his insomnia this time was quite different and much less enjoyable. There was a problem with the drug. Yes, that bloody wonder drug. The one he had spent his whole working life dreaming of. A problem only Will knew of because it was he who had hidden the incriminating data far away from the prying eyes of the regulatory authorities. A finding that the drug could potentially be burdened with unpredictable and maybe even life-threatening adverse effects on human subjects. A gnawing secret he usually managed to bury deep down in the pit of his bowels and far away from his thoughts. But today was different. A day when all his guilt would rise to the surface. It was the morning of the day of a symposium that he was hosting. A bitterly cold day in early January. A scientific meeting where his talk on the drug would be the plenary lecture keenly listened to and likely picked apart by some of the sharpest minds in the medical profession. And then there was the media to also worry about, but Will only had himself to blame for the latter, having gladly prostituted himself to several popular talk shows. The big networks lapped up this visually appealing scientist so adept at unravelling a complicated subject to a ley audience with humour and modesty. He had become a media darling. Not that he would ever disclose the flaw in his drug to his new media followers nor even to his scientific peers. The fear and the worry that had ruined his sleep was that he would somehow be found out by his fellow scientists, many of whom were jealous of his success and fame and would welcome the ruination of Will's career and legacy that would surely follow if the fraud was uncovered. It had become a recurring and inescapable nightmare. The fear of his secret being discovered was the horse behind him on the relentless fairground carousel that had become his life. Will was clinging desperately onto his own horse with all his might, so fearful of falling, being caught and his secret discovered. The horse in front of him was the true contentment he would never be able to reach.

*

What would have made Will even more worried that morning was something he was yet to find out. You see, he was not the only one who knew of his dark secret. There was someone out there who not only understood the possible consequences of what he had done but was also prepared to do something about it.

    Me.

THE TRAP IS SPRUNG

The Hilton Hotel, Cambridge

*A*nd there I found myself the very morning after the symposium of the day before. Lying naked next to a certain Dr Will Jeavons in a hotel bed. So just how did that happen?

*

I must have been awake for no more than an hour, but at the time it seemed like many more. What was the time? If only I had not left my watch and my phone on the dressing table at the far side of the room. I dared not climb out of bed to retrieve either, fearing I would wake my snoring bedfellow. Anyway, time was needed to gather my thoughts before taking the step that would irretrievably change my life forever. Even without the company of my watch – a thoughtful Christmas present from my ever so thoughtful husband – the intensity of the sunlight forcing its way *through the carelessly closed curtains suggested that we had already missed breakfast on this winter morning. The night just passed had all been a rather flustered rush of frightening and unpredictable events. At least for me.*

There he goes again. A flurry of loud, seemingly final gasps of a dying man followed by breathless silence and then a loud snort. The telltale signs of too many corporate dinners. But this time, it was not only me he had woken but also himself.

Once awake, Will paused for a handful of seconds, no doubt trying to remember where he was and who he was with. "And a wonderful time was had," he commented to the same hotel roof that was also enjoying my full attention. I didn't immediately answer what I perceived from the tone of his voice was an unquestionable statement of fact rather than even a rhetorical question.

His reputation had all stacked up, at least, on the evidence of last night, even though he was allegedly with a long-term partner. Although his body had probably seen better days, Will remained a physically and facially attractive man as well as an experienced, considerate and passionate lover. And he knew it. As I'm sure Will also knew that much of this was new to me despite my age. The consequence of a faithful marriage. But, yes. I had to admit that I enjoyed the sex despite it being, or maybe even because it was, my 'virginal' infidelity. Despite it being with a man I truly despised – to this day, I have still to reconcile my conflicting and counterintuitive thoughts. Despite thinking constantly throughout the night of the desperate actions I would enact in the hours to come.

I turned towards Will, and he angled his head to face me in response. "I suppose so," I teased. "Some tea or coffee to start the morning?" I was keen to get on with what I had originally planned to do the night before. You see, the sex was never have meant to have happened. The Rohypnol I slipped into his whisky nightcap was meant to make him too sleepy to even think about sex, so I was either short-changed by the dealer or my bedfellow is a sexual monster. I wouldn't rule out either scenario. Although it was at least guiltily enjoyed at the time, did I later regret the sex? I should. I really should have after what he had done to my family. I was trying to convince myself that 'using' him for sex was just the icing on the cake to my retribution, my vengeance. I was the one with the power. It was me who was the one who not only called the shots last night but would also dictate what would now happen this morning. I'm not sure I really believed my flimsy attempt at self-deception, but it was the best I could come up with.

"Black coffee with just a half teaspoon of sugar, if you are offering," was just the answer I wanted to hear. Sliding out of the warm bed, I self-consciously rushed to pick up the dressing gown I had dropped beside the bed the night before and wrapped it tightly around my nudity. "Shy all of a sudden?" was a question I didn't think needed answering as I disappeared into the bathroom to fill up the parsimonious hotel kettle that I had snatched en route from the dressing table.

With the filled kettle safely returned to its electrified base and switched on, I quickly made my way back to the bathroom and firmly closed the door behind me. I needed time to further compose myself as well as trying to avoid engaging in too much conversation with my imminent victim.

"Everything OK in there?" shouted my companion.

"Of course. Won't be a moment." I hoped that had sounded less flustered and frightened than I was feeling.

I glanced at the smudged mirror above the sink to check if it was really me in that hotel room and it was really me who was preparing to add the powdered mixture of diazepam and zolpidem to someone's coffee whom I had only first met socially less than a day before. It was. Now time to act, but would it be fight or flight?

I edged out of the bathroom, having transferred the polythene sleeve containing the drug from my washbag to the right-hand pocket of my dressing gown. The zolpidem I used was from a prescription I had teased out of my GP for a sleep problem I didn't have, and the diazepam was a common drug we used in our labs and so easy enough to sneak a few milligrams home. Being caught taking drugs out of the workplace would be the least of my problems if my plan was to be successful.

With the kettle having boiled, I glanced over my shoulder to make sure my actions were not being scrutinised too closely. As had been the case for much of yesterday evening, little seemed to be more important to my lover than what was going on in his phone.

Recalling a vision of my husband surrounded by banks of life-preserving equipment in a soulless hospital room was all the motivation I needed to vigorously stir in the drug with more than double the amount of sugar requested. My mouth was sickly dry at the thought of what I would have done if I had overdosed. I had booked the hotel under a different name and had paid by cash, but any half-decent police investigation would surely find me quickly enough after discovering his body.

The drug cocktail was duly delivered to the healthy patient, and I then walked around the king-sized bed to place my drink on the bedside cabinet next to where I had been lying. But would he actually drink it? "This is almost as sweet as you are, my dear," was the sickly comment I received as I sat down on the bed ready to drink the black tea that I had poured for myself. A hot drink that I hoped would ward off the nausea that was gathering in the pit of my stomach. "You did only put in a half teaspoon of sugar, didn't you?"

"Sorry. It was a full teaspoon of sugar," I lied. It was two. At least Will didn't pick up on any drug-related tastes. He didn't strike me as someone who dabbled in drugs. "I can make a fresh cup," I offered.

"No, no. This is fine. Reminds me of my decadent youth."

"Well, we've missed breakfast so we should make the most of these drinks," I suggested in the hope that Will would be getting the full dose. His coffee was consumed before I had managed to gently lie back into the bed. "Didn't that burn your mouth?"

"Believe me. I'm an expert in bolting back hot drinks. A great way to end a boring work meeting, and I can think of more interesting things to do this morning than just drinking coffee." And with that, he swung round in the bed to face me. "So, where were we? Not with your dressing gown still on, that much I know."

With that, I sat up and disrobed with as much decorum as the situation allowed but then came up with an excuse to waste a little more time and allow the drugs to take effect.

"You know what. Second thoughts. I think I'll have a quick shower before I get back into bed."

"Oh. Do you have to?"

"I feel really sweaty and greasy after last night." It was only a half lie.

"Not a problem. Why don't I join you?"

Why did I know he was going to say that? "No. That's OK, if you don't mind. I hate having showers with other people."

"Sounds like an area you have some experience in."

"I used to. Right up until I stopped enjoying the experience." I smiled back at him over my shoulder as I self-consciously walked over to the bathroom, having left my dressing gown on the bed.

"All depends on who you're with," Will shouted after me as I closed the bathroom door.

How long could I make this shower last until my one-(and only) time lover became restless for some more of what he seemingly enjoyed last night. My hope was that the drug cocktail would take about half an hour to kick in and maybe a little longer than that for him to become completely unresponsive. But we are all of us different. I had finished my shower and stepped out into the bathroom to dry and brush my hair. I reckoned it had been about twenty minutes before I heard him knocking on the locked bathroom door.

"What are you doing in there? We have to be out of here in about an hour or so. Just how clean do you need to be?"

"OK. Two minutes and I will be out." I switched off the shower and waited until I heard him slump back into bed before unlocking the bathroom door. I smiled at him as I quickly walked to the bed and dived under the duvet cover.

"At last! I thought we would never meet again."

We were both naked in bed once again and he wasted little time in making his predictable moves. I sensed that this was not going to be the quick and lust-driven ride we had both enjoyed in the early hours and was still fresh in the memory. He was going to make this into a slow burn. In his mind, he was going to make beautiful love to a beautiful woman, as he had done with so many others. Or something like that. I forget now his exact words. There was nothing for me to do other than lie back and smile about the revenge I was soon to enjoy and count down the minutes to when lover boy needed a little rest. Maybe another ten or fifteen minutes tops for some sort of drug effect?

OK, let's call it at about ten minutes. "You know what, not feeling too well," he murmured as he suddenly disengaged from his thoroughly cleaned partner to lie on his back, probably in an attempt to gather his senses. "Not well at all." With that, he gingerly moved to sit up on the side of the bed, slowly rose to his feet like an arthritic old man and walked rather unsteadily towards the sanctuary of the bathroom.

"Are you OK in there?" I shouted after him in my best attempt at a caring voice. It was my turn to ask a question to which the answer didn't really matter. A prolonged retch suggested otherwise. Please, God, don't let him throw up too much of the medication. I decided to find out for myself if that was going to be likely by following him into the bathroom. "You don't look good," was the rather obvious comment I made to the poor mite as he hovered over the toilet bowl, but at least he hadn't vomited. Yet.

"Must have been that bloody shellfish I had at the conference reception. I knew I shouldn't have taken the chance. Bloody Cambridge caterers!" If only Will knew. "I'm really sorry about all this. What a fucking state."

"Could be. Who knows, but whatever it is, it's not your fault," which was indeed very true, "and nothing much you can do about it other than rest up for a while. Why don't you come back to bed with me?" I carefully backed out of the bathroom to provide a clear path for my lover to retreat to the comfort of our still-warm bed.

"It's as if I have been on the piss all night," he breathed just before almost diving onto the, by now, extremely tousled bed. "All I had was that white wine at the reception, which was practically non-alcoholic anyway, a couple of pints at the Anchor and that nightcap you bought for me. I'm so sorry. I'll make it up to you. I promise," he said, knowing he wouldn't.

I pulled the duvet back and lay beside my very sorry man. I pushed my right hand through his hair to soothe him and to try to rush him off to sleep. Hair that he always spent so much time on coiffuring but had now become shapeless and dry. "No apologies or promises needed. Just get some sleep and I will sort us out somewhere in town for brunch to make up for the breakfast we missed."

"What a sweetheart you are. Give me half an hour and I will be up and running again." That was the last I heard from my lover-cum-future victim before he fell into a deep sleep that I hoped would last for far longer than the thirty minutes it took for him to lose consciousness.

By all rights, I should have castrated him right there and then. No less than he deserved, and many women and their husbands would have rejoiced at the news, but the closest thing I had to a sharp blade was a hotel teaspoon. Anyway, I believed that I had something more than painful enough to give to a man who was long overdue some suffering. That *would all happen in due course and with a fair wind. But, at that very incredulous and frightening moment in my life, I had in front of me a man who was almost as comatose and helpless as my poor, wretched husband, who remains a long-term guest of the NHS not more than a handful of miles away from where his vengeful wife was contemplating her next steps.*

*

But that was back then, and this is now. A smidgen over a year since that night and I can still remember every little sordid detail, every stomach-churning emotion. Even the unremarkable watercolour vistas of Cambridge city on the hotel walls. Just as I will never forget those terrible, terrible few days that followed. I wonder if Will also has such vivid memories of the life-changing moments that we shared.

I would say things are pretty much back to normal for me these days, or, at least, what normal is for my little family. Apart from those flashbacks, of course.

"To be expected and might go on for a few years yet," lamented my psychiatrist, who has thus far proved to be of little help.

Will? Maybe you should ask him yourself how he is coping, as we were hardly likely to meet up again to reminisce over old times after what happened. As far I know, he is still alive and still not behind bars.

But just how did we both find ourselves in that Cambridge hotel room on that night? A long old story, I suppose, with more than a few twists and turns along the way. Now, where exactly should I start?

TO BEGIN AT THE BEGINNING

July 2021

The unannounced, energetic strike of a brass gong visibly surprised those in the reception area who had not before attended a formal dinner at a Cambridge University college.

"Dinner is served," shouted the butler to the ceiling of the sunlit atrium. A man who could shout very loudly indeed but with a certain reservation. Very formally suited and long experienced in what he now viewed as the tedious college traditions, the butler dutifully followed the fellow, resplendent in his gown, to the top table of the Wolfson College dining hall. The trailing conference attendees searched for their name tags, as directed by the seating plan advertised in the atrium reception area, and stood to attention behind their allocated chair and dining place. The college fellow glanced across the long tables spread out before him and patiently waited for the excited chatter to die down to a handful of persistent whispers.

"*Benedictus benedicat.*" Grace had been given for this evening's dinner by Dr William Giancarlo Jeavons, who was the first of the diners to take their seat.

"I do so enjoy these lovely quaint traditions you have at some of your universities," were her first words after the dinner guests had settled into their rather uncomfortable chairs and introductions made between close neighbours. "And thanks for inviting me to the top table for the conference dinner and a University of Cambridge experience. Well, sort of." She smiled. "A very pleasant surprise indeed. Thank you. And what a very interesting talk you gave this afternoon," was the final comment she squeezed in before reaching for what was left of her glass of fizz.

"My pleasure." Will smiled; he was delighted that Ms Celeste Simmonds of Myers-Stratton had not only accepted his invitation but also seemed genuinely pleased to be there. It was clear to at least the fellow's eyes that his dinner companion considered this an important enough event to have taken great care in the demure but stylish clothes she had chosen to wear, the meticulous way she had applied her make-up and tied up her hair to a still young-looking and pretty face. Myers-Stratton's director of business development looked at least ten years younger than the forty-six years old Will knew her to be from the research he had done through her background. Maybe the chin was as not as taught as it used to be and perhaps the eyes were a little careworn, but Ms Simmonds was undoubtedly an attractive woman.

He had been ignored out of hand by several other business development representatives from pharmaceutical companies over the years and so was looking forward to an opportunity to make an informal dinner-table pitch for more investment into his biotech start-up company to someone who had actually accepted, even if Myers-Stratton was far from being one of the big US players. His company, Granta Pain Therapeutics, was running out of money and likely to fade into insolvency and from corporate memory within months unless Will could secure significant new funding. However, maybe his pitch should wait until after he tried to make a personal connection, which was a competency he prided himself on, especially with more experienced women such as the elegant businesswoman who was sitting next to him that evening. Will much preferred the description 'experienced' rather than 'mature' or, perish the thought, 'old'. *And you know what,* Will thought to himself rather ungraciously, *she's not half bad, this one. I've certainly been with far worse.* The CEO of Granta Pain could never be accused of being an introverted, dusty, old bachelor academic with no interests other than his scientific research. Women and sex were just far too important to him.

"The gongs, butlers, gowns and the pictures of all the crusty old masters on the walls?" Will waved indiscriminately at the dining hall walls. "The least we can do to show our conference guests a bit of the University of Cambridge life. And death, I suppose, or should I say history. But listen, great that you enjoyed my talk and found it useful, although it was only just a review presentation really. One of those things I feel obliged to do from time to time even though I would much prefer to talk about our latest research, but, unfortunately, that is still under wraps and confidential." Will had baited his hook in the hope that Celeste would bite.

"Of course, of course," she added quickly to emphasise she wasn't some sort of starstruck undergraduate new to science. "But I always find such reviews very useful, even though I am supposed to know it all. Always good to remind myself of the many things I have forgotten! And I must also complement you on your very well-run conference. Definitely some new and thought-provoking science going on and all topped off by dinner in a Cambridge college. What's there not to like? My colleagues back in Boston will not enjoy seeing the photos!" replied Celeste, taking in a panoramic view of the dining hall decorated with painted oars and baffling coats of arms.

"Really, thank you again," responded Will, trying to even up the gratitude score. "But maybe next time we will be able to enjoy dinner in Kings or maybe even Trinity. Much nicer than here and more history, but please remember that I didn't say that!" whispered Will in confidence as his eyes briefly spanned to long tables full of scientists desperately trying to prove to their dinner companions just how much more important their own research was. "Talking about photos, would you like a photo to commemorate your visit here and copy to a few selected Bostonians?" He gestured over to the conference photographer, who was busy annoying a conglomerate of balding men before waiting for an answer. Their slender glasses of the cheapest prosecco that Will thought he could get away with buying for the conference dinner collided as both smiled for the photographer.

"I will get the photo off to you next week. To your good health and future success, Ms Simmonds."

"And to the continuing progress to clinical trials of

your fascinating breakthrough pain medication. But, please, it's Celeste."

The photographer grimaced involuntarily as he took one last photograph of the dinner table, raised champagne flutes and the smiling couple seated under the grand portrait of a long-forgotten vice chancellor.

Will paused to consider his guest's last comment before calling over one of the waiters who, without any expression or comment, topped up both of their glasses. Who would be a waiter at a college dinner? *She has clearly done her research before getting here and so there might just be some real interest from Myers-Stratton. I think I've got a big'un circling the hook here. Don't fuck it up, son. Just don't fuck it up.*

"So, it sounds like you know just a little bit about our little company, Celeste."

"But only a little bit for sure, as it's difficult to find out much about your company. Not much out there in the public domain that I could find," she answered, trying to stifle a grimace upon suffering the aftertaste of the prosecco.

Will took in a deep breath to avoid trying to argue otherwise through pointing out to Celeste the publications and many company presentations that he had personally contributed to in the last two years. It would not help his own cause if he were to make it too obvious that she was not doing her job properly.

"Well. That's maybe where I can help you, Celeste." Will smiled, switching to semi-flirting mode whilst congratulating himself on suddenly coming up with, in his opinion, a rather good idea. "Why don't you pop by our labs tomorrow morning and I can make sure you get back on that plane with a much better understanding of what we are working on than when you arrived?" Will followed up his smile by gently touching her forearm. "Oh, but please forgive me. That is, if you are free tomorrow."

Celeste glanced at her arm and returned her dinner companion's smile. "I would be delighted to see your place of work and find out some more about your research. That would be great. Thanks for the offer." She paused to take the smallest sip of her drink, not least to confirm for sure that the refill was as poor as the original. "I had earmarked tomorrow for some sightseeing around this beautiful city of yours. Flying back to Boston on Friday, but I guess I will have more than enough time to do both." Celeste thought it unnecessary to tell him that even prior to leaving Boston, she had every intention in arranging a meeting with Will and finding out more of Granta Pain Therapeutic's research so as to update her spreadsheets. But she considered it best, at this early stage, not to give him any notion that Myers-Stratton would be interested in funding Will's company. Celeste did not want to lead him on and leave him with any expectations. All standard business practice for Celeste.

"That's sorted then. I'll come and pick you up at wherever you are staying. Say about 10am, or maybe a little later, if you prefer?"

"The University Arms, and 10am would be fine."

"Let's drink to that," ordered Will, raising his almost-empty glass towards her. "But let's first enjoy the conference dinner tonight, maybe finding out a bit more about each other as well as our research interests." Will had switched to full flirting mode.

*

Celeste was rushing down a hotel corridor through to a busy reception just as Will was asking the concierge if they could ring Ms Simmond's room. "No need. Here she is." He waved dismissively to no one in particular. Will's take on the smart but casual business suit she had chosen to wear that morning made him wonder if his choice of jeans, baggy white summer shirt and boating shoes was entirely appropriate for the occasion. *Doesn't look too good, does it? Hardly a top-CEO look. Pretty thoughtless and disrespectful of me. But too late now. Just as well I picked out my best pair of jeans*, he mused.

"I'm so sorry," gushed Celeste, trying to steady her breathing and brush down her jacket. She was trying her best not to look flustered but failing hopelessly. "I would like to put my being late down to jet lag but we both know that it was caused by one too many cocktails at the hotel bar last night. I really should know better at my age and with my experience, but I did enjoy the night. And your company, of course."

Through an enjoyable and intriguing evening sharing their potted careers and even life stories across colourful, ferociously expensive cocktails, he found out that she was in the process of going through a messy divorce and she had been made aware that he was single and unattached, although she struggled to believe the latter.

"No more so than me. A thoroughly enjoyable night

out in Cambridge. Some fascinating science discussed in the finest of company," argued Will as he helped her to turn over her collar. *Maybe that was a little bit too forward and presumptuous?*

"Thanks." Celeste was a little bit taken aback by his familiarity but far from offended, and maybe she was even a little bit flattered. She paused to try to find the appropriate words to justify her choices and actions from the night before. "You know, I'm sorry not to take up your suggestion of a nightcap in my room, but another drink would really have pushed me over the edge and maybe also you coming up to my room would have been more than just a little bit inappropriate." She was putting down a marker for any future potential business relationship they may have, even if it sounded less than convincing to either of them.

Over a late and rushed breakfast, she had mulled and even fantasised over scenarios of how things might have played out if she had brought him back to her room. Would she have regretted doing so more than how she had regretted not doing so this morning? It was clear to Celeste, as she thought it must surely have been as equally clear to Will, that there was a sexual chemistry they enjoyed during the long evening visiting a few of the city pubs Will had suggested and which ended with cocktails at the hotel bar. It could, for Celeste, have been a sort of one-off holiday fling with no strings attached for either party, although it would have been far from the most professional of endings to her conference meeting. With nearly fifteen years' experience in business development, Celeste had been more than used to men coming onto her and also how to handle them. There had been several occasions when she had been tempted and the opportunity had been there for the taking, but she had remained faithful to both her husband and her employer. But this William Jeavons fellow! Young, ambitious, a rising star in his field of research, deliciously handsome and with a PhD in how to charm women. And, of course, she was well aware that he might just be chasing after Myers-Stratton money and not what else a mature woman could offer. Ms Simmonds really had her hands full with this one.

Will wondered how best to respond to her bringing up last night's rather forward suggestion he had made to enjoy a nightcap back in her hotel room. *Probably wise to not dwell on the matter. Yet another example of too much drink mixed with too much libido.* "A very sensible call indeed. I'm not sure one more drink would have done me much good either," he lied. "On occasion, conferences can rather take on a life of their own."

With the hope that he had managed to avoid irreparably damaging their business relationship before it had even started, Will turned his attention to getting Celeste over to the lab and making that pitch. Will was angling his body toward the revolving-door exit of the hotel in the hope that Celeste would follow his lead, which she did. The University Arms was his favourite hotel in Cambridge. Not that he could ever afford to stay there, of course, and he winced at the thought and memory of how much the cocktails cost last night. *Why did I ever offer to pay for them?*

Acknowledging the hotel porter as they left the hotel, they walked out into bright sunshine and onto a busy Regent Street. A Cambridge city street which is always busy but maybe no more so than this first post-Covid summer. "Where have you parked your car?" probed Celeste, looking up and down the street for a car she would not have recognised anyway.

"I'm afraid Cambridge is not a place for cars, so I hope you don't mind walking over to the labs. Probably a ten-minute walk at most if we walk very slowly, and the sun is actually shining for a change. Ready to go?"

"Walking? Really? One learns something new every day," added Celeste, maybe only half in jest.

But walk they did. Battling to cross over Regent Street, they made their way up to the Downing College main gate, which was literally no more than a stone's throw away from the hotel. Regent Street was full of summer tourists brought out by the fine weather mixing with irritable locals commenting on how the place had been infested with visitors even more than usual. As they walked through the grounds of the picturesque college buildings, Will did his best to say something interesting about the place but could only come up with that John Cleese had been a student there and that the Heong art gallery was well worth a visit. He remembered that he didn't really know Cambridge very much at all despite having lived there for nearly ten years. "Of course, the best way to see the city, and especially the colleges, is by punting on the River Cam. Interested? Ticks your box of wanting to do some Cambridge sightseeing."

"What? Today?" asked Celeste, temporarily coming to a halt.

"Why not? If you've got the time, I've got the punt. A benefit from our links with the university. You can't visit

Cambridge in the summer without going punting. It really is de rigueur. How about after lunch? Why do you think I have come dressed like this?" he asked, sweeping his hands over his body. *That little fib will hopefully rescue the situation and overcome any lack of respect she might think I am showing.*

"OK. You have convinced me. Why not indeed," answered Celeste, stepping forward once again whilst struggling to find a good reason as to arguing why not. "Do I need to go back to the hotel to get changed first? As you said, you have come dressed for boating or punting or whatever you call it, but I'm not sure I have."

"No, no. You're fine. I've yet to capsize a punt," lied Will.

A full day ahead already planned, they walked out through side exit past the Department of Pathology, turning left into Tennis Court Road. "And here we are," announced Will, stopping outside an unremarkable, functionally styled five-storey building beside the narrow road. "Behold, Granta Pain Therapeutics! Just the first phase. Not the whole building, of course. We hire a few labs on the second floor from the university, but we hope to be moving to a place of our own sooner rather than later. All depends on our next round of funding, as you can imagine," hinted Will rather clumsily.

"Still in Cambridge? I mean, are you only looking to relocate locally?"

"That's our hope, as is maintaining close links to the university." Which Will knew was a strong selling point for his fledgeling company.

They walked to the far side of the building to a small courtyard and an entrance door, which Will held open for his guest. "Let's go up to my office for some coffee before we get started on the tour. I have also taken the liberty of booking a meeting room to give you a short, non-confidential presentation of where we are with our research if that's OK with you." Will took a smiling nod from Celeste as a yes as they made their way up the stairs.

Those experienced in such matters would say that one lab is typically pretty much like any other lab. The background hum of the fume hoods and refrigeration. The bright lighting illuminating long white benches made untidy by equipment and glassware. That was certainly Celeste's experience, and this occasion was really no different as she was ushered by Will through into Granta Pain's only laboratory space, although this was clearly an academic lab lacking the newest equipment typically on show in Big Pharma. She suspected some of the older equipment on show had long ago depreciated in value to the point of no longer being considered as company assets. There was also the unmistakable smell of chemicals because of inefficient fume hoods and non-matching, less-than-white lab coats of varying designs worn by the staff. Yes, indeed. This was not Big Pharma. Celeste had to smile when she saw a battered old CD player poorly hidden under one of the benches. No music to be played when there are important visitors to entertain. Nevertheless, Celeste did enjoy the chance to meet the few staff who worked at the company, despite it being obvious that they had been tipped off about her arrival that morning. The combination of a small team and limited equipment suggested that the company likely relied heavily on using contract research organisations for at least some of their research. *Expensive!* concluded Celeste to herself.

"No one joining us?" asked Celeste as Will closed the door of the small, fifth-floor meeting room sharply with his foot as his hands were full carrying his laptop and a coffee refill for his audience of one.

"Ehm." Will breathed as he focused his attention on connecting his computer to the ancient projector. "Ehm, no. I never let the little buggers leave the bench," was a comment uncomfortably close to the truth although was meant in jest as well serving as a throwaway distracting comment meant to cover up a potential oversight he might have made in front of Celeste. Granta Pain Therapeutics was Will's company. No one else's. An attitude that was perfectly aligned with his ego but did not always play well outside the confines of his own head. A flaw in his personality, which Will was very aware of, but sometimes he just couldn't help himself.

He took a seat opposite Celeste in the so-called meeting room, which would be more truthfully described as a dumping ground for various IT equipment that had experienced better times and was unlikely to see action ever again.

Please don't fail me today, baby, whispered Will to the notoriously moody projector known by all in the company as Geoff, although no one was quite sure why. "Good," announced Will to no one in particular as the title slide gratifyingly appeared on a magnolia-coloured wall masquerading as a screen. "As I said earlier, we have not yet signed a confidentiality agreement so this slide deck will just be a short summary of non-conf data. That OK?"

"Yes, that's fine and understood." Celeste smiled. "We can follow up with a confidentiality agreement if we think it is worth moving to the next stage." She was making sure that Will fully understood that Myers-Stratton only funded a small proportion of the research proposals they reviewed. It was the default approach Celeste made to all her wannabe money-grabbers.

It took less than thirty minutes for Will to close out his presentation, skipping through the acknowledgements highlighted on the final slide, pausing only to call out the names of his current investors and himself, Dr William Jeavons. Celeste had to admit to herself that Will really was onto something and was championing just the sort of project that Myers-Stratton and probably other companies were looking for. That mythical Holy Grail that many had promised, but no one had delivered on. A novel, non-addictive therapeutic to treat moderate to severe chronic pain. The likelihood would be that this project would fail just as all before had done but at least the rationale was scientifically plausible, and a potential candidate drug had already been identified.

There was only one question Celeste had after Will had fielded her gentle probing into the science. "Of those four scientists you have listed in your acknowledgement slide, is there anyone who is crucial to your efforts moving forward?"

Interesting question, Will mused to himself. *Is she fishing for what would be a minimum size of company that Myers-Stratton would be willing to fund?*

"Well, as you might expect, I would say all four of the names you see here on this last slide have been essential in helping us get to where we are today. You met all of them in the lab earlier this morning." Will took in a deep breath to at least give the impression that he cared deeply about his staff. "But, if I have to make a shortlist of those with the skill sets needed for the next phase of the company then I would say Grace and Neville. Especially Nev, who was the first to join the company, has been there and done that with many other companies and who I often seek a view from. He knows his stuff."

"Hmm," responded Celeste pensively as she wrote something down in her battered, ever-present notebook, which Will could not quite see. *Was it three additional staff needed?* "Grace did come across as a bright little spark." Which Celeste seemed to emphasise by crossing her legs.

I really wish she wouldn't keep doing that, hoped Will, trying not to imagine what lay beneath the neatly pressed trousers. He was so pleased that she wasn't wearing a short skirt.

"Yes. And only a few years out from a postdoc year in Schneider's lab. She will go far and hopefully with us if we can attract more funding and keep her interested."

Celeste nodded her head rather agitatedly after hearing yet another reference to money. Yes, she had got the message loud and clear. The company needed funds and now.

Will recognised the sign. Time to close out the pitch. "So you see, Celeste. Our strapline, if you like, of where we are with the project as of today. We have used AI to identify a known drug that has previously gone into clinical trials for depression, but which also hits our target receptors. As I explained in the presentation, drugs acting on the combination of these receptors - maybe synergistically although that remains to be proven - have to the best of our knowledge, never previously been linked to a role in modulating pain. These findings add to what we believe is the core property of this drug, which is its unique action in potentiating the efficacy of the endogenous opioids, the enkephalins and, as you know, an area my lab has focused on over several years. This exciting novel mechanism of action and, until now, undiscovered profile of the drug is proprietary to Granta Pain Therapeutics and will be patented once we have secured further funding. As much as I would enjoy revealing more about our breakthrough non-addictive treatment for moderate to severe pain this morning, I'm sure you understand why we are keeping confidential the identity of the receptor targets as well as the drug. All will be revealed if, and hopefully when, we sign a confidentiality agreement!"

"Of course, Will," responded Celeste, looking down intently on the notes she was scribbling down.

"We have clear freedom to operate on the repurposed drug as its original patent has long expired and we have identified a novel therapeutic use. As you saw in the slide deck, the drug shows similar in vivo efficacy against pain as do the standard opioids such as morphine and fentanyl, but, most importantly, unlike the opioids, our drug has no abuse potential. Given what we have seen so far, it should not be addictive in humans. Thus, we are proposing to repurpose an original drug for a new indication, which I know is an approach Myers-Stratton has taken with several of their marketed products. We have a fully costed clinical development plan in place and are now looking for further funding of around twenty million dollars to take the drug candidate through Phase 2a clinical trials targeting pain." Will was keen to emphasise the close links with the University of Cambridge. Always a winner with overseas investors. "And, as you saw, we plan to continue leveraging the expertise and capability of the world-class AI team we have here in Cambridge in designing cost- and time-optimised clinical trials and maybe back-up drug candidates if our investors have the appetite." Will paused and looked across to Celeste. "Any other questions?"

"Thank you, Will. All very impressive and the basic rationale does seem to hold up, at least with the preclinical research you have done so far. You did mention that the repurposed drug showed an acceptable toxicity profile, but I'm guessing the guys back in Boston will want to go into more detail on that as well as drug product." She carefully placed her pen on the table and closed her notebook. "I don't suppose you could give me a copy of the slides to take back to Boston?"

"Of course. Not a problem and please send over any other questions your team back in Boston may have."

"I will as long as I don't drown before the day is out." Celeste smiled.

"Drown? Oh, of course. Punting! How could I forget," responded Will, a little disappointed that the chance to go punting seemed more important to Celeste than talking further about 'his' work. Perhaps this was just going to be yet another one of those wasted pitches. But he was not going to give up that easily. There was still the afternoon for him to work his magic. And maybe even the night.

*

"This is not unusual, I'm afraid." Will breathed heavily through clenched teeth, narrowly missing colliding with a punt of shrieking Italian students. "A typical late-July day on the River Cam. Not a good look. The plan is to get past all this and take the punt upriver to Grantchester and from where we pinched the company name - well, at least from the pub," he joked, "and some peace and quiet for us to enjoy that bottle of cava I have tucked away in the wicker basket." Celeste looked down on the smudge of grease that had already appeared on her trouser suit and smiled rather nervously whilst making a mental note to ensure that the next small boat she would step onto would boast of at least one outboard motor.

Will was true to his word and Celeste became a little less nervous as they moved out of the city-centre waterways and flotillas of excitable landlubbers and through the relative tranquillity of Grantchester meadows.

Far enough, thought Will to himself as the meadows started to come into view. The punting was getting harder, the sun hotter and there was no one on the punt who was going to take them back to the city centre other than the one who took them out. "This OK for you, Celeste?" pleaded Will, pointing to the riverbank to his left.

"That would be lovely. I do so like being near cows," joked Celeste. "Blue skies, long green grass and a free afternoon in Cambridge. Let me take a photo of you before we dock or whatever it is you call it when in one of these things," she suggested. *The man is so annoyingly photogenic*, thought Celeste, looking back on her phone at the photos she had just taken. *With those dark Mediterranean looks, he would not look out of place on a gondola. Dress sense apart, naturally!*

Disembarking onto a riverbank just a little bit higher than was sensible was never likely to be pretty. And it wasn't, but Will was content that both of them stayed dry, although he now started worrying about them getting back into the punt almost three feet below where they were now standing. But that tricky moment could wait. Will unfolded a woollen blanket for them to sit on, opened the cava and poured out two drinks into plastic cups. "Apologies for the tableware but cheers and to your good health, Celeste." Now for part two of the pitch.

Before getting much beyond Will mapping out a new potential site for the Granta Pain Therapeutics labs, Celeste held up her hands to stop him in mid-flow. "Sorry to interrupt you, Will, but I think, thanks to your presentation and all that we have discussed both last night and today, I now have a pretty good understanding of your business and your science and where you want to take it. My brain is now full, and any more information will just spill out over the top and into the river," she joked, pulling her hands up and away from her head as illustration. "Why don't you tell me about this Dr William Jeavons. Not a verbal dump of your CV. Not what you have already done in your research. Tell me what *you* want to be. What you want to do. Your hopes for Granta Pain. What will Dr William Jeavons' CV look like in five years' time?"

She wants me to talk about my favourite subject, mused Will. *Me. No problemo.*

"First and most important of all, I will be looking for a much bigger head in order to accommodate my rapidly growing ego!"

Celeste's response to the remark was a thin smile but no more.

Look. I know I have a massive ego but at least it is not so big that I can't also send myself up.

"But maybe I should be a little bit more serious for a moment," offered Will, desperately trying to appear professional. "In five years, Granta Pain will have moved to one of the science parks around Cambridge. Our lead drug will have shown efficacy in several pain indications in humans without showing abuse potential. We will have series of patents defending both the drug candidate and the unique mechanism of action. If we get additional funding, we will also have brought through a number of novel back-up drug candidates targeting pain ready to start clinical trials, and Myers-Stratton will have followed up their initial investment by acquiring Granta Pain Therapeutics!"

"Is that all?" Celeste laughed. "I thought you would have at least been featured on the front cover of *Forbes* magazine as the man who discovered the first non-addictive drug to treat severe pain and solved, at a stroke, the opioid epidemic."

"Oh, I was rather taking that as read," answered Will. This time they both smiled. "Let's drink to that."

And they did, with the next two hours filled with effortless conversation fuelled by the contents of a bottle of cava summarily returned empty to the wicker picnic basket Will had borrowed from Grace.

"You know, I'm not sure I am up to taking you back up into Cambridge on the punt. It's been a long week at the conference topped off by a long day today. Why don't I get one of my students to come and take the punt back and I will walk you across the meadow, through Newnham and back to your hotel. A bit of a walk, I'm afraid, but a pleasant enough route and you will get back to base much quicker than if we went by punt. Another part of Cambridge ticked off."

"Do I have a choice?" asked Celeste, looking up to Will, who was already packing away their belongings.

"Well, if you commit right now to funding Granta Pain then I am prepared to carry you all the way back to the University Arms. How about that?"

"Nice try, Will. Nice try. But no cigar, I'm afraid."

Celeste stood up with the aid of Will's offered hand and they made the first step of the many needed to get the Myers-Stratton employee back to her temporary base. A slow walk through meadows full of late-summer flowers past groups of prone university students taking in the sun as a reward for finishing their exams. Cambridge was showing off the best side of its face. After almost half an hour of walking, Will slowed as they approached the grand entrance to the hotel, and she turned to face him.

"Thank you so much, Will, for our business chat this morning and entertaining me this afternoon. It was very kind of you and maybe you will allow me to reciprocate. If you are willing and able, perhaps you will let me treat you to dinner here at the hotel this evening. Let's say 7pm at the bar?"

"Nothing I would like better, but if you really want to taste the finest food Cambridge has to offer, then may I be so forward as to suggest Midsummer House. I should add that it is ruinously expensive and so I couldn't possibly expect you to pay for dinner, but I guarantee it will be an occasion you will remember and maybe even more photos for you to take back to Boston."

"Funnily enough, someone back in the office in Boston did tell me about that place. Why not?" Celeste beamed at the thought of getting one up on Nat, her boss. "Will that be another long walk for me?"

Will smiled. "Maybe not this time," reassured Will. "If you don't mind booking yourself a taxi at the hotel reception then I will meet you in the restaurant at around 7pm. That is assuming I can book a table, as it's really popular. Two Michelin stars last time I looked, but don't quote me on that."

"That sounds fantastic," gushed Celeste. "A very nice way to finish a very useful and surprisingly pleasant week. See you at 7pm, then."

And with that, Will said his goodbyes and walked off, heading for Parkers Piece and the scenic route back to his apartment backing onto the railway station. *Still a chance. The door is still just about open*, hoped Will, marginally avoiding a cyclist determined in finding the quickest way across the park. *I will try not to think too much about how much dinner will cost. And the wine? Well, fuck me. The woman is certainly no teetotaller.*

*

He thought she was late once again, as he had been waiting at the front of house at the restaurant for some ten minutes after their agreed meeting time, but then he caught sight of Celeste talking earnestly to a tall and worryingly thin woman at the far edge of the reception area near the window. By coincidence, she had simultaneously glanced around the room to catch his eye. Celeste raised her hands to her companion, begging forgiveness for breaking off their conversation. *I wonder who she is? Maybe someone she met at the conference*, thought Will.

As a smiling Celeste walked towards Will, the words 'elegant', 'sophisticated' and 'mature' washed through Will's mind. She was wearing a simple enough little black dress with a halter neck covered by a perfectly fitting jacket. Her hair was tied up to show her sharp jawline and high cheekbones. Will had also made no little effort in *dressing to the max*. Although dressing to the max for Will was rather a subjective description. Shoes – with laces. Socks – not white. Trousers – not denim and held up tightly with a belt. Shirt – long-sleeved and clean. Jacket – whatever he could borrow. Tie – *I don't think so!* He had to buy a suit when he arrived in Cambridge and that, in Will's mind, was what he would fall back on if he really had to for business and college dinners. Will just 'didn't do' nice clothes, although he had the looks and the body to fully justify the expense.

Now for the part that Will more often than not got wrong. How to compliment a woman on her looks without causing offence.

"I hope you don't think it inappropriate for me to tell you how nice you look tonight," asked Will as Celeste drew near.

Nice? Did I really say nice? asked Will of himself. "I of course meant to say how beautiful you look." Although he would have preferred to have added the words 'drop-dead gorgeous' and 'too sexy by half', but even he knew that would be going too far.

"Maybe a tiny little bit inappropriate given that we hardly know one another, but I do appreciate the sentiment." The smile came across as a little bit patronising to Will but perhaps he was imagining it. "Maybe a word of advice for the good," was the start of Celeste's postscript. "Not the sort of thing that will go down all that well when you come over to see us in Boston." Celeste bent her head forward quizzically. "I meant if, of course. If you come over to Boston."

Very promising. Maybe a little slip from the unreadable Ms Simmonds.

Will could just about remember the one and only time he had been to Midsummer House before, but he might have been fooling himself. They were led to a small, cloth-covered table and seated in maybe not the most comfortable of chairs the dining companions had experienced. A strong evening sun was bathing the diners through the conservatory ceiling. He had chosen well. A perfect venue for entertaining a potential investor in his company. Both were looking forward to dinner after a busy day.

The meal? Out of a show of solidarity and hoped - for display of good taste, Will decided to mirror his companion's choice of poached John Dory decorated with herbs he was struggling to name and so didn't even try. *Nice enough*, he thought, *but hardly worth the cost it is all likely to add up to*. Despite being fortunate enough to have experienced fine dining at many university functions, Will disdained of all the 'crap' and pretention surrounding 'good' food. He cared and knew more about wine, reckoning that he could pick a good one out when he saw one, and the bottle of Bourgogne Blanc that they managed to polish off between them was one such bottle.

"That was truly special. Memorable," announced Celeste as she scraped out the last spoonful of an exotically named sorbet.

An almost perfect example of style over substance, Will silently considered, toying with the option to call into that wonderfully reassuring kebab emporium on Regent Street on his walk home. *Now that really is food fit for the Gods.* Will smiled to himself.

"What did I tell you. Food to die for," lied Will sincerely.

"Thanks, Will, for today and this evening. I really appreciate your time." Maybe her gratitude needed an addendum. "And your company for a whole day, of course. I insist on me picking up this one," finished Celeste, pointing to the bill that had been left on the side of the table and that Will had done his best to ignore.

Will protested meekly, although both were fully aware that he had no intention of contributing to the obscene cost of their evening out in Cambridge.

"Is your apartment much of a walk from here?" probed Celeste, who was starting to feel the chill of the cooling July evening as they waited outside Midsummer House for the taxi pick-up she had booked at the hotel reception.

"Thirty minutes. Maybe forty," fabricated Will, hoping for the offer of a share of Celeste's taxi.

"So you will come with me to the hotel, and I will ask the taxi driver to take you on from there and back to your apartment. No arguments, please."

However, the closing throes of the evening didn't quite turn out that way. This time, it was Celeste who suggested that they finish up with a nightcap just before the taxi pulled up outside the University Arms. Will didn't need a second invitation to see the inside of Celeste's hotel room and the chance to find out how the night might end.

"Just the two lumps of ice, please," Will advised as he leaned forward on his chair to accept the tumbler of Irish whiskey. "Great. Thanks. What a fantastic suite you have been staying in." He was genuinely impressed with the hotel stocking miniatures of Irish whiskey in the minibar.

"I have to admit that Myers-Stratton does treat me very well when I am overseas on business," she admitted. "I have argued and argued rather successfully for the importance of our people feeling comfortable and refreshed whenever away from home."

"Seems like you got your way, but aren't you also going to have the nightcap you invited me to come back for?" he asked, noticing that she was sitting back in the sofa at right angles to his armchair but without a drink to place on the shared coffee table.

"I don't know why, as heaven knows how many times I have been over in the UK, but I'm always surprised at how much you Brits drink."

"You clearly have yet to meet my Scandinavian colleagues."

Celeste smiled at Will's comment and leaned forward towards him. "What I'm trying to say but clearly not doing very well is that I don't want to do anything else tonight I might end up regretting. I don't want drink to be the reason I spend the night and tomorrow morning with you."

Celeste had shocked even herself. This was not her. She was never so forward, even with men she knew well, and was now regretting inviting Will to her room. Whatever was she thinking? What did she imagine was going to happen next? This was not the wife and the ultimate career professional she had always considered herself to be. Not the sort of person who invites potential clients back to her hotel room. Never would she ever risk mixing business with pleasure. But there was something undeniably special about the man now sitting in front of her. Something so very different. Yes, he was attractive, intelligent and attentive, but there was an aura about him that she just couldn't quite put her finger on. An unfathomable intangible. Or was it only her once again falling for a serial philanderer as she had done with her husband? Her mind had become an inescapable maelstrom of confusion, indecision and regret that she had put herself and Will into this awkward position. This was not her.

What the fuck? were the words emblazoned at the front of his brain. "Anything else you might regret? What else?" asked Will, rather too loudly, leaning forward almost on his haunches.

"My other regret? Asking you up here for a nightcap and perhaps coming over as a bit of a sexual predator, which I can assure you was not my intention. It's not who I am. Far from it. The day and the night… the half bottle of wine… being away from home… my poor excuse." She paused to allow Will to respond. Which he didn't. "Look, Will. Let me be frank and honest with you. Maybe too honest. However much I might enjoy a one-night stand with you to finish off what has been a perfect day, it would clearly be a very unprofessional thing to do. You are a prospective client, after all, and I can't afford to appear biased in my opinion of Granta Pain. On top of that, I'm just not ready to have any other relationships. Not now."

Will knew that his chance to avoid having to walk back to his apartment had passed and answered, "But aren't you practically divorced and, if I can be a little blunt, back on the market?"

Celeste could have explained that she was still some way away from formalising any divorce proceedings but now was not the time for such detail. "I know, I know. Difficult to explain but hopefully you will never have to find out for yourself how going through a messy divorce screws up your mind. I hope not forever. Let's please not talk any more about this tonight. I'm not divorced yet." An overwhelming feeling of remorse and guilt for something that Celeste had not even done had flattened any lingering desire she had to take Will to her bed.

Both parties fell silent in order to fully contemplate the rather awkward place they had found themselves.

"I may not have gone through what you are going through, but I think I understand and, of course, fully respect your thoughts and wishes, but maybe you will allow me just one indulgence."

"As long as that indulgence doesn't involve me taking my clothes off," was her reply, half in jest.

"No. Of course not. I hope you consider me a gentleman. But maybe not so much a gentleman to stop me from letting you know what an absolutely perfect ass you have got!"

The shared laughter was genuine. "Something else you should never consider saying out loud in Boston!"

"I very much look forward to not saying such things when I am in Boston, but could I be granted just one further indulgence? Just a teeny, tiny, small one."

Celeste leaned forward, looking up accusingly at her companion. "I'm not sure you are allowed two indulgences on the same night, but what the hell."

"That you will now join me with that nightcap, after which I will wish you goodnight and a safe journey for your flight back to that rather prudish place you call home."

She crossed the room, opened the minibar, poured out a miniature of brandy and returned to the sofa with her nightcap in hand. "Let's drink to that, Dr Jeavons, and to the memory of a very pleasant day indeed in old Cambridge town."

Walking back to his apartment in a still and muggy July night, the time had arrived for Will to try and make some sense of the last few hours. "I mean, what the fuck?" That commentary was supposed to be just for Will's own benefit but was mouthed loud enough for a young couple passing the other way on Parkers Piece footpath to glance at each other and quicken their pace away from yet another drunk. "She might have claimed to not be a sexual predator, but I honestly couldn't tell the difference. But never mind, Will. Never mind. You sold her the science as well as you could and, for a change, we might actually get somewhere with this one. Boston, here we come!" announced Will to himself, clenching his right hand tightly at the imagined future success. Will quickened his pace as he left the park and started up the Mill Road drag, which was still busied by its cosmopolitan dwellers despite the relatively late hour. Will decided that he should be pleased with the events of this summer's day, so why not a quick one in the Swan to finish off a rather nice day?

HARD TIMES

I thought it was unusual for Mum to ask me to go out with her so late in the night. When she did go out, which was often enough, she always left me on my own and usually with a little treat – a bottle of pop, crisps, sweets – a kiss on my forehead and forcing a promise from me to go to bed before 10pm. I got another kiss and sometimes my mum would even lay down in bed with me for a while when she got home from wherever she had been. Such sweet memories will remain with me for as long as I will live. But sometimes she wasn't home even when I woke up in the morning. I so hated those lonely days when I had to get myself ready in the morning with no Mum to see me off to another day at school. She was all kisses and tears and 'sorrys' and 'it will never happen agains' when I got home after school on such days, and I sometimes got the odd book or even a DVD from Woolworths as a present. As if that would erase the memory of me being left all alone in that tiny flat with strange, frightening noises or loud, swearing arguments overheard from the other flats around us often keeping me awake through the night. So, yes. It was unusual for my mum to take me out with her at night.

"Look, son," she said to the top of my head as we queued to pay for the bus, "as I said when we left the house, I wouldn't drag you out this late unless I really had to, but your mum really needs your help tonight."

She held my shoulders and gently guided me to an empty pair of seats near to the back of the bus. I sat next to a chilled window with winter darkness and a steady drizzle on the dimly lit streets outside for company. Mum budged me up tight to the window so that she could place a large, empty carrier bag between us.

"Right," started Mum as she stroked the back of my head. "Right. What I am telling you now and what we will be doing tonight has to be a secret just between the two of us. Top secret." The bus lurched forward out of the bus stop and then stopped suddenly to allow a gesticulating cyclist to pass. Even this mother and son sitting towards the rear of the bus could hear the torrent of swear words unleashed by the bus driver. My mother leaned out into the aisle to stare malevolently at our driver. Mum was strange like that. Hated swearing and bad manners and then there were all the bad, much worse things that she herself did. Things I knew for sure, even at the age I was back then, that other mothers just didn't do.

She turned back to face me. "Don't tell anyone. Your friends," not that I really had any, "your favourite teacher, Mrs Singh, and not even Grandma or Grandpa. Do you understand? This is very, very important." My mum looked frightened.

"Yes, Mum. Of course I won't, Mum," I replied, adding emphasis by crossing my heart, although that really didn't mean anything to either of us.

The bus driver had now calmed down and was making slow progress through the evening traffic. "You know all about the medicines I have to take for my back pain that sometimes mean I have to lie down in bed. I know you do because you take such good care of me when your old mum is not feeling so well." She once again stroked my hair, peering strongly into my eyes. "You are such a sweet and thoughtful little boy." She hugged me tightly for what seemed like minutes. Another precious memory I hang onto.

"Can you tell me where we are going now then, Mum?" I asked when she finally released me from her embrace.

"Just down to Wandsworth. Won't take us more than half an hour. We just need to pop into the chemist's to pick up some medicine for your mother's back pain."

"But why do we have to go all the way to a chemist's in Wandsworth? Why can't you get the tablets at our chemist's in town?"

Mum stared forward to nothing in particular and said nothing for what seemed like minutes. Her thick blue coat, which she wore everywhere she went in the winter, looked as old as her careworn eyes.

I was almost too afraid to ask. "But why, Mum? Is our chemist closed?"

Then she smiled and looked round to face me. "Sort of, I suppose, son." Mum paused as if she was trying to remember something she had forgotten. "This is the secret I want you never to tell anyone." Another strange pause and a grimace. "OK. Your silly mother has run out of her medicine, and she really needs some right now. My pain is really, really bad." She reached down to the small of her back to provide context. "The only place right now they have got the sort of tablets I want is in a chemist's in Wandsworth and that's why we are on the bus. I will have to wait another week for them to come into our chemist's and I just can't wait that long." A lie that I was too young to pick up on.

I was apprehensive of the mood my mother was in as she seemed agitated and nervous. I needed to be careful of what I said. Maybe it was best to keep quiet for a while and just stare out through the window into the dark and wet streets as we made our painfully slow way to Wandsworth.

It had been nearly forty minutes since we got on the bus and almost all of it spent in silence. "Right, this is us," she proclaimed, grabbing the carrier bag and waving me out into the aisle and down to the door at the front of the still moving bus. Thankfully, the drizzle had decided to leave and find someone else to annoy, which was just as well since I had never seen Mum with an umbrella.

We walked down an unremarkable street that had clearly enjoyed better times. She clutched me tightly across the shoulders as we made our way past closed shops and seemingly towards a shop from which light cascaded out onto a wet pavement. The chemist's. Mum decided to stop walking just a few shopfronts before the chemist's, undo her embrace and turn to face me. She bent down slightly to meet my height and held my shoulders.

"This will be our secret. Remember what I said?" I nodded yes. "Our secret to be kept forever."

"Yes, Mum. Yes, Mum," was my reply, which must have appeared a little nonchalant as she then gripped my shoulders uncomfortably tight.

"I'm serious, son. This is very serious." I don't think she saw the nervous gulp I took. This was not how my mum usually behaved. Now she was frightening me. "I am going to have a very private chat with the chemist, which I don't want anyone else to hear. So, what I want you to do is to close the doors at the front of the shop after I have gone in. Can you see them over there on the right? Two doors that close together. Then I want you to stand outside and not let anyone in."

I decided to panic. "How will I stop grown-ups who want to buy something?"

"Look, I won't be more than a couple of minutes and I doubt if there are going to be many people who need to go to the chemist's on such a horrible night." She paused. "But if someone does turn up… just say… just say that your father has had to close up the shop because he has to sort out a burst pipe. Tell them to come back in an hour."

"The chemist is my dad?"

"Don't be silly," was the stern reply. "You know your father left us years ago. I want you to pretend it is your father." Her stern face was replaced with a comforting smile. "Look, I know this is difficult, but it really is no big deal and we will soon be back home."

"But what if the chemist is a woman?"

"Good point. If you see that it's a woman behind the counter, just say it's your mother," she answered rather tersely. "Doesn't really matter anyway because you won't be letting them in, will you?"

We briefly resumed and then finished our walk, stopping just before the doors of the chemist's. Mum looked inside, presumably to see if there were any shoppers about. There weren't. She turned towards me again. "Remember the plan. Stay outside the shop until I come out. Understand? And don't let anyone in." She looked up at the 'Open' sign hanging on the inside of the door. "That'll help. See that sign? I will flip it round to 'closed' when I get in."

Which she did as I took my position outside the middle of the door. I can still remember the fear of those long minutes as I peered up and down the street literally praying to God that no one would want to go to the chemist's this night. Please, God, help me and Mum. I didn't dare look behind me and into the shop. I had been given a job to do and that was what I was doing. It wasn't for me to turn round to see what the shouting I could hear behind me in the shop was all about. I didn't even turn around when I heard a woman scream. It didn't sound like Mum, but I couldn't be sure.

After what seemed like hours, Mum opened the door behind me breathing very heavily and pushing me in the direction from where we arrived and the bus stop. "Quickly," she urged as we half trotted, half walked down the street. I noticed that the carrier bag we brought with us was no longer empty. After we had passed the corner, Mum pulled me down a narrow, dark side street and we paused to catch our breath. She pulled open the top of the carrier bag and gazed at all the little boxes inside, taking out a few to read the labels under the faint light coming from a closed hairdresser. "That should do." She sighed. "Just what your mum asked for." She smiled, looking at me.

"But what was all that screaming I heard?" was the question I dared to ask.

"Screaming? Oh yes. The shopkeeper. Yes, the chemist. Well she had to climb a stepladder to get to my medicines and she nearly fell off and that must have been the scream you heard."

I peered into the bag. "That's a lot of medicines, Mum."

"She was very helpful indeed. Much better than our local chemist. Now I've got enough tablets to keep me going for a long time. Helps us both." She smiled, putting back the samples she had taken out of the bag and linking her arm with mine but not before taking two tablets out of one of the boxes and swallowing them without even a drink to help. "Time to go home."

Mum was in a great mood that night, letting me stay up late to watch a DVD of our favourite film, *Indiana Jones and the Temple of Doom*, before tucking me up in bed with sweet kisses. That was the last time we watched a film together. The last time she snuggled up to me in my bed. The last time she kissed me on my forehead. The last time I saw my mum alive.

The morning after is still a jumble of very confused memories for me and I'm sure some are just imagined or were planted forever deep in my mind by others. No doubt the brain trying to throw out traumatic recollections as best it can. What I think I do remember? Waking up and getting ready for school like I did every school day. But that day, no sign of Mum, who was usually woken up by me clattering around the bathroom and the kitchen. Not always, though. Shouting through her bedroom door and then knocking it. Nothing.

"Mum. I'm coming in. Are you getting dressed?"

She wasn't. And this is the picture that will surely be burnt on my brain for as long as I get to live. Her lying fully clothed across the bed and on her back. Her head laid to one side and her pallid face had vomit stains coming out of her open mouth. Her eyes were half open and staring through the bedroom window at a winter's day struggling to start. I must have checked to see if I could somehow bring her back to life and I must have phoned for an ambulance, but I can't remember any of that. Nor can I remember all the people who must have turned up or even who took me somewhere afterwards. All I can remember is my mum lying all alone on that bed.

*

It definitely wasn't the case that Will woke up every morning with the memories of being that abandoned little boy, but it was often enough, even now, for him to rarely look forward to sleep. It was only in the years that followed when Will could better understand the emotions and frailties of adults that he was able to gradually piece together what happened on that dreadful, life-changing night and how it had all come to that sorry end for his mother.

But what really happened that winter's night all those years ago, and why? A young mother desperate for the next hit but without any money to pay for it. A kitchen knife in the carrier bag that Will hadn't even seen which his mother had used to threaten that poor woman in the chemist's. One prescription drug too many on that night for an addict not used to such a smorgasbord. Years of drug abuse brought upon her after the death of a young daughter made worse still by then being left by her husband to fend for herself and their son. Should anyone be surprised or cast blame on such a poor unfortunate? Certainly not her son, whose love for her probably grew still further after her death. He conveniently chose to forget her many failings as a mother.

Will was much better these days than was the case when he first moved to the Midlands to live with his foster parents – his new mum and dad – where he was often consoled by them both whenever he woke up in the middle of the night calling for his old mum. His real mum. These days, for Will the man, it was more a case of recognising and accepting the raw emotion for what it was and using the coping techniques to get over his anguish that the psychiatrist had taught him as a boy.

How lucky he had been to end up living with the best foster parents in the world. Ed and Lindsey Jeavons doted on a sweet but troubled little boy their ungrateful God had never let them have for themselves and very soon embarked upon the long and painful process of becoming adoptive parents. A God who was dropped soon enough when Will arrived at their small but immaculately kept semi-detached house in Edgbaston. For his part, Will was the person responsible for holding their marriage together, as he became the centre of their attention rather than the growing inadequacies they saw in each other after fifteen childless years.

Will was always quick to credit his new mum and dad for making him the person he was now. For their part, they soon realised just how bright their little boy was and were tireless in making sure he had all the support and encouragement he needed to excel at school. It was his dad, an astute and intelligent man whose abilities were undervalued and wasted in his job as a junior-school administrator, who managed to get Will into the local boys' grammar school. Doorstepping his teachers at junior school. Appealing to the local authorities to look favourably upon a disadvantaged pupil. Meeting the headmaster of the grammar school, who he was fortunate enough to know through the local bowls club. So it was indeed a special day when that long-awaited letter appeared on the mat underneath the letter box of the Jeavons household.

Ed looked at the markings on the envelope as he bent to pick up the letter and walked through into the tiny dining room to join his wife and his son at the breakfast table.

"I think this is it, Will. This could be it," he nervously announced, taking a chair between wife and son. He paused before pulling out the letter and paused again before unfolding the typed reply from the grammar school. His lips moved gently but he said nothing before handing it to Will. Not even a smile or grimace passed his lips.

Will had suddenly lost interest in the half-eaten bowl of cereal in front of him. "I'm in!" shouted Will to the ceiling. "I got in." He beamed as Lindsey walked around the table to give him a hug, followed by Ed, who picked him up off the floor with his trademark bear hug.

"Today, this Saturday, we will always remember as the special day where this little man takes the first step on his way to becoming a future Prime Minister of Great Britain!" shouted Ed to his little family. At that moment, Will couldn't recall if he had ever been more happy.

"A special day like this demands some special celebrations. At least dinner out at Will's favourite place. Might that be McDonalds, Will?" teased Ed. "Then off to Will's other favourite place. Dudley Zoo. And then back here to see the night away watching a DVD of our very clever boy's choice. What would you like to watch, Will?"

"*Indiana Jones and the Temple of Doom.*"

*

Ed had got him into grammar school through a combination of Will being near the top of all his classes in junior school and his own wheeler-dealing with those in authority. It was now up to Will to make the most of the opportunity he had been given.

It was a slow start at his new and rather scary grammar school, which was not helped by being put into the bottom set when he arrived. His early years schooling in an inner-city primary school just didn't compare to the public-school experience of most of his classmates. However, it was not long before Will's natural intelligence and appetite for knowledge won over his teachers. There were not many in the school who asked the sort of probing questions that

Will often posed. That was no less so in science, where more than one teacher found themselves struggling to feed Will's thirst for knowledge. This made Will an uncomfortable pupil for some of the less-able teachers, but not so his biology teacher, Dr Anton Nilsson. Nilsson was a rarity amongst the staff at Will's grammar school in that he had worked in industry before becoming a teacher in his later years. It was he who fully realised Will's raw potential in science and perhaps rather selfishly pushed him into biology, as Will was also equally capable in both chemistry and physics. So, it was much to Nilsson's delight that biology was the subject that Will had chosen to study in university. A BA in natural sciences at Cambridge. Will's heart was set on it. Or was it his teacher's that had been set on it? However, whoever it was who chose the course, it was not to be. That was to be the last time that the University of Cambridge would turn him down.

Will's second choice was Imperial College and it was back 'home' to London he would go in the dying days of September 2002 to begin his study for a BSc in biological sciences. This was shortly after an underwhelming farewell night out celebration with the few friends he had made in his grammar school and the tears and hugs from his mother and father as he stepped onto the London-bound train to start the next chapter of his life. Will was surprised at his own warm tears as the train slowly left the crowded suburbs of Birmingham. Tears for the parents he was leaving behind and maybe also because he was returning to the place of the parent he would never see again, even if he was no longer that little boy William Giancarlo Messina, but the man who would be William Giancarlo Jeavons. *Why ever did my 'new' parents insist on me keeping that middle name?* was a thought that bothered Will for many more years to come. It was through those tears that he opened the letter he had kept for this moment. Leaving his home again and this time probably for good. A letter from Dr Nilsson.

I know you will work hard, Will. But don't forget to also play hard. To be successful in our world, you will not only need to be a brilliant scientist but also someone who can empathise with others regardless of their backgrounds, abilities and personalities. You will need the common touch, and you will only assimilate that vital trait by meeting people. Lots of people. Throughout your career as a scientist, you will undoubtedly meet people more talented, more driven and more successful than you can ever imagine but don't underestimate the contribution you can make. You are a remarkable person, Will. Be incredible. Do incredible things.

"That's just what I needed," spluttered the crying university student, catching the attention of a similarly red-eyed student on the other side of the train carriage.

"Your first year?" She smiled, recognising a fellow sufferer.

"How did you ever guess that?" Will laughed, wiping away his tears with a handkerchief embroidered with his initials that he had been given as a going-away present by one of his aunties. Just one of many presents Will had received from the Jeavons family in the weeks leading up to starting university.

His crying companion, Ann, turned out to be the first friend he made at university. A platonic relationship that they maintained throughout their three years of study – a history degree for her and biological sciences for him – despite them both losing their virginity one clumsy and underwhelming night spent together in her university accommodation after a freshers' ball. Will learnt so much about women from his new friend over the years that followed, allowing the young man to make full use of his striking Mediterranean good looks.

"The only thing that my Italian father gave me before he fucked off back to Naples when I was six," he sometimes drunkenly joked to the many admirers who asked of his appearance, although the anecdote brought back the memory of dark times in his life. Of his mother falling into depression and becoming hooked first on benzodiazepines and then painkillers. Of his delicate, tiny little baby sister fading away in a hospital bed, riddled with cancer. Of losing a father he had not seen again since that terrible, violent argument with his mother in their London home. The last vision Will had of his father was him looking back at his son with a darkness and sadness in his eyes that Will had never seen before. Not a word was said between them as he pushed his suitcase in front of him and slammed the front door closed behind him. But that was not before he had battered his wife and Will's mother into a hospital bed.

Ann rather regretted that their sexual relationship did not go beyond that one drunken night, but she was far too reserved and proud to ask any more of her one-time lover than friendship. She was also fearful of losing a warm friendship if her advances were turned down, which she had convinced herself would be the case. In her mind, she was just not in his league. But whatever league he was in, Will always enjoyed being with his dearest friend. He found the company of girls so much easier and less annoyingly competitive than socialising with his male contemporaries.

Dr Nilsson's script on how to become an incredible person who does incredible things was followed almost verbatim as Will sailed through university. His lecturers quickly realised that Will was going to get a top first in his degree course and so was treated accordingly, with several of them inviting him to interview for a PhD at Imperial as the course came to an end. And although he did at least turn up to one of them, his heart was set on Cambridge, just as had been the case when he had applied for his first degree. Few of his lecturers were surprised when Will was accepted to study for a PhD in Cambridge with the world-renowned pharmacologist Professor Johan Kritansky. The Neuropharmacology of 5HT7 Receptors and their Role in Pain. His choice being a consequence of his mother's addiction and death. The beginning of his steadfast and enduring conviction to find a non-addictive treatment for pain that would have prevented the painful life and death of his mother and so many other victims of opioid abuse. But before that lifelong quest could start in earnest, there was a summer of celebration and hedonism to look forward to. The second part of Dr Nilsson's script.

The summer of 2005 was everything that had Will hoped it would be. Confirmation, if it was needed, that he had earnt a first and the top mark of his year according to the head of biology, who whispered the unrewarded accolade into Will's ear after the graduation ceremony in the Royal Albert Hall. A truly unforgettable occasion for the graduate and his parents, the latter of whom were a little surprised that nearly all the friends he introduced them to at the lavish reception were girls.

"You seem to have had a rather good time at university, son." His jealous father smiled after meeting a statuesque Indian friend of Will's. "Weren't there many boys on your course?" was a question that remained unanswered as he introduced his best friend, Ann.

"But are you courting, Will? Do you have, you know, a proper girlfriend? That Ann seems a very nice girl and seems to know you so well," remarked his mother.

He didn't. And hadn't throughout the three years he had been in London. According to his envious male flatmates, he took to his bed more than his fair share of female companions, although few of the relationships survived beyond a few weeks and this was almost always Will's choice. The result of a confusing fear of commitment that was to remain with Will long after his time at university had passed. Was it his own selfish pursuit of the pleasure of new sexual experiences or the impossibility that anyone could ever replace his real mother? Will even wondered if it was a reflection of his competitive nature. Prove that he could have the girl others couldn't and then drop them after the conquest. The typical answer he trotted out to himself and to anyone who questioned why he hadn't settled down with one girl was that work was too important to him and any long-term commitment to a relationship would only get in the way. But he never believed that answer. Will would never really get to fully answer that question to his own satisfaction. Until it was too late.

The long, hot summer then drifted onto graduation balls, a very basic holiday in Greece, which put him off camping for life, and a bar job in a pub near his parents to pay for the holiday he quickly tried to forget. Could life ever be as enjoyable and carefree as the one Will experienced in that memorable summer of 2005? He would soon enough get to answer that very question.

WE ARE ALL SO DIFFERENT BUT THE SAME

For example, I guess you could say that Will and I are similar in some ways and yet so very different in others. Maybe I should explain. Who would not have at least some sympathy for what must have been the traumatic childhood that Will suffered? Almost impossible to imagine what that frightened and lonely little boy must have gone through. My childhood doesn't bare comparison to Will's shocking experience, although mine was not without tribulations that would leave a lasting mark on my mind as I grew into the woman I am today.

Like Will's, my little family also struggled to eke out a hand-to-mouth existence in a tiny flat, although ours was on the wrong side of Corby – if there is a right side, of course, but I shouldn't run down the place that at least gave me my education. Not that there weren't some good times enjoyed, but after our father was made redundant at the local steelworks, we had to move out of our house with its tiny back garden, where I spent so much of my time as a little girl, to a two-bedroom, third-floor flat with not so much as a window box of daffodils to look out on. It was a desperate place and a desperate time for us all. As young as my younger twin brothers and I were at the time, even we could see that our family was falling apart about us in that stifling flat. Our father was changing in front of our eyes. No longer was he the dad who used to whisk his children out to local parks and lakes for adventures and give our mother a break from her boisterous children. No longer the man who would patiently sit down with us telling stories of all the wonderful inventions that were made from the steel made with his very own hands. A once-proud man who just could not deal with the indignity of being long-term out of work and, in his eyes, on the scrapheap of life. He slowly but steadily withdrew from family life, spending as much time as he could walking everywhere but nowhere. Anything to avoid being at home all day and having to face up to a jobless existence. He was a man of a generation where unemployment brought feelings of shame and weakness. A man considered by society to be incapable of caring for his family.

Our poor mother was effectively left alone to look after us all. Husband and children as well as working as a cleaner when we children were at school. It breaks my heart now to think how she suffered through what should have been one of the best times of her life but how proud I am of her for making sure her children wanted for nothing. She was and still is my inspiration, even though Mum died at far too young an age.

My first day at secondary school was the very day my father died. Found, maybe perversely, by an old colleague of his from the steelworks, lying face down near a stream he used to spend so much time sitting next to watching and listening to the water trickle by. A massive, un-survivable heart attack. He was just forty-three years old but going on sixty.

As I said, not nearly as harrowing a childhood as suffered by Will, but we both took indelible scars into adulthood. However, our experiences also moulded us into the relentlessly determined characters that we are today. Fired in the kiln and battle-hardened. We were ready for the worst that life could throw at us.

I don't think Will could have been any more driven than I was in making a success of my life. No one could have worked harder than me at that terrible secondary school I ended up at. A school taking children from that desperate catchment area I was unlucky enough to have lived in. Looking back at those days, I wonder if my working so hard was also a distracting activity to show my mother and two younger brothers that our family could overcome my father's death and our poverty. To my reckoning, I got the A level grades I needed to be able to study biomedical science at the University of Hertfordshire despite my teachers and not because of them. Looking back, I think my father's death was also the inspiration for me to choose medicine as a career and try, maybe somewhat naïvely, and, as it turned out, very naïvely, to make some sort of contribution to discovering new life-saving medicines. Will and I indeed may well have been naïve in our dreams, but I hope few would criticise our intent.

So, you see, Will and I are perhaps not all that different. We both suffered losses early in our lives, although I was lucky enough to keep my mum. We both had a passion for the subject we had chosen for our careers and worked hard at trying to be successful scientists. We are both as determined a character as you are ever likely to meet, and it would be unwise for anyone to get in the way of either of us chasing after what we want.

So how is it that Will and I are any different? I hear you ask. Families. My little family is why I exist. It defines me. I can just imagine the howls of anguish from the feminista hordes shocked at why such a seemingly intelligent woman can be so subservient, but anyone who knows me would never consider me subservient, least of all to my husband. I just happen to think my family is the most important thing in my life. Am I really so wrong to believe that? Would it be better to devote my life to a career that is so dependent on people I am unlikely to ever meet? That's where Will and I are different. His life was his career. It is what defines him. He used to say to those who asked that his family were his adoptive parents and very rarely mentioned the existence of his birth mother, less still his real father. He just wasn't interested in relationships or families.

BOSTON – HOME AGAIN

"**D**addy," she said rather resignedly into her phone.

"Celeste. It's your dad." She wondered how someone who struggled so badly to have a phone conversation could ever became a partner in a large investment fund management company, although she did find his little eccentricities endearing. But not today.

"How's my favourite daughter? Are you back home yet from your conference in Cambridge?"

"Your only child is in a limo on the way back from Logan to see my dear husband," was her reply, with a rather too obvious venomous emphasis arriving at the end of the sentence.

"Whoa! Don't forget what we decided about how to handle this. We are not actually filing for a divorce. Just talking it all through and hopefully you two will be able to sort out your differences."

"First of all, Dad, it's not *we* who are going through a

divorce. It's me. Me and Charles. Not you. Not Mom. And not even his parents. Don't forget, it's Charles who had the affair – sorry, affairs – and it's that little bastard who is now trying to blame me for wanting to break up the marriage." Celeste immediately regretted swearing. The Simmonds don't do swearing.

"No need to swear, Celeste," was the exact response she was expecting to hear from her ever so prim and proper father.

"Look, Dad. I just don't want to talk about it right now. It's been a very long week away and I just want to get home and catch my breath."

"Of course," replied her father in the most conciliatory tone he could muster. "How was the conference and, more to the point, did you get to see that Jeavons man you were keen to meet?"

"Conference was fine. Cambridge was as beautiful as you told me it would be and Will Jeavons was certainly worth looking up," answered Celeste, playfully biting her lip. "Clearly a very capable scientist and he has an interesting asset that I will follow up with the guys in the lab on Monday."

"Sounds promising and maybe something we board members will get to hear about soon."

"Maybe you will. There is certainly not much else out there in pain that Myers-Stratton is likely to be interested in from what I have seen of late, so who knows. Look, Dad, better go, just coming up to the house." She never enjoyed lying to her father, even little ones like this, but she needed time in the car to compose herself to what she thought would be an inevitable confrontation with her husband unless she was lucky enough for him to be out when she got back home.

"OK. Not a problem. Maybe speak to you on the weekend. Make sure you rest up, sweetie. Bye, Celeste."

Celeste ended the call with a weak farewell and laid back to enjoy the comfort of the executive travel that Myers-Stratton afforded its top employees. She smiled at the thought of her father. Of the sweet and patient man he still is and how on Earth he ended up marrying her mother. Difficult to imagine two so very different personas. She a rather strait-laced but very successful academic at Harvard. A professor of biochemistry before she hit forty. He, yes, very successful in his own right, but even he couldn't deny that he had effectively been parachuted into a biotech-focused venture capitalist company by his ridiculously wealthy father, a financier who had power and influence over such institutions. Bob and Barbara had first met at a lavish reception sponsored by his company, Boston Pharma Ventures, which then became the start of an on/off relationship that eventually ended in marriage and, just two years later, the arrival of their only child. Celeste's parents could easily have afforded to retire years ago but she wondered if either of them was really looking forward to spending all that time alone together. And there was always the thought of just how her mother would cope with the perceived loss of status and kudos by becoming an ex-professor.

Despite Celeste's mother moving mountains of paper and annoying far too many middle-aged white men to get a legacy place for her daughter in Harvard, Celeste was always Daddy's little girl. He doted on the couple's only child in a way that her rather unaffectionate mother wouldn't or, perhaps more likely, couldn't. Her father also took more interest in their daughter's career, not least through getting her the business development role in Myers-Stratton just as his father had helped him. Celeste had struggled badly in her biomedical science graduate studies at Harvard despite working so hard to try to match her mother's achievements. But she was not her mother. Celeste had always set her mind on going into research, so it was with no little trepidation that she took the role her father had won for her through investing in Myers-Stratton and taking a place on their board. No one was more pleased than Bob seeing his daughter work her way up through Myers-Stratton to become Director of Business Development. He was so proud of his 'favourite daughter', but then again, he always was.

Celeste stopped at least trying to catch up on all the emails on her mobile phone just before the electronic gates made way for the limo to drive up through the long, gravelled driveway, stopping outside the mock Georgian façade of the marital home. The portly driver struggled to get out of the car before putting on his company hat and opening the rear door for Celeste to crunch through the gravel as she stood up to face the house.

"If you don't mind me saying, ma'am, you do have a magnificent house."

"Well thank you, Jesus. So nice of you to say so. You know, I have become rather attached to it myself over the years."

It was indeed a magnificent house. A ten-bedroom house set in almost twenty acres of meadows around a small lake in Lexington, some fifteen miles outside of downtown Boston. A wedding present to Charles Lewis Amos III and Celeste Grace Simmonds (she insisted on keeping her father's name for business reasons) paid for mostly by his father, Lewis, the long-term CEO of Boston Pharma Ventures. And therein lay the problem for poor Bob Simmonds. A marriage made in heaven helped by the support of work colleagues and close friends now turning sour. Celeste's father was very concerned as to how the potential break-up of the marriage would affect his position at Boston Pharma and his relationship with the CEO. He couldn't really afford to be angry with his son-in-law's repeated infidelities, although he should have been. Bob was fully aware of his failures as a protective father and felt very guilty in letting his daughter down.

Celeste walked up to the heavy black door, waved goodbye to her driver and turned keys into the two locks before opening the door onto a sunlit atrium. Her pleasure at not having to deactivate the burglar alarm was tempered by the realisation that her husband must therefore be somewhere in the house.

"Charles," she called as she took off her jacket and parked her suitcase next to a coat stand. "Charles," she called out again. "Where are you?"

Without waiting for an answer, she made her way out of the atrium, down the hallway and into the kitchen masquerading as a restaurant, such was its size. Charles was standing next to the wine chiller with a full glass of white wine in his hand, watching intently his wife walk into the kitchen.

"Why didn't you answer me? You must have heard me calling," asked Celeste once she saw her husband.

"And good afternoon to you, darling. Would my dear wife like a drink?"

"Hardly past lunchtime and you're already pissed," she commented, reaching down to take off her shoes.

"Nasty swear words from his daughter's mouth. Whatever would Daddy say to that?"

She placed her handbag onto the pine-top table in the centre of the kitchen. She ignored his latest cheap shot. "If only my father could see you for the person I know you really are, then he might not be so keen in trying to keep us together."

"I'm one hundred per cent with your dear daddy on this, as both he and you well know." He refilled his glass to an unhealthy level. "You sure you don't want any, darling?"

Celeste walked to the other side of the table to buy time for her to keep her composure. "Yeah. Just as we all know that you are trying to blame me for asking for a divorce and breaking up the marriage when it was you who was caught at work between the legs of your teenage PA."

"Old news, my little darling, old news. Everyone makes mistakes and I have apologised to all for my little error of judgement." He downed almost all of his glass of wine in one. "And for the record, she is twenty-two. Cheers!"

Celeste was genuinely baffled as to why he wanted to stay with her. Was there some sort of financial benefit to him or his father from avoiding Charles being the one to ask for a divorce? He wasn't staying with her for the sex, as he had given up on that, at least with her, after the tests revealed that Celeste was infertile. Was it just because it was an easy life allowing him to jump from one sexual conquest to another with impunity because of Celeste's job involving so much travel? Or was it just the grand house? Trying to make her appear as the one who was looking to break up the marriage and so Celeste to be the one moving out of the marital home. All she did know was that she could no longer stand the presence or even sight of her serial cheat of a husband.

He finished his drink and reached over the breadbasket to pick up his car keys. "Must dash, darling. Places to be. People to meet. You know what it's like." He walked the long way around the kitchen to offer, in passing, a sarcastic kiss to his wife. She easily avoided his lunge.

Celeste composed herself and followed her husband down the hallway to the front door, which he then opened. "Have you got everything, dear? Wallet, phone, condoms? Hope you get to enjoy pulling down the panties of the latest tight-assed blonde you are abusing."

He finished his drink and reached over the breadbasket to pick up a monogrammed leather pouch containing his car keys.

It was that very afternoon when Celeste finally convinced herself that she would formally file for divorce despite her father's reservations and regardless of any potential financial consequences that may befall her. It was her life, and this was the moment when she was going to take back control. Her only regret was that she hadn't made this decision years ago instead of hoping that he would somehow change into a man he was never likely to be. Celeste might be, in her own eyes, the wrong side of forty, but she knew that men were attracted to her and so there was no reason why this moment and this decision would herald in a lonely journey through to the end of her life. But there was one thing she knew for sure. It wouldn't be easy.

*

Celeste prided herself on being able to prepare and give concise presentations. Her review of the Granta Pain Therapeutics opportunity presented to the Myers-Stratton business development team was no different.

"If I can summarise. Granta Pain have compiled a convincing preclinical dataset which largely substantiates their claim of identifying a potent but non-addictive treatment for moderate to severe pain. Their proposed drug candidate is postulated to work through a proprietary mechanism of action on which the company is ready to file a series of patents. The drug candidate is a known drug that has been into Phase 2 proof of concept clinical studies for depression but was pulled by its UK manufacturer because of lack of efficacy in that indication. It's an old compound that Granta Pain has renamed GPT107 but its identity remains confidential to the company until CDAs are signed. The patents on this old drug contained no claims on being able to ameliorate pain and have now lapsed. A potential quick win, for us as we should be able to quickly get this into a Phase 2 trial for pain and get an efficacy read out without having to fund any discovery or preclinical development activities. Maybe a few fill-in toxicity studies at most depending on how well the drug has been profiled and how easy it will be for us to find that data." Celeste looked over to her audience and paused for the inevitable question from the COO and her boss, Nat

Stevens, a gnarled veteran of the pharmaceutical industry who almost seemed to revel in being a caricature of a silverback.

"So, Celeste. According to what you have just presented, the science checks out and, from what you have said, our guys in the discovery lab have already ticked off all their little boxes. There's a plausible rationale and reasonable confidence that there will be some defendable intellectual property, although I thought it a little bizarre that Granta Pain have yet to file any patents themselves, if I understood you correctly, Celeste. It looks like the headline costs for us to get to clinical proof of concept should not be too much of an issue, although detail is still lacking at this early juncture. Plenty of big questions and judgement calls still likely to come, of course, as is the nature of the beast. But what is this Jeavons fellow like? Is he someone we can work with or is he going to give us a hard time like has been the case with some of the Brits we have had to deal with in the past?" The COO smiled and looked around to the faces of the other members of the team. "Do you remember that Andrews guy? At least, I think that was his name. But I suppose that he did at least have a pair of balls on him." Most of the audience thought it prudent to appreciate the sharp wit of their boss by at least attempting a smile.

Celeste winced at the laughter and the memory of a great opportunity they had walked away from because of Myers-Stratton's rather conservative views. "Jeavons comes across as a very capable scientist and seems to thoroughly understand at least the subject matter of the asset he is trying to fund based on the written answers he provided to our questions. Maybe exactly as you might expect given his background. A biology first degree at Imperial College in London. A PhD with Kratinsky in Cambridge, which included some formative publications on the role of 5HT7 receptors in pain. A postdoc year in Stanford and back to Cambridge again before taking tenure as a research fellow in the Department of Pharmacology in Cambridge. It was only seven years later that he founded Granta Pain Therapeutics with some seed funding from the university and local business angels. So, I would say, a pretty impressive guy."

Nat held up his hand to pause Celeste's monologue. "He sounds great and the money he is asking for is not unreasonable given what they are trying to do, but, as I said, is he a Brit we can work with?"

Celeste couldn't stop herself thinking of that last night at the University Arms when she had so much wanted him to share her bed. "Well, he's half Italian if that helps," which received the laughs she had hoped for. "I was only with him for a handful of hours," she lied, "but he didn't come across as some sort of psycho. At least not to me."

Nat smiled. "OK. It sounds like we could do worse, but are there any issues we should be concerned about and what do we need to focus on when we get him over here to give his pitch?"

"Well, yes. As is almost always the case with these early start-ups, Jeavons may well be on top of the science, but he has only a very basic awareness of what is needed to take a drug through into the clinic. He will need some serious support, advice, hand-holding and probably also ego massaging. There is also the potential issue that the asset is just one compound. We will need to commit to finding extra funding if we want a back-up drug or two to reduce our risk." She ended her summary by broadcasting a smile across the boardroom.

Nat shuffled his copy of Celeste's presentation to signify the end of the meeting. "Good stuff, Celeste. We might have a live one here and we really do need some interesting and compelling options to present to the board before the end of the year."

Celeste jumped in as Nat was drawing breath. "And the beauty of this opportunity is that we should be able to arrive at a decision very quickly indeed and not with the usual six months plus we typically need to complete a deal. Granta Pain's only assets are the compound itself, GPT107, and their knowhow. I can't see there being much in any data room for us to review so I would hope that we could turn round our due diligence in weeks rather than months. Maybe target a term sheet in October if we want to go ahead?"

"All sounds very promising provided that our scientists are still happy after trawling through the raw data and yes, a potentially quick one to boot, so see what you can do and get him over here for us all to meet ASAP. Could I have a quick word, Celeste?"

Celeste waited until the chattering executives had filed out of the room to leave only Nat and herself. He walked over to where she was standing. "Too early to get overexcited but I've got a good feeling in my water about this one. As I said, get him over as soon as you can and maybe also push the boat out a bit socially speaking. You know the drill. I will work on some of the non-execs to find time to meet him. We need to move quickly in case there are some others sniffing around this. Well done, you!"

He laid his hand gently on hers and Celeste did her best not to pull it away too quickly and cause offence. She smiled weakly before slowly pulling her hand from under his. "Thanks, Nat. I will do my best." Celeste had had to put up with more than her fair share of lecherous men over the last few weeks.

*

Celeste was surprised that someone was phoning her on her early morning drive into work. She didn't recognise the number. "Hello. Celeste Simmonds speaking."

"Celeste! Great to hear you. It's Will. Will Jeavons from Granta Pain Therapeutics."

"Will. How nice to hear you. How can I help?"

"Just phoning about your email inviting me over to Boston to present our work. I guess I could have replied by email, but I just wanted to make sure that I thanked you in person - well, sort of in person - for your generous invitation. Very much looking forward to meeting you again and discussing the project with your team. Hadn't heard back from you after the conference so I had assumed that you weren't interested in what we've got here."

Celeste could not suppress a smile. "Business development moves in mysterious but very slow ways. Glad to hear that you can make it over here. Do those dates in early September I suggested work for you? We would like for you to spend a couple of days with us if possible so that we can squeeze as much out of you as we can," she half joked.

"Never been to Boston before so I might actually add an extra day to your itinerary. At my expense, of course."

"I think you might find our Cambridge a little bit different to yours. No dangerous little boats around here!"

"Very much looking forward to finding out, Celeste, and thanks once again for the invite. See you soon enough."

"Oh, one last thing before you go. Would you find it useful to bring any of your team over? Neville? Perhaps Grace?" She was hoping he would say no.

Which he essentially did, as Will thought that a contrarian Mancunian would have been unlikely to go down well in front of an American audience and Grace was far too young and inexperienced to be risked – rabbit in the headlights came to mind. Also, there was Will's ego to consider. It was his company. "Thanks for the offer but I don't think so, although I'll give it some thought. I should let you get on with your day. Bye, Celeste."

He hung up first. Celeste spent the remaining twenty minutes of her drive to work thinking of the ideal places to take her English business associate and maybe even friend. A lover? Not now. Not while she was still married to her husband and Myers-Stratton. But not never?

Celeste eased off the throttle after noticing she was driving rather too fast.

BACK IN THE LAB

There were not many days that Neville Chamberlain – a joke of very poor taste made by his father, which his son had to endure throughout his forty-five years and counting – did not wake up without having some issue with the world or, more specifically, the people who inhabited it. This morning was a little different. Worse, even, than just normal. At least, Nev's version of normal. The unfortunate vibe had been picked up earlier in the morning by his equally unfortunate wife, Li, who was busying herself with making tea in their kitchen-diner.

"What's the big problem this morning then, Nev?" asked Li, immediately regretting that she had once more opened Pandora's box but probably best to get it all out of the way early rather letting him come to the boil.

Nev returned his spoon to an empty cereal bowl and looked up as his wife sat down opposite him at the small, well-used table. He would have liked to have complained about the muesli he was 'forced' to eat every morning and the hordes of August bank holiday tourists he would soon have to battle his way through on his way to work, but there were more important things to discuss this morning that were also ruining his life.

"Not good news at work," began Nev.

"Any different than the usual not good news at work?" Li immediately regretted poking the bear.

"I always appreciate your unwavering support," he answered, disappointed that he could not think of a more cutting remark.

"Come on, Nev. Lighten up. You know that I'm always here to listen."

"Anyway." He paused before unleashing his diatribe. "The boss actually came into the lab yesterday and told us a few home truths, although there wasn't anything that he told us that we had not already assumed. Our funding is running out – no shit – and if we don't cut back our spending right now then Granta will be no more by early next year."

"Oh, Nev. Not another change of job. I really couldn't face upping sticks and moving again, especially with Anthony having his GCSE exams in a couple of years." She finished her tea and looked out blankly through the kitchen window and to the small back garden, which, as always, needed urgent attention.

Nev realised that he was maybe painting rather too dark a picture. "We shouldn't panic just yet, but it would at least be sensible to get myself back onto the job market. Won't be easy to find another job like this one at my age."

Li remained silent, caught up in her own thoughts and

memories of all the moves they had made over the last twenty years as Nev, or more typically his employer, found reason for him to leave a job. With her breakfast duties completed, she undid her apron and smoothed down her work uniform and slim figure. Li often wondered how she ended up with a balding curmudgeon with an addiction to real ale.

"Jeavons told us that he still has one iron in the fire, although he was a little concerned that he had not heard anything back from them. Some American company on the East Coast. I suggested he got off his arse and chased them up, but he seemed reluctant to do it. Can't understand the man. If it was my company, I would be full on chasing up all options. Too much up his own arse, if you ask me. Thinks he's better and more important than everyone else."

"Lots of arses, there, Nev. Should you really be talking to your boss like that?" asked Li, worried that Nev might have once again overstepped the mark with an employer.

"Just a manner of speaking, Li. I didn't really tell him to get off his arse. But I should have, for all our sakes. The man at least owes us that for all those extra hours we put in during Covid. No other fuckers in the department were in the labs when we were working our fingers to the bone. They were all at home watching Netflix. You would think that sort of loyalty is worth more than the meaningless handful of shares he deigned to throw our way after the pandemic."

Li could sense that her husband was building up a good head of steam and perhaps now would be a good time to end this morning's little chat. "I'd better get off to work, as I'll be late. Let's finish this up when we get back home tonight." *Please, Jesus, Mary, Joseph, God and the Holy Ghost, no*, Li whispered to herself.

Without waiting for a response or receiving even a tacit acknowledgement that she was leaving the house, Li stood up from the breakfast table, stuffed her house keys into an oversized blue handbag and walked towards the kitchen door leading out into the hallway. "Back at the usual time. See you then. Don't go slamming the front door when you leave, as Anthony is still in bed."

"And that's something else we need to talk about. That lazy git needs to…"

His last words drifted into the distance as Li rushed to exit stage left, gently close the front door behind her and venture forward to the normality, sanity and sanctuary that was her job as a dental receptionist.

*

The roads out of Cherry Hinton were mercifully almost traffic-free as Nev cycled on and off the various cycle paths that the local council had built at huge expense and maximum inconvenience to the few motorists who had the patience and temerity to take their cars into Cambridge. The almost pleasant ride under a warming August sun soon, however, came to an irritating halt when he reached the United Nations outpost that is Mill Road. Worse was still to come as he battled his way past even more irritated motorists getting across from Gonville Place to Lensfield Road. His mind was too busy plotting what to do when he arrived at work to allow him to engage in his favourite commuting pastime: 'accidently' bumping into expensive

German cars. He reached the narrow street haven that was Tennis Court Road not long after 9am and, at last, work.

And just who said that I would find commuting in Cambridge so much easier than my travel to work when I was living in London? he muttered to himself as he double-locked his bike in the alleged cycle enclosure and entered the university's Department of Pharmacology. Neville briefly considered tucking in his shirt before taking the stairs up to the lab but thought against it. He wasn't paid enough to dress smartly for work, even if that was possible for a man who could never find clothes that actually fitted.

As was typical, Nev was the last one to arrive in the lab and his three colleagues were already well into setting up that morning's experiments when he opened the heavy fire door to be greeted by the usual, tired odours.

"Morning, all. And another fine day begins at Granta Pain Therapeutics."

The self-appointed head of the laboratory's usual call to arms received its usual apathetic response of muffled acknowledgements of his arrival. "OK. Time for tea."

Grace turned round to protest without diverting all her attention from the job in hand. "But we've not long got in ourselves and need to get these assays up and running. Why a tea break now? Can't it wait?"

"Not really, Grace, I've got some important things I think we all need to talk about before the boss clocks on but OK, upstairs in the tearoom in twenty minutes. Everyone alright with that?" Nev turned towards his own workbench without bothering to elicit any feedback from the team. *Why didn't I bloody clean all this crap up before I left last night?* A rather common lament for Nev.

The tearoom at the top of the department was no more or less unpleasant than any other room in the building, although it did boast of allegedly the world's largest stainless-steel teapot – very unlikely, but to be proven otherwise. If tea was your bag, one was advised to have one's tea break earlier rather than later so as to avoid the steeped, hours-old washings of the seemingly hundreds of teabags that accumulated at the bottom of Alice's teapot. Alice was the sort of scary and rude member of staff that would only be considered acceptable in British academia. If only Nescafé were aware of how many people Alice had converted to drinking instant coffee.

Nev and Alice just did not get on – birds of a feather – and so it was with a mug of coffee rather than his preferred beverage with which he joined his colleagues at their usual table at the far corner of the departmental tearoom. Nev sat down with an air of resignation, or at least that was what he hoped it looked like he was doing.

"I walked past his office and the boss was not there, so we have a little time to talk."

"What's all this secrecy, Nev?" asked Grace. "Do we really all need to be up here to talk about whatever?"

"Just hold your horses there, Grace." Nev often found it difficult to handle or even understand his ambitious colleague. He also felt intimidated by her youthful beauty. "I'm just trying to help us all. Pass on some advice and come up with some options before they get taken away from us."

"As long as we don't have to listen to your slagging off Will again. The man is trying his best. At least, that's my opinion," finished Grace, looking over to the faces of her tearoom companions for support.

"Far from it, Grace. But we should be prepared to push back against him just getting rid of us one by one to keep the company alive. Believe me, I've been here before." Both Grace and Nirmala raised their eyes at hearing that line once again.

Nev almost considered standing up to try to reinforce his viewpoint. "No. Listen to me. Hear me out. Instead of us taking turns to walk out of that front door and never return, we should come up with some money-saving options to at least delay that scenario."

Even Grace was beginning to pay attention to Nev's reasoning but without yet showing any sign that she was convinced. "OK. Like what? Bearing in mind that Will has never given any inclination that there will be any redundancies anyway so why suggest to him ways of saving money other than those he has already mentioned? Doesn't make sense," finished Grace, looking over at her nodding colleagues.

"Believe me, we'll be the last to find out about any redundancies. Money-saving options? Well, we need time to work on that but, off the top of my head, how about at least taking a look at how much we are spending on consumables. There must be other suppliers we should consider other than Jeavons' mates. Cutting down on the number of assays we are running. I don't know... maybe even working a shorter week but surely anything is better than being made redundant. And don't forget, we would be getting jack shit as a redundancy pay off."

Just as Nev was sitting back in his chair, content that he had got his arguments across to the team and looking like the elder statesman he considered himself to be, they all saw Will rushing into the tearoom looking flustered. Maybe he should have taken more time in the bathroom and made a better selection of clothes from his wardrobe before leaving for work that morning. He walked quickly up to where his Granta Pain staff were sitting.

"I really shouldn't be disclosing this in front of everyone here but who gives a fuck." Two senior lecturers who had fallen out with Will several years ago looked up from the table they were sharing near the tearoom door. They appeared mildly interested in the unusual commotion. "Just talked to Myers-Stratton this morning after an email I got from them last night. It's on!" Will clenched and raised his right fist. "I have been asked to go over to Boston to discuss our project with them. Isn't that just fucking brilliant!"

Even Nev seemed genuinely pleased to hear the news.

"That's just wonderful, Will. You must have made a great impression on them. Well done, you." Grace was learning fast how to get on in business.

"Obviously we are a very long way from securing any funding, but it all has to start somewhere," added Will, in order to provide some perspective for his inexperienced team. "Something to celebrate, I would say, so the drinks are on me at the Panton Arms at about 12.30pm. We should always be mindful of celebrating our successes."

"Great news, boss," added Nev. "Will you be taking anyone over with you to Boston?"

MY FAMILY AND I

*P*erhaps I should introduce myself properly before we go any further, but where do I start? Maybe an easy one first. My name is Lydia Goldberg, but I was christened in Northampton with the name Lydia Mortimer. A heads-up: please don't call me Lyds or Lids or whatever. My name is Lydia. It's not often, but it's also not unusual, to get a funny look whenever I tell people I'm a Goldberg. After over twenty years as a Goldberg, I can see why Luke renounced his faith before we got married, although a Catholic wedding did not go down at all well with his parents, I can tell you!

My age? If that's important to you. Well, I won't see forty again and that's not me being modest, although many, if not most, people think I look younger. And I don't have a problem with that! Nor do I any longer have a problem – but it was really tough when I was 'growing' up – with being a little bit on the short side, which I like to label as petite. Much better than what my husband, Luke, calls me. Midget. Although he no longer does so in public after that particular word became yet another 'banned' one. Around our home, and always in our bed, I am his little midget. That was, of course, until he recently left me for another's bed. One owned by the NHS.

Fashion? I must admit that I have a passion for clothes, although Luke calls it a weakness – but he's just thinking about the money I 'waste' – and our daughter insists that the clothes I wear are 'not befitting a woman of my age'. In my book, if you've got it, then you should flaunt it, and I think I've still got it! There will be plenty enough time still to come to start dressing like the old woman I will soon become. And anyway, how would I ever reach the giddy height of five and a half foot without an impressive selection of high heels? Perhaps my attraction to the finer things in life is just a reaction to not being able to afford them when I was young.

My hates? Not many, I would say, but I do hate the arrogance of a bully, and I have no time for lying. In fact, I detest liars with a passion.

Right. What next. Family, I suppose, although I really should have written about that before babbling on about my appearance because, as I have already explained, there is nothing more important to me than my family. They are my world. Our daughter and our only child, Samantha, or Sam, was born in 2003. Just two years after Luke and I married. She hit us like a hurricane and that storm has never abated. That girl is a force of nature. It has never been a case of me and Luke having to push her and encourage her, but more a case of trying, but usually failing, to temper her expectations. So how proud were her parents when she won a place at Berkely to study her oh so complicated obsession, mathematics. I don't think I have ever cried so much. First at the news that she had been accepted at Berkely, then when we waved her off at the airport and for weeks and weeks after she had left us. Our little baby. Over five thousand miles away.

Now to the only man in our little family. It was while I was at university that I met Luke. Not that he was a student. Luke was a 'townie'. Unlike his student contemporaries, Luke had the nerve and the corny lines to chat me up at the end of my first year at university at a Town and Gown disco in Hatfield. It was only as our relationship grew that I learnt his funny, cheeky-chappie chat-up lines were all bravado. Him trying to look the big man in front of his friends. We were each as bad as the other when he finally got into my knickers. All legs, arms, pleases, sorrys, do you like thats, which way round do you put on the condom, etc., etc. How nice it was to learn these things together and we did get better as the months went by and I have never looked at another boy or man since and, if he knows what's good for him, he had better have behaved himself as well.

If only my Luke could be with me right now. Stopping me ruining the pasta-bake dinner I will be eating alone tonight through crying all over the sauce. If only I could look forward to falling asleep lying next to him this very night, waking up with me in his arms tomorrow morning. My poor, poor Luke. I will make it all better. I will make it all go away. I promise, my darling. Just you see.

So, I hope you get the vibe that life was once good for our little family. If there was anything worth worrying about then we were certainly not aware of it. That was right up until when Dr William Jeavons came into our lives. That was when things changed for us. That was when our lives would never be the same again.

AMERICA, HERE I COME

Will never looked forward to flying and this was especially so for long-haul flights. He actually used to be scared to board a flight, although it was now really just a case of it being an annoying chore in trying to avoid picking up any respiratory diseases. But this was different. Business class. *Now this is what I call flying*, thought Will, opening the bag full of goodies he found on his seat. *And I can even stretch my legs. My God, I won't even need to touch elbows with a stranger.*

The opportunity to experience this sort of luxury was one of the drivers for him escaping the penury of academia. The chance to have the life he saw those in industry enjoying. The pharma and biotech movers and shakers. The people he saw attract little crowds of groupies at conferences. These were not the scientists, or at least they weren't anymore. These were the C-suite executives. Almost always society's bêtes noires; middle-aged white men. This is where the proper money hung out. The houses. Socialising at country clubs. The kudos ánd respect. The power. Will was, at the very least, a highly capable and consistently innovative scientist but he wanted more than that. Much more. A place in first class would have been a good start.

To start on this journey to money and fame and get anywhere near such lofty aspirations, Will would need to make a big success with Granta Pharma. A *big* success! That would not only raise the possibility of him being parachuted into a senior role in Big Pharma after his company had been acquired but, at the very least, would firmly put him on the radar of those with influence that he was a young, up-and-coming successful entrepreneur with a promising future.

To have any chance of selling Granta Pharma, the pain project they were working on would almost certainly have to show convincing data, ideally including demonstration of a lack of abuse potential. Just to be able to start clinical trials, Granta Pharma needed significant extra funding. To get funding, he needed Myers-Stratton to open their wallet and soon, since not only was Will's company fast running out of money but also there was no one else interested in their project, at least as far as he was aware. Will knew that he would have to make the best pitch of his life over the next few days to get anywhere near their money. *Easy*, thought Will. *Piss easy.* But he was not even fooling himself.

He decided to hasten away the last few hours of his flight to Boston by falling asleep listening to the 'Classic '90s' playlist he had collated on his phone before being cruelly woken from a bedroom scene involving Celeste in a ridiculously spacious Boston penthouse suite overlooking the harbour.

"We will be landing in ten minutes, sir," was the wake-up call from the smiling, formidably manicured member of the cabin staff who brought Will to full consciousness.

The tender touch of her long fingers on the back of his hand reminded him of one of his unfulfilled fantasies. *Aeroplane cabin crew. I really must do something about that one day. But perhaps not today, my boy. Priorities.*

His next priority was to dig out from his handsome but well-worn briefcase a paper version of the itinerary of his visit that Celeste had composed. The plan was unburdened by detail, with less than a handful of events with only approximate timings.

Tuesday 13th September

4.30pm	Limo shuttle pick up at Logan Airport
5pm	Arrival at InterContinental Hotel
7pm	Limo shuttle pick up at hotel for dinner at Sorellina

Wednesday 14th September

8am	Limo shuttle to Myers-Stratton main office block
8.30am	Meet with host Celeste Simmonds
9.30am–4pm	Meetings with scientists and management team to include presentation of Granta Pain Therapeutics research
4.30pm	Limo shuttle return to hotel
7pm	Dinner (Venue TBD) with Celeste Simmonds and senior executives

Thursday was left blank for Will himself to complete, as he was staying on in Boston until his flight home later that evening to do some sightseeing at his own expense. *Not a great deal of detail*, mused Will, turning the piece of paper over to see the blank page he was expecting to see. He suspected the lack of detail for what was to happen on Wednesday was to allow for flexibility in seeing, hopefully, the principal decision makers at the company. Dinner that Tuesday night with Celeste was something he was looking forward to, but he vowed to himself that, for the sake of his company, he would not be anything other than one hundred per cent professional. *Unless she comes onto me strong, of course*, was Will's somewhat predictable and wholly unprofessional caveat.

What was perplexing Will, as he once again braced himself for the catastrophic landing he had still to experience, was why it was Grace who helped him create his vitally important presentation slide deck rather than his usual confidante, Nev. *Definitely something a bit different about Nev of late. A bit on edge, perhaps*, considered Will whilst tightly gripping onto his armrests as the plane landed without any obvious injuries to passengers or crew. Maybe his reluctance to volunteer to help Will was something to do with a perceived sleight arising from him not being invited to Boston to support his boss. Will was not the sort of manager to go digging into the grievances of a disgruntled employee unless he had to and, in this case, there was no need to as Grace almost literally jumped at the chance to help prepare the slide deck. *And what a good job she made*, thought Will as the captain of the aeroplane apologised for a delay at the gate. Will's slide deck had never been so organised, concise and professional-looking. Grace had completely revamped the design such that it no longer came across as the ramblings of an easily distracted academic. Perhaps Celeste had really seen something in Grace that Will himself had not picked up on other than she was another woman. But Nev? *Maybe I need to keep an eye on the old man.*

Will decided to overlook the brusqueness of his welcome to the good old US of A he experienced going through passport control and instead looked forward to enjoying transport on four wheels rather than the two he had become so used to back in Cambridge. He guessed Mexican when Will first saw in arrivals the uniformed holder of a laminated A4 sheet of white paper bearing both his and his company's name. After some perfunctory words of welcome, the rather squat and powerful-looking chauffeur sporting a magnificent moustache guided his passenger to be to the Myers-Stratton company limo. It was a mode of transport that was all Will had hoped for. Unashamed door-to-door ostentatious décor showcasing more technology than would ever likely be used by its many lucky passengers. It even boasted of a range of free drinks for its thirsty passengers. *This is what I need*, thought Will as the limo escaped from the airport underpass to allow him to take in the sights of downtown Boston.

What a room! I mean, what a room! Will quickly parked his suitcase near the closed door to his hotel room. Spacious? *Well, what do you expect from an American hotel room?* Luxurious? *I should co-co.* View? *Never mind. But who needs a view when you've got all this?* The large window afforded only a partial view of the harbour he was hoping to see. However, the pièce de résistance, and what he just *had* to take a photo of, was the large window above the headboard of the bed which could be opened out onto a large bath and the bathroom beyond. *What can one say!*

After unpacking, Will spent the next few hours stretching out on the bed, going over the presentation he was to give the next day whilst neither hearing nor seeing whatever was on the random US TV channel he had turned on. A quick shower to freshen up before going out to dinner with the delectable Ms Simmonds but only after doing something he certainly wasn't looking forward to. Wearing new clothes and shoes for the very first time. After his poor fashion showing at the dinner in Cambridge with Celeste the month previous, Will decided that he needed to start dressing at least something like the professional he imagined himself to be. Even he knew that he couldn't just wheel out the ancient suit he bought when he first arrived in Cambridge. That conservative outfit was maybe good enough for formal dinners in college but not for such an important meeting as this. So it was with a heavy heart that he devoted one whole afternoon in Cambridge to searching for and, in his mind, gratuitously overpaying for his new 'international executive man's' wardrobe. So very different to the rest of the clothes that could be found in the rather small built-in wardrobe back at his apartment. His biggest shock and the resulting moral outrage were caused by the best part of £100 he ended up paying for shoes. *Just one pair of shoes, mind.* If only he wasn't such a soft touch, so easily allowing himself to be coerced by those two ever-so-nice young ladies at M&S who convinced him of how good he looked in their shoes. "Women will be the death of me," he muttered as he struggled, for the third time, to attach his tie to any degree of satisfaction.

The limo ride to the Sorellina restaurant was mercifully quick after all the travelling he had done. On another day he would have preferred the walk. During the short drive, he found out that his 'beginning to be more friendly' limo driver for his stay in Boston was Jesus and that he could be contacted through the numbers on the Myers-Stratton business card he gave to Will, should he need to be taken anywhere in the city. Will also learnt that his driver's employer does not own a private company jet. "How sad, never mind, what a shame," murmured Will.

Will was expecting Celeste to meet him at the reception desk and so was temporarily struggling for words when he was questioned by the person on front-of-house duties.

"I'm sorry, sir. Could you please say that again? Do you have a reservation for this evening?"

"Oh, sorry," spluttered Will. "Ah there," he pointed out to a table at the far side of the restaurant where Celeste was sitting. "I am a guest of Celeste Simmonds of Myers-Stratton. My name is Dr Will Jeavons, if that is any help to you." Will always liked using his title whenever he was faced with anyone who he suspected had even the merest hint of pretension.

Will's adversary thought it necessary to double-check the booking before briskly walking his English guest over to the table that had been reserved.

"So nice to see you again," was the first thing a smiling Celeste said as she stood up from her table to shake Will's hand. "Welcome to Boston."

"Great to be here in your city and better still to see you again," smarmed Will, taking his seat opposite the host.

"I hope you don't mind me getting here early but I have an important family occasion I need to get back home for later this evening and so I'm afraid that I will have to be on my way by about 9pm." This was, for the most part, a lie. Celeste needed to be back home by 9pm but not for a family occasion. She wanted to get back early to try to catch her husband in bed with his latest mistress, the last nail in the coffin of their marriage and final proof to both fathers that Charles would never change his unfaithful ways. Charles would never make any sort of spy and Celeste could always spot when he was lying or up to something. Or both. From the strange comments and suspicious looks she had picked up earlier in the day, she concluded he was up to something and probably trying to take full advantage of her being out for the evening. As much as she had been looking forward to having dinner with Will, tonight was all about divorcing her husband. Getting the proof that was needed to make divorce inevitable and unavoidable even to her own father. Will can wait. He will just have to.

"Really. You should have said, Celeste. I could easily have found somewhere for dinner myself."

"Nonsense! We couldn't ignore you and leave you on your own after having travelled so far to see us. I'm just so sorry that I will have to leave earlier than I would have liked to. Anyway, the big dinner will be tomorrow when we will be joined by Nat and a few of the company's senior executives," Celeste hoped. "That is, providing said senior executives eventually agree on where to go! I should have said, Nat Stevens is my boss and the company COO."

Will was encouraged that at least one C-level executive thought Granta Pain's research worthy of devoting some of their free time to. "Fine with me and thanks for your hospitality both tonight and tomorrow. I'm sure you would rather be somewhere else to spend your free time. I guess we had better get started on making the most of the time we have tonight," added Will, picking up one of the menus that the waiter had obsequiously placed on their table.

"I picked out my favourite Italian restaurant in honour of your heritage, Giancarlo Jeavons."

Will smiled in reply but chose not to tell her of why he had done his best to forget any connections he may have with his father's country. Maybe a story for another day. Will Giancarlo Jeavons is, and will always be, one hundred per cent English regardless of his middle name.

The dinner and the company were pleasant enough. but, at least to Will, Celeste seemed distracted. Not the engaged person he had met only one month earlier when conversation between them was so natural. Not the same person he was no more than a few words away from staying the night with. Frankly, she was hard work. *Could it be that something has happened very recently at the company that means I am wasting my time being in Boston?* he thought as Celeste rushed to finish the last of their surprisingly pleasant bottle of Soave.

"I'm so sorry, Will," announced Celeste within seconds of Will taking his final mouthful of a halibut dish he had been so looking forward to but had slightly disappointed. "I really must go. I had planned to drive you back to the hotel but I'm afraid you will have to chase up Jesus to take you back. You do have his contact details, don't you?"

asked Celeste, seemingly not really all that interested in what Will's reply might be. "Alternatively, just order a cab at the front desk. Really sorry about this. Make sure you claim the money back off us if you take a cab. Very much looking forward to catching up on your research. See you first thing tomorrow morning. Goodnight, Will." She paused, standing by the table looking down on her dinner guest. "And, Will. I will make this up to you. I promise."

Will rose from his chair, saying goodbye to Celeste's back as she picked up her plain white clutch bag and made her way out of the restaurant, stopping at reception to pay the bill and retrieve her jacket. *Was that all a bit strange or is it me?* pondered Will. *At least there was some real emotion in those last words. More than the whole night put together.* Will just couldn't work out what was going on with her. With them. Perhaps there really wasn't a them. *So now what? It's not even 9pm and I need to keep awake for a few hours to help change my clock. I know! I'll phone my good friend Jesus.*

And it was his new off-duty best friend, who was actually Portuguese, who not only picked him up in his limo but also joined Will for a quiet nightcap at the InterContinental after a very long day for the Englishman with likely an even longer and more stressful day still to come.

*

Celeste had left her car on the roadside outside the marital home and walked the several hundred yards leading up to the front door on the grass verge to avoid noisily crunching up the gravel driveway. She stole around to the back of the house to find a door that was unlocked so as not to risk alerting Charles and his unlikely muse by using any noisy keys to get in. Her finding an open door, lights on in the house and his car in the garage amounted to robust evidence that Charles was somewhere in the house. The big question was whether or not he was alone. A bedroom would be the obvious place to look first but which one in a house where there were ten? Would he really want to insult his wife so much by choosing to use the marital bed for his affairs when there were so many other bedrooms he could have opted for? Celeste thought so, because it was such a sumptuous room, and so it was to their bedroom that she was carefully making her way towards when she heard a voice just as she neared the top of the stairs.

"Celeste!" called Charles from the foot of the stairs. "What are you doing back home now? I thought you were out for dinner."

She turned round, catching her breath deep down in her throat. Celeste struggled to think of a reply. "I had a headache and so came back early. I was just going up to bed and get an early night." She had regathered her composure. "If that's OK with you, of course," she added with more than a little edge.

"Why wouldn't it be?" Charles recognised the tone of his wife's voice. "Look, Celeste, we need to talk. I'll come up with you to our bedroom and we can chat awhile."

Celeste suspected he was trying to hide something. Hide his mistress. Head her off from one of the bedrooms, but which one had they been using if not the marital one in this latest blatant example of infidelity?

"OK, where is she?"

"Where is who?" replied Charles, holding out his arms and shrugging his shoulders to accentuate innocent confusion as he slowly made his way up the grand, feature staircase.

"Don't mess me around. Don't waste any more of my time. You know damn well who."

"Whoa. More swear words."

"And don't fucking try to patronise me, Charles. Not tonight."

"Sorry, sorry. Stupid comment. But there is no one here. I promise you." He moved his hand to cover his heart.

"Since when have your promises meant anything to anybody? Lying comes so very easy to you. It's one of your few gifts. We both know that I won't be able to wipe that permanent smile off your face as you could easily hide your whole damn harem in this place without me ever finding as much as a pair of crotchless panties."

"Look. I deserve it all," was the reply that Celeste was least expecting. "I've been selfish for far too long. Had a long chat and a fair bit to drink with your father and mine last night with lots of home truths made very clear. Home truths that I am the only one at fault here. Home truths that if I don't get my act together, you will leave me." Celeste picked up a scarcely believable sincerity in the way he spoke, how he emphasised certain words, and from the morose look he had on his face. Could this all be genuine? "You and I have spent a lot of time, a lot of sweat and a lot of money getting to where we are now. Altogether, a big chunk of our lives. We have a fabulous lifestyle most people can only dream of. No money worries now nor ever. I, for one, don't want to give up what we have now and what we will have in the future and that's what I told your father. And mine. I don't want to give up on you, Celeste. On us."

Celeste was struggling to know what to say. She wanted to believe that her unfaithful husband was sincere, but could she trust the man who had let her down so many times before?

Charles filled in the silence. "Will you give me one last chance? A chance to make it up to you. To be the husband you deserve. To enjoy the future we always thought we would be enjoying. To be that loving couple we once were."

Celeste wondered whether he had been copying lines out of wedding cards. Is this the man who has treated her so badly over the last two years, almost living like a sex-obsessed single man?

"I'm struggling to take this all in. I'm sorry. I just can't trust you anymore." They were both standing on the landing at the top of the stairs and outside the marital bedroom. She couldn't gather the nerve to look him in the face.

"And I don't blame you, Celeste. Like I said, I don't deserve any more from you. You have every justification for walking out of this house right now, ending our marriage right now. That is, unless you give me one last chance. A chance for me to rebuild that trust. It won't be easy for either of us. It certainly won't be quick, but will you grant me just that one more chance? And if I don't change? If that trust never returns? Then is the time you leave me."

When Celeste woke early the next morning, she turned round to face her sleeping husband. The first time that they had shared a bed for more months than she could remember. His soft face. His almost-perfect body. The dimple in his chin. His downy chest. How he had made passionate and unrelenting love to her throughout the night, just as he used to in those early years. She remembered how she knew he was the one when they met all those years ago. How her heart leapt whenever he walked into the same room. This was the man she had fallen in love with and had married. Not the man whose personality had changed so much when they found out after years of trying that they could not have children of their own. But was she really so gullible as to fall for his latest presumed trick and a likely angle he or his father had found to screw even more out of her? Perhaps she was. She certainly wouldn't have been if Charles had not been the first one to find Naomi's deodorant in the en-suite bathroom of a bedroom at the far end of the third floor the very next morning.

*

His big day started much as how Will had predicted. Awake not long after 5am and unable to get back to sleep because of the jet lag. The nightcap Will had enjoyed the previous evening did nothing to help his adjustment to the new time zone, although he did get some interesting and rather indiscrete low-level background on the Myers-Stratton senior executives who Jesus often chauffeured around Boston. Those who didn't ignore their lowly driver completely were apparently, at best, deeply boring. Marginal benefits from the far too early morning rise included another chance to go through his presentation and a more leisurely breakfast than Will had anticipated, although it brought a reminder of how it was impossible to find good bacon on American breakfast tables. Back in his hotel room, he was updated almost every ten minutes on the local TV news channel that it was once again going to be an unusually hot day for September in downtown Boston. Will wondered how many times it took for the unusual to become usual. Not that he needed to be bothered by the 30C-plus temperatures as he was transported from one air-conditioned hub to another.

The day itself was, to Will, a contrasting mixture of the expected and unexpected. The expected included the imposing company reception area, vast office spaces (*do all managers need their own drinks cabinet?*) and pristine labs, which showcased scientists wearing lab coats that were matching and spotlessly clean. What did surprise Will, and what he hadn't expected to find, was how sharp and knowledgeable the scientists he met were, having previously laboured under the somewhat patronising belief that all the top scientists worked in Big Pharma or Academia. There were some very incisive questions they posed after his presentation, several of which Will didn't have an answer for. *Maybe I should have brought Nev along with me after all. Grace?*

"That's a really good question," would be Will's opening gambit to buy him some time to think of a worthy response. An often-used trick by many. But he prided himself in not being like many in that he was not a bullshitter. If he didn't know the answer, he would always be truthful. "I'm afraid I can't answer that one off the top of my head, but I will make sure we come back to you after I have spoken with the team, even if it is with the answer that we still don't know!"

More a realisation than a surprise, but it was made painfully clear to Will that Granta Pain lacked the capability and experience, never mind the means, to take a drug candidate into clinical development and pass muster with the regulatory authorities, even with a drug that had already been tested in humans. Granta Pain would either have to pay for such support or it would have to be directly provided by Myers-Stratton. *Food for thought,* considered Will as, if by example, he failed to provide an answer to the very basic question as to whether there were any potential issues with drug product stability. Will had learnt a great deal about drug development and the industry he was working in from that day he spent at Myers-Stratton as well as being made to appreciate just how much more there was to learn.

Whilst in the shower back at the InterContinental, Will was trying to sum up his overall thoughts of the day so far. *An eye-opener for me. A good learning experience as to what I should expect in future such meetings. I think I came across well. Although I would say that, wouldn't I! There will always be gaps in knowledge and unanswered questions. That's research for you. The biggest problem? Coming over very amateurish on our plans for clinical development. But what do you expect when you are backed by a bunch of tight-arsed shysters who pretend they are venture capitalists?*

Will didn't have enough experience to know whether to be encouraged or disappointed as to the turnout of

Myers-Stratton's 'senior' executives at dinner that night. The predictable over representation of white middle-aged men went some way to explain why a carnivore-loving French eatery had eventually been chosen. The rather bizarre and grandiose titles of some of his dinner guests suggested that his companions for the evening were really not very senior at all. Will at least took some comfort from Nat making the effort. The only C-level executive present that evening. Will was a self-confessed schmoozer and one skilled in the art of making engaging dinner conversation after all his years as a University of Cambridge academic and far too many top-table dinners. This was his gig. He went to work making sure Nat was the centre of most of the conversations, which the COO was only too happy to be. Nat thought Will was his sort of tie-wearing, old-school scientist. None of the lazy business-casual look most of his Myers-Stratton colleagues were allowed to get away with. If only he knew.

Result! I think that went rather well. Will smiled to himself as he took care to shake hands and make some private and bespoke conversation in turn with each of the middle-aged white men as they left in their separate taxis lined up in a neat row outside the restaurant. There was just Celeste remaining to wish goodnight to.

"I really do owe you some time and attention after you were so kind to take me out punting. What a lovely and memorable day that was. But I'm afraid we have another company visiting us tomorrow," she lied, "and so I just haven't got the time. To try to make it up to you, I have asked our driver to take you wherever you want tomorrow at our expense, and I have asked one of the PAs to send you a list of some places around Boston you might want to visit. I'm sure Jesus will have his own opinion as well."

"Of course, I understand, Celeste," Will replied, wondering if this was a muted signal that her company were unlikely to be following up with any offers to fund Granta Pain and that she no longer had any interest in him personally. She seemed even cooler to him than was the case at dinner the previous night. *Just what is going on? Is it something I have said or not said?* "I'm very grateful that you gave me the opportunity to present our research to Myers-Stratton. Hard work, but a couple of enjoyable days and great for me to be able to meet the team. You certainly have some smart cookies in your discovery team." Will thought about an embrace but instead went with a handshake.

"And thank you, Will, for coming out to see us. I know from my own experience how exhausting it all can be." She paused. "Moving forward. I will, of course, circle back with the team to get some views on what you are doing at Granta Pain, and I would hope to get back to you with our thoughts by the end of the month, although I can't promise that. Is that OK with you?" she finished, knowing full well that he would be very unlikely to argue otherwise.

Will was aching to get some read from Celeste as to how the meetings went, but he knew she was far too professional to give anything away. "Of course. Absolutely fine with me. I will get those answers to the points your guys brought up over to you early next week and please get back to me if there is anything else we can help you with."

"Goodbye, Will, safe journey home," were the last few words she spoke as Jesus opened the car door for Will.

Will peered into her eyes to see if he could see anything. Even the merest flicker of emotion. There was nothing. He gave a weak wave to Celeste as he climbed into the limo. Will waited for his driver to settle himself into his seat before suggesting what to do with the rest of the Boston night. "Right, my good friend. How about a proper drink? Your city. I'm open to wherever you think is the place to drink around here."

"I thought you would never ask." Jesus smiled back towards his passenger as he fastened his seatbelt and engaged drive.

STRATEGY

Will spent the whole weekend following his trip to Boston trudging around his apartment half-dressed, surrounded by feelings oscillating between disappointment and resignation. It was perhaps the inevitable and unavoidable uncertainty that was uppermost in his mind. Will they, won't they? A decision he had little influence over now that he had presented Granta Pain's research and answered the majority of their questions. Will hated not being in control and this was something that he had very little, if any, control over. *But I'd better get used to it, as they are not likely to come back with their decision anytime soon. Definitely not until the end of the month, according to Celeste. Unless that decision is no. Fuck!*

He was also unnerved as to how Celeste behaved on a personal level when they had spent time together. It was as if they had never met before. That those late nights back in her hotel had never happened. He thought he was a good 'reader' of women, but he had to admit that he found Celeste an unfathomable conundrum. Maybe it would be best that he should now forget what had happened between them in Cambridge and instead be professional and focus on their business relationship. Getting funding for his company was all that really mattered and was why he had met Celeste in the first place. But that didn't mean that Will could stop completely at least thinking of her as a potential lover. He just wasn't made any other way. *What the fuck happened? Has something changed in her personal life?*

Will only once left his apartment on that weekend. He bravely ventured outdoors late on Saturday morning to buy a carrier bag full of unhealthy but life-sustaining ready meals, several bottles of coke to keep him awake when he should be awake and ibuprofen to hive off the edge off a fierce headache he had been suffering from ever since he got off the train at Cambridge station on Friday afternoon. A fully justified headache after a delayed flight and the cancellation of two successive trains because *those bolshie train drivers could simply not be arsed to turn up to work.* Now was the moment for him to be professional. Focus on how to respond to and what plan to put in place following his meeting with Myers-Stratton and not how to react to Celeste's apparent indifference to him. What to reveal to the board and staff and what to keep to himself.

As his headache faded and the feel-good benefit of a chicken jalfrezi with egg fried rice had kicked in, Will could feel at least the notion of a strategy forming in his mind if not yet on paper. Drill down to addressing the main issues that were raised by Myers-Stratton and slow down Granta Pain burn by finding cost savings. The former should hopefully make Granta Pain Therapeutics a more attractive proposition to Myers-Stratton and the latter should buy time and help keep the company solvent, at least through until end of the first quarter of the following year. Stretching out the timeline for the company to remain as a going concern would provide insurance to cover Myers-Stratton walking away and the chance, no matter how unlikely, that another suitor would appear. *Now try and tell the staff all that without completely freaking them out.*

∗

"Thanks for getting up here at such short notice. I hope I have not completely messed up your schedules for today, but I thought you would all appreciate a debrief on what happened in Boston last week." For some reason, Will felt a little distracted and on edge. "Antonio. Do you mind moving that box of crap over to underneath the window. Thanks. I thought this so-called meeting room was supposed to have been cleaned up. Sure!"

Will rattled through his brief slide deck without any questions being posed by his employees. *Is no one interested in this? Surely that can't be the case. These are clever people, and what is happening right now might well define their future careers.*

"Take-home messages? I am quietly confident we will get a term sheet from Myers-Stratton," he lied. "Maybe by the end of the month. We'll see. But we should be ready for all possible scenarios, as I highlighted in my presentation deck. Firstly, how can we make ourselves as attractive as possible to Myers-Stratton? What can we do to address the key issues I picked up in Boston?" Will looked around the table and remembered, with the exception of Nev, just how young and inexperienced his team were. *Maybe I am just expecting too much from them.*

Nev held up his hand.

"Yes, Nev." *Finally*, thought Will. *A smidgen of interest from someone I really should expect to get more from.*

"Given that you came back on Friday, and it is now only Monday morning, I'm guessing all this has not yet been put in front of the board."

"Good question, Nev." Will was busy trying to concoct an answer to a question he really should have anticipated. "If I may be blunt. Clearly not. These are just some ideas I fleshed out over the weekend, and I wanted to get your inputs early before requesting an extraordinary board meeting." *What a brilliant answer, Will! Well done, you. Ticks all the boxes.*

"Consequently, the jobs I am going to dish out now are just a heads-up and not anything you should start working on until I have got approval or otherwise from the board. Everyone clear on that?" No one said anything to suggest otherwise. "Good, OK.

"The jobs. Grace. Can you chase up Liz Hughes in the patent office to see if we can book some time to discuss filing at least one patent? Probably two to include covering the mechanism of action. I don't think we should wait any longer to get this rolling based on the feedback I had from Myers-Stratton. Nev. Can you go up and see your friends at Biopharmaco? We need to find out what holes there are in the safety pharmacology and tox package we have already got on our drug, GPT107. What other tests do we need to carry out on the compound to make sure we have profiled it sufficiently, at least in the eyes of Myers-Stratton? You OK with that, Nev?"

"A bit on the edge of my comfort zone, boss, but I will give it a try."

"Thanks, Nev. Appreciated. I think it will be useful to get Ron's opinion at Biopharmaco as he has been really helpful to us in the past. Now, one for all of you. Get those research reports looking professional as they are likely to be needed for a data room for due diligence purposes. Now, moving onto some money-saving efforts to help fund the extra studies at Biopharmaco. Nirmala and Antonio. Can you share between you looking into other suppliers for the key reagents and consumables? I'm sure we can find some useful cost savings." Far too early for Will to talk about staff working from home and winding down bench work to cut consumable costs, never mind potential redundancies, not least because of first needing approval from the board and also because the team would definitely be spooked.

Will wanted to bring the meeting to a close and avoid any tricky questions about any potential redundancies. He was relieved, but also a little surprised, that Nev had not asked his usual probing questions, which could easily have undermined Will's tentative plans.

Finish on a positive, Will. Try to stir up a bit of motivation.

"Important times for our little company. I am hopeful that there will be a transformative deal with Myers-

Stratton, but let's do our very best to make sure we leave no stones unturned in further profiling and protecting our key asset. Onwards and upwards!"

That meeting seemed all a little bit flat, thought Will as he made his way back to the office. *My fault, I guess. Must hide my moods a little better.*

*

Not for the first time, Nev was disobeying one of the house rules. Rule three, subsection two – no mobile phones to be used at the breakfast table. He glanced up momentarily from his banned item to take in Li standing over the dinner table staring at the miscreant.

"Yeah, OK, OK. But I've just got an email back from Ron at Biopharmaco about my job query, but, hey, if you don't want to know what he said then I can just crack on with this disgusting muesli," finished Nev, putting his phone down in the centre of the table.

"You really are an annoying little man, Neville Chamberlain," replied his wife partly in jest, taking the seat opposite him. "Spit it out, old man. Judging by the fact that you are not scowling then you might have some good news to tell me for a change."

Nev regathered his phone and scrolled down to the email in question and read it out loud in a good impersonation of Ron's Edinburgh burr. "Great to hear from you after so long, Nev, hope you are keeping well. If you are interested in working here then good timing, my old friend! We are just about to go live with a recruitment campaign to help staff an expansion of our pharmacology department. Why don't you pop in for an informal chat if you are interested in following up on this? Regards, blah, blah."

"Very good, Nev." Li smiled. "About time we had some good news. But isn't this just a back-up? Do you really want to leave Granta Pain?"

"The way I'm feeling at the moment? Yes. Have never trusted Jeavons and I very much doubt he will show me any loyalty if Myers-Stratton buy us and look to cut headcount. Which they will. I've seen all this sort of thing before…" He paused. "No need for you to nod your head so vigorously, Li. You're no better than those at work. And if Myers don't buy us then we are fucked anyway. If Biopharmaco do offer me anything half decent, then I will bite their fucking hands off. But not until I see if it's worth hanging on for a redundancy payment from an oh-so-sorry Myers-Stratton." Nev finished his little tirade with a smug, self-satisfied little smile. He was going to be the winner for a change.

Li rose from the table carrying her empty mug to the sink to clean later and when she had the energy. She replied over her shoulder. "Just be careful, Nev. You might think that you are the one calling the shots but little nobodies like us never get to call the tune. Like you said, Nev, you've seen all this sort of thing before so you of all people should know how all this could end. Us in the shit. Not them."

Nev pushed back his chair and harumphed theatrically. "I guess we'll just have to see. Won't we? I'm going to work." Which he did soon enough, although leaving the house even later than normal.

His later-than-usual arrival at work merely demonstrated, at least in Nev's mind, who was really in control of the situation.

"Nev!" called Grace as he put on one sleeve of his lab coat. "Will dropped by earlier this morning asking where you were," she said, with no little glee in Nev being caught out arriving late. "He asked if you would go up and see him whenever you got in," added Grace, determined to milk the situation as much as she could.

Nev did his best to feign indifference at the requested audience with the boss, but he was fooling no one.

Will turned round to see the source of the heavy clumping footsteps approaching his tiny, deliberately cluttered office.

"Nev. Take a seat. Any seat." A too-often-used in-joke. There was only one seat. "Late in this morning, Nev. Everything OK at home?" Will's rather clumsy opening gambit on trying to find out if Nev had any 'issues' he wanted to talk about. *Sometimes even I can see a reason for HR or whatever they call themselves these days.*

Nev was taken aback by the question. Not the sort of thing he thought Will would have any interest in. "No. At least I don't know of one. No. Why do you ask?"

Fair question, thought Will. "I don't know. No big deal. You just don't seem to be your usual self these days. But as I said, no big deal," answered Will, trying to scramble down from his opening lines and regretting why he had raised the subject in the first place. "Anyway," inserted Will in an attempt to avoid any further awkwardness, "what I really wanted to discuss is what we do with Biopharmaco."

Nev straightened up in his chair, fearing, somehow, that Will knew about him applying for a job. "Oh. You mean the toxicity studies. Right. Got you. Right. What were you thinking of?"

There really is something different about the man.

"Just some guidelines for your chat with them. Priorities? Share with them what we already have on GPT107 and ask them what holes we need to fill. What new assays have appeared over the last twenty-odd years or so since the drug was first profiled that we should be considering. As usual. Costs and timeline approximations. On top of that, their thoughts on manufacturing a drug product that is likely to be the rate-limiting step. Bottom line. We need a fully costed plan to get over to Myers-Stratton PDQ. Something to impress them, Nev. In the meantime, I will go back again to those hard cases who originally made GPT107 or whatever they labelled it as. See if the scent of some potential incoming funding will help open their mouths and databases to see if we can winkle out any data on the compound that is not in the public domain and save us some money. Should also help you in your discussions with Biopharmaco."

"As I said at yesterday's meeting, boss, not my sweet spot but I trust the people at Biopharmaco not to pull our trousers down on this one."

"Brilliant, Nev. One last thing before you get back to the lab. This is your top priority. Don't hang about and don't fuck it up!"

"Yes, boss." What else could he say?

*

Will always considered board meetings a definitive example of how to stretch what should be a short and informative meeting into the exact opposite. What added to his dismay was the deeply annoying shortcoming that he had to hire and pay for a room in Cambridge as well as paying for catering and travel expenses of board members out of company funds. *They go on and on to me about me saving money but are perfectly happy to blow a few hundred quid on a meeting they could have easily held online. Roll back the good old Covid days!* At least there was something meaty for the gathered non-executives to discuss at this particular board meeting. Myers-Stratton.

The chairman urged silence to the chattering members of the board and invited Will to update the assembled on recent events. *I assume that's the last we will hear from that useless old buffer today. Just how much do we pay for his 'services?'*

"Thanks, all, for finding time for this hastily scheduled meeting, but I have an important update after my recent trip to Boston and some proposed changes in strategy I would like to present for discussion this afternoon. And thanks to Himari for rushing to provide me with some budget projections that I will also go through this afternoon."

The part-time consultant CFO, Himari Yoshida, was an appointment that Granta Pain's lead investor, Mordor Capital Investments, had insisted upon. She was on the board of several of Mordor's portfolio companies. A ferociously bright and hard-working accountant who had Will's respect not least because she did all the heavy lifting with the company accounts and audits. Will tried his best to understand what she was talking about whenever they met for a catch-up, but detailed 'financial stuff' buried below the top-line numbers went way over the glazed eyes he wore during such meetings in much the same way that the science usually proved to be beyond Himari's grasp. Hence the mutual respect that they had for each other. Will's problem with the CFO was that he believed that he was very much second in line after Hirami had first briefed Mordor. An assumption that wasn't so very far from the way things actually worked.

In Will's opinion, the presentation and follow-up discussion went well. The board was genuinely appreciative of Will's efforts in finding a potential acquiror of Granta Pain – *so they bloody well should be* – and his proposal to focus efforts on getting GPT107 ready for clinical trials. Will was grateful that the board did not pass comment on Hirami's financial projections for various redundancy scenarios. A discussion for another time.

The chairman called an end to the meeting after he deemed that there was no other business to discuss, leaving Will to bid his farewells to the smiling board members. He left the meeting in a much better mood than he had found himself the weekend after he had returned from Boston. He had done all he could to position Granta Pain closer to the opportunity he believed Myers-Stratton were looking for than had been the case prior to first meeting Celeste. Will had taken back a little control. But was it enough?

CAREERS

I, for one, certainly don't envy the career path Will chose for himself. The CEO of a small biotech. Am not sure what I would hate the most. The seemingly endless uncertainty of how long the funding would last and always striving to extend the timeline out as far as possible to the point when there is just no money left to remain solvent. I would also not fancy one bit having to always be on top of the science. Presenting complex science to experts, many of whom focus on finding fault with the research you are doing and can't wait to explain to you your big mistake. It is referred to as the scientific method but all too often becomes subjective rather than objective. But what would be worst of all for me? The constant worry of being responsible for the livelihoods of the staff and their families. Will is very welcome to it all, including his eye-watering salary. He deserves it. His is not a stress-free job.

Our career paths diverged when we finished our first

degrees. It was onwards and upwards for Will as he chased his dream of first being an academic research fellow and lecturer and then onto starting his own company. Me? If I'm being honest, I guess I had fully realised my potential in almost getting a first-class degree. Now I needed to get a job and finally earn some money. Luke and I were going to set up home together and we needed an extra income to top up Luke's earnings as a self-employed plumber. We had it all worked out. Well, I had it all worked out. Our first home was to be in Cambridge and a short bus ride or even bicycle ride on a good day to my first, and up to now my only, job. I was one of the first scientists to be taken on by a new start-up contract research company called Biopharmaco. A brilliantly lucky choice made by me at the time, as the company has since grown to over two hundred scientists and is considered to be a service provider of choice by many in the industry. However, even more important than that, it is a truly wonderful place to work. The managers actually listen to you, and I have made many good friends. I have managed to find my career, even if I will never be that inventor of a life-saving medicine. I have found what people refer to as the perfect work/life balance. Lucky old me.

DECISIONS

"Come in," called Nat Stevens, at first not bothering to look up to see who had knocked gently on his office door. "Ah, Celeste." He glanced up at the clock directly above the door. "It's really late. Shouldn't you be at home with that splendid husband of yours? Such good company is your Charles."

Celeste winced involuntarily. "Charles? He's old and hairy enough to look after himself. I hung around to see if you had a chance to discuss in this afternoon's board meeting the Granta Pain term sheet I had drafted for you to present."

"Yes, of course. I really should let you know what's going on, shouldn't I. Why don't you sit down." Nat paused to order his thoughts in a logical sequence and perhaps soften the blow Celeste's ego might suffer when he told her about some of the board's more aggressive demands. "Well, as always with our board, there is the good and the bad. That is an opinion to be kept between you and I, of course.

And also, please keep the rest of what I am going to say to you now to yourself until the minutes of the meeting have been circulated." Celeste nodded in reply. "The good? The board were keen to follow up on this opportunity and get a term sheet over to Granta Pain Therapeutics at your earliest convenience." He smiled. Nat then went onto to exaggerate a comment from one of the board members. "They were also very complimentary about your efforts in bringing this project to their attention."

"That *is* good news." Celeste smiled in response to both the news and the compliment. "I'm not going to like the bad news, am I?"

"And nor do I, Celeste." He stood up and walked towards the window, which looked out towards a busy Boston city street many floors below now finally calming down for the evening. "The term sheet the board finally agreed upon has kept much of the technical detail of your original, but the headline numbers are pretty different. In fact, very different, I would say. They ended up with a valuation of about a third of what you proposed."

"And my valuation was not much more than half of what Granta Pain had muted," she blurted out, trying to calculate in her head what the final number was.

Nat returned to his seat. "That's about it, Celeste. We're essentially expecting Granta Pain to take it up the ass and say thank you." He could see that Celeste was not appreciating his old-school language. "In a manner of speaking. Just trying to get my point across."

"Point taken, Nat. But why? Don't you think it shows a lack of respect for a company we want to work with rather than screw into the ground?"

"Of course it does, but how much does that really matter? It's not like we are merging with another large company and taking on their staff. We just have Jeavons to be concerned about, and we will make sure he is looked after. I don't care the tiniest iota if we upset their board of nobodies. Look, Celeste, we're both grown-ups. It's not the first nor the last time a company running out of money will be lowballed and shafted. The board's view is if we don't make an offer then Granta Pain will fold, as the current investors haven't got deep enough pockets to take the drug into the clinic and, as far as we can tell, there are no knights in shining armour waiting in the wings to rescue them."

"So we're a bit like a charity then, helping those down on their luck," replied Celeste in her best sarcastic tone.

"Think what you will, but I can guarantee you one thing. Granta Pain's investors would do exactly the same to us if the boot was on the other foot. In this business we all have to be prepared to be bottom feeders whenever the opportunity arises. This is a game for big boys."

"And big girls, Nat. I can't see Jeavons hanging around too long once we've finished trampling over all his ambitions. It's going to be very difficult to get full value from this asset without Jeavons being involved."

"Which the board is well aware of, thanks to me. Don't you go worrying about your man Jeavons. Like I said, we'll look after him. He'll be made an offer he'd be foolish to refuse. A very attractive remuneration package and share options that will keep him honest moving forward. I should add, and I fully agree with the board on this one, a lower valuation will free up budget to spend on clinical development which will benefit all parties. I think that should be a strategy you need to focus on and a message to get over when you get to discuss this with Jeavons. Myers-Stratton is not Big Pharma. Our revenues don't allow us to compete with the behemoths when looking to in-licence assets. Better to spend the money on getting the drug into the clinic rather than lining the pockets of shareholders and do it quick and now before any behemoths come circling."

Celeste was struggling to push back any more, not that anything would change even if she did. "Thanks for giving me the heads-up on this, Nat. I appreciate you taking me into your confidence. I guess it is what it is and the big news here is that the board has bought into this opportunity and one which I personally think is a very exciting programme with a lot of upside."

"Exactly, Celeste. Now up to you and me, but especially you, to make this happen. For all I know, they might turn our offer down, but I personally don't think so, as they are fast running out of runway and options. We'll talk about next steps when the board minutes are out. I predict lots of international travel coming up for you in the weeks to come so let's call it a night so you can get back home to spend some time with your husband. Goodnight, Celeste. See you in the morning."

"See you tomorrow," replied Celeste as she made her way out of his office and back to her own office, at least happy that the board had agreed to make an offer to acquire Granta Pain but feeling a little bruised at how her term sheet had been battered. She also worried about how the aggressive offer would be received by Will and his company's board. Egos will need to be managed.

Celeste waved weakly to her husband as their cars crossed on the driveway of their house. She was not sure if Charles had seen her, as there was no return wave of recognition, although it seemed he was in a hurry to get somewhere quickly given how his two-seater Mercedes convertible was snaking across the gravel driveway. If Charles had told her that he was going out that evening, then it was news to her.

Another long day at the office over and so a perfectly valid excuse to leave the car directly outside the front door rather than go to the trouble of parking it up in the garage. As she paused outside the front door to search for her house keys in her briefcase, Celeste rummaged through her mind as to how the last two weeks of marital 'reconciliation' had gone.

As she entered the kitchen to make herself a life-restoring mug of black coffee, Celeste recalled the scene of the morning after that night when Charles somehow convinced her to give their marriage just one last chance. He had certainly made a good start in the bedroom, both during that night and again in the early morning, but it was at breakfast before Celeste left for work and her meeting with Will that she found the more remarkable. Genuine tears from Charles. At least, she hoped that they were genuine. Tears as he pleaded for her forgiveness for all that he had done and tears as he once again begged her for one last chance. Celeste couldn't remember if she had ever seen Charles cry. Certainly not at their wedding and not even when they found out that they couldn't have children. It would take a heart of stone not to be convinced by this new version of Charles, and Celeste's heart was not one carved from stone.

Although not nearly so dramatic as that first morning and the night before, the next two weeks were a revelation. At least for Celeste. Several quiet dinners for two nights out in Boston. A much less quiet evening out at a nightclub as a nod to old times, although not an experience to be repeated if Celeste had a choice. Even a lazy Sunday afternoon spent with Celeste's parents at the family home. One thing even his wife had to admit was that Charles knew how to socialise. He could charm the birds from the trees. And then there was the sex. Not every night but often enough and good enough to convince Celeste that she was wanted. That he still found her body attractive. Maybe she was wrong after all, and Charles could change his ways.

With the coffee in hand, Celeste pulled up a chair to the kitchen table and decided to catch up on her phone messages as a distracting activity from having to make herself dinner. But it wasn't her phone that was making a noise; the ringtone was from Charles's phone. The ringing had stopped long before she found his phone in the usual place on the low table in the orangery. There was a message lit up on Charles's phone.

Missed call from Naomi

Celeste felt the need to sit down in the wicker armchair. Then almost immediately a text from Naomi, which she opened courtesy of the PIN Charles had shared with Celeste the previous week. No more secrets.

Where the fuck are you? You're supposed to meet me outside the hotel at seven.

Celeste could feel bile collecting in her throat. Perhaps she was jumping to conclusions. It might all be something to do with his work. An evening dinner with a client, although the language used might argue against such a scenario. She should at least wait until he came home and was given the chance to explain something that might be completely innocent. A WhatsApp short video follow up from Naomi changed Celeste's original course of action in a heartbeat.

If you don't turn up at room 618 in the next thirty minutes then I'm putting all this back in the box.

What followed was a sex act that Naomi demonstrated on her naked body which left no doubt as to why and where Charles was hoping to be that night.

Celeste was surprised to feel hot tears streaming down her cheeks and onto the bed as she hurriedly packed a suitcase with enough clothes to see her through the rest of the week. She wasn't sure if the tears were from the realisation that her marriage was now finally going to be over or from the realisation that she had once again been humiliated and made to look a gullible fool. Whichever it was, now was the time to get out of the house as quickly as she could and before Charles realised that he had left his precious phone and incriminating evidence at home and return to collect it. At that moment, Celeste just didn't want to be in the same house let alone the same room as her husband ever again.

As she banged the heavy suitcase down the stairs, she paused to consider leaving him a handwritten letter, but there was no time. She could send something on her phone when she arrived at the sanctuary of a hotel she would stay for the night.

Writing an email to her husband was the first thing she did when she sat down at the table in her hotel room.

Dearest Charles,

Just a short note to say that I won't be staying the night in 'our' house tonight. Nor any other night. I am assuming you are fully aware of the reason why and a reason that you will see explained in more detail when you hear from my lawyers.

I wish I could say that it's been a blast. But it hasn't. I wish I could say that I still love you. But I don't. I wish I could say that we will part on good terms. But we won't.

Please don't try to contact me, my family or my friends. If there is something you need to say, then say it to my lawyers. Expect one of my friends to drop by 'our' house in the coming days to pick up the rest of my clothes and important belongings. I will give them my house keys.

I can't wish you well but neither do I wish you ill. I just no longer care.

Your ex-wife to be,

Celeste

PS Please do pass on my compliments to your latest young beau on her wonderful body and astonishing flexibility. I wonder what she sees in the multimillionaire that is Charles Lewis Amos III.

THE OFFER

It was now the second week in October and Will had still not heard anything more back from Myers-Stratton. Not even a courtesy call. He was beginning to get twitchy. Checking his emails and texts far too regularly like a teenage boy yearning to hear from his sweetheart. It had got to the extent that it was beginning to interfere with the work he was actually supposed to be doing. *I'll give it until Friday and if I haven't heard anything by then, I will email Celeste even if it is just to show some sort of enthusiasm.* He didn't have to wait that long.

"Will. It's Celeste. Celeste Simmonds from Myers-Stratton. Can you talk?"

At the shock of the sound of her voice, Will managed to obliterate a digestive biscuit he had hovered over his mug of afternoon tea into many pieces, the largest of which splashed into the tea covering his hand with scalding-hot beverage.

"Will? Are you there?"

"Sorry, Celeste," he answered, biting back the pain, "you sort of caught me a bit by surprise there." He mopped up the remainder of the tea with his handkerchief.

"Not a problem," added Celeste, unsure what to make of the noises she could hear in the background. "Some news for you. Myers-Stratton is going to make an offer to acquire all Granta Pain Therapeutics shares, and you and your chairman should have a non-binding term sheet in front of you before the close of business today."

Will scrunched up a piece of A4 paper he had been making notes on and let out what he hoped was an inaudible cry of *YES*.

"This phone call is just to give you a heads-up and some context on what is in the term sheet but please don't share what I am going to say to you with anyone else, and that includes your chairman. Understood?"

"Of course, Celeste," replied Will, although he was still very much in celebration mode to listen too carefully to what she was saying.

"We are offering a small upfront payment with the remainder in milestone payments based upon successful progress of GTP107 through the clinic. We hope that the upfront will be acceptable to your investors but frankly, Will, although plenty of upside, there is no obvious value in Granta Pain at this point. You don't have a novel compound, and you haven't even filed a patent, which, between you and me, Will, was something your investors really should have insisted upon."

Will's mood was starting to darken. "But what about the novel mechanism of action that we have discovered? Surely that must be worth something."

"That is clearly a key aspect of this project but much of it has already been disclosed in the publications going back to your time at the university. The real value inflection point will be when you are able to demonstrate efficacy in treating pain and lack of abuse liability in the clinic, and we have proposed a generous milestone payment to be triggered when, hopefully, that key objective is realised."

Will was not sure what else to say in the defence of his company. "Obviously I haven't seen the term sheet yet, but from what you have told me, this all seems rather underwhelming."

"I completely understand, Will, I really do. Perhaps I can provide some context to how we have arrived at the numbers on the term sheet. Myers-Stratton is no less keen than are you to get a drug out of this project. To achieve such a tough objective, we must ensure that the clinical trials are carried out to the highest possible standards, and this is obviously not going to be cheap. Thus, we would prefer to concentrate our spending on progressing the asset rather than, if I'm being brutally honest, rewarding shareholders at such an early stage of the company. I hope that makes sense, Will."

It did but that didn't help assuage his feeling of disappointment, which Celeste could feel seeping through the phone.

Time for the coup de grâce. "Now, this really is strictly between you and me and not to go any further, even after the term sheet has been sent. The deal is dependent on you remaining as CEO of Granta Pain Therapeutics. No Will Jeavons, no deal. Now, we obviously can't make you stay or go anywhere, but based on your current salary, I think you will be very pleasantly surprised by the salary and share option package we will be offering for you to stay on. Think US CEO salaries," she teased.

Will involuntarily stubbed his toe on the ancient pipework underneath his desk. "Sounds good, Celeste," he squeaked. "Looking forward to seeing the actual numbers."

"Yes. I think you probably will. I imagine the board will want to chew over this and arrange some sort of meeting with our team, but I would urge you to make this happen as soon as possible. Our board have a very short attention span. If everything works out as well as I hope it does, you might be seeing me again sooner rather than later, which I am very much looking forward to. But could I please ask a favour of you, Will?"

Will was a little bemused as to what favour he could possibly provide. "But of course."

"Don't get me wrong. I'm really grateful for you taking me out to Midsummer House and for the experience, but next time, can we please go somewhere where I don't still feel hungry afterwards!"

They both laughed at a shared memory. "You know what, Celeste. I think I know just the place."

"Until then. Take care, Will," were her last words before ending the call without even giving him chance to say goodbye.

Will sat motionless, smiling at the pieces of biscuit spread across his desk and at the thought he might just be very soon the comfortably wealthy scientist he always wanted to be. The freedom to think about science rather than worrying about money and funding. All he had to do now was try and convince the board to take the only offer they were likely to get for the company. *Surely even they can't be so fucking stupid as to walk away from this.*

During his walk into the city centre for a well-earnt after-work alcoholic drink, he mulled over what to make of Celeste's behaviour. The return of the old Celeste he met in Cambridge back in the summer? *Please let it be the old Celeste who next turns up in Cambridge.* He was unsure as to exactly why he was so much looking forward to seeing her again. He just was.

What Will really wanted to do that evening was celebrate and drink the city bars dry, even if the celebrations were rather premature. It was on such special and personal occasions that Will realised that there was no one important person in his life that he could share such secrets with. No lover who he could go back home to who could enjoy his happiness and success. Maybe his life wasn't as complete as he thought it was.

WOMEN

"Will. Will!"

Consciousness was gradually returning, and he slowly turned his head to the source of the disturbance. Standing next to the bed holding a mug of something in one hand and two digestive biscuits in the other was a completely naked brunette.

"From what I have seen you drink from afar in the tearoom and what you have in your rather bijou kitchen, I'm guessing you drink white coffee. Would you like me to add some sugar?"

His memory was just filtering in. Amy Stevens. Works in admin in the pharmacology department. Married with three grown-up children. Husband works in the city – works away from home a lot. She obviously doesn't know him that well, as he drinks tea in the morning.

"Come here, you," he grumbled, trying to pull her body back into bed.

"Whoa, tiger. Plenty of time for all that." She smiled whilst deftly avoiding his lunge. "Time now is for morning refreshments," announced Amy as she walked around the bed, put her cup of tea on the bedside table, and slid back into her side of the bed.

A synapse or two in his brain were fired into action. "You've been spying on me in the tearoom? Really?"

"I'm far from the only one, I can tell you, and that includes a few men."

Will smiled a little uneasily at the thought of who those men could be. "All very flattering, but why?"

"I can only speak for myself, but take a look at yourself." Amy half pulled down the duvet to reveal a fully naked Will lying on his back. "Voila, exhibit one. Exhibit two." She pointed to his head. "All that clever stuff going on inside there. And on top of all that, there's your reputation, of course. So with all that going for you, why exactly do you settle for dried-up old women like me when you seemingly have free access to getting into the panties of all those gorgeous undergraduates who hero-worship you? It's not like you're teaching them anymore apart from the odd lecture, so not a problem with regards work rules, I would have thought."

"I really do think that requires a very careful answer," replied Will, sitting up his haunches in preparation for drinking his coffee. "Funnily enough, I was only thinking the other day about my sex life and how it is that I have nearly arrived at forty and still don't feel the need to settle down. But do you really want to hear about my selfish introspection?"

Amy smiled. "What on earth else could I possibly want

to do with my time sitting next to a naked man over ten years my junior than to hear all about Dr William Jeavons' sexual preferences?"

"Point well made, so please do shout out should anything you would rather do comes to mind," added Will, gently caressing her right breast as a reminder of an alternative to listening to his monologue that she might want to consider. "But first of all. You yourself know that you are far from a dried-up sexual has-been and I would so much enjoy adding to the evidence I enjoyed last night at some point this morning. If you will allow me to, of course."

"Definitely a smooth operator, aren't you. Last night was OK, I suppose," teased Amy, "but it's not easy for me to be out overnight for obvious reasons. Days and evenings are much easier. At least for me."

"I think I could manage that. Your place or mine?" he joked.

"So that's the rest of our lives sorted, what about you now telling me about your selfish introspection?"

"Fine with me but don't say that you haven't been warned. You may want to make yourself comfortable, my girl."

Amy wriggled her hips and pulled the duvet up to cover her breasts in her best *Watch with Mother* pose.

"The few male friends I had as I travelled through my teenage years used to make fun of me for being a late starter when it came to girls but, with the benefit of hindsight, that was of course just macho bravado from them. I guess you could say I broke my duck not long after I started university with my good friend Ann. Sweet memories of an innocent age. There were others who shared my bed when I was at Imperial and later during my PhD and postdoc years but none who lasted more than a couple of months, really."

"Why was that, Will? Couldn't they put up with you for any longer?"

Will took this in the good humour that it was meant. "If I'm being honest, and maybe also a little immodest, it was usually me who broke things off. Why? At the time, I used to fool myself that I didn't want anything to get in the way of my work and I think that, at least to a certain extent, I am still clinging onto the same excuse. Maybe that plus the rather selfish and shallow belief that life just couldn't get any better for this bachelor about town. But yes, I think selfishness is the big theme here. My preference for steamy assignations rather than having to adapt myself to fit with someone else's life, to like their friends and pretend that we are destined for one another for the rest of our lives."

"There's no deep-down urge to have a life with just one woman? No desire for children or family? Perhaps this conversation is now getting a bit heavy. Don't feel that you have to answer that."

If he was being truthful, Will would have at least touched upon the deep and confusing emotions his birth mother had left him with, but he had never felt close enough to anyone to reveal those still-raw thoughts and feelings.

"Doesn't look good, does it? But it gets worse," added Will in a mock-serious tone.

"Why don't we stop now?" asked Amy, looking concerned.

"I'm just teasing you, Amy. Heavy stuff over. I was going to finish with how I eventually developed into the fully paid-up, card-carrying cad that I am now. How I find married women like the rather delicious one I am lying with now so irresistible. Pray, may I continue?"

"If you insist, but only providing that you keep the compliments flowing."

"I recall a few postdocs I went out with when I took up my lectureship here in Cambridge but none of them reported to me. All above board, you see. And definitely no undergraduates. Cross my heart."

"Like sure! You never fancied any of the endless examples of leggy blondes we always seem to have around the place? Not sure I believe you."

"I can't *make* you believe me. And there were chances. Offers. But it just didn't feel right. I know, it hardly sounds credible. But it's true. I always preferred to date mature, experienced women. Those who knew what they wanted in bed and willing to ask for it, but it wasn't just sex that was the driver for me. I wanted to go out with women who I could really talk to and knew about life, people, music, literature, fine wine. Someone I find fascinating as well as a good shag, I suppose. Not really asking for much, am I?"

"And I'm such a someone who knows about literature, music, wine, etc., etc.?"

"Frankly, my dear, you're the exception. I've just got you shacked up here to shag!" he added, dragging his hand up the inside of her thigh. "But joking aside, my real move over to the dark side came when I upgraded from just mature women to mature married women. The cad I have become. Why the preference? On top of all the advantages of being a mature woman, they have no expectations or interest in heavy duty commitments. Usually. They just want to enjoy the company of a new, no-obligations lover. No strings. And the choice is almost endless. All those middle-aged women with grown-up children who have left home and a raving sex drive unsatisfied by a husband more interested in chasing after the new brunette who has just started in the office. Why would any heterosexual man want or need to look beyond all those desperately unsatisfied married women?"

"You make a compelling argument, Dr Jeavons. Looks to me that you think you are supporting the community. Providing a service for us poor unfortunates. A sort of social worker of our times for those married women so frantically craving male company and a good leg over."

"Bingo!" replied Will, holding out his hands in front of him in the shape of pistols. "However, I must add one important caveat. I would never risk breaking up a family, no matter how rotten the marriage might have become. I am discreet to the point of being anal and am never the one who makes the first move. I rely upon people such as yourself to come after me!"

Amy could see so many holes in his flimsy attempts at self-justification. He was simply delusional if he really believed that he wasn't putting marriages at risk by his selfish actions and had probably already done so without even realising. It also occurred to her that his obsession with more mature women had something to do with him searching for a replacement for his mother, not a theory Amy would ever dare share with him. Nor would she dare share with him her belief that his need to be with so many women was reassurance for him and proof to others that he was liked. That he was not the worthless person whose father had walked away from and that he was not the person even his own mother had often left to fend for himself. He wanted to feel wanted. He seemed to Amy like he probably seemed to many other women as a man who was lost and was hiding behind his work ethic to avoid confronting the deep holes he had in his life. Something needed to change, and it would probably take someone else to change it.

But now, in bed next to a naked man she wanted so badly, was not the time for such an uncomfortable debate.

"As you said yourself, Will. Never knowingly modest!"

"What can I say? Guilty as charged."

"I should say so. Anything else the defendant wants to say in their defence?"

"Maybe actions can sometimes say more than mere words. Now, where were we?" asked Will as he rolled over to take up his smiling lover into his arms once again.

THE DEAL

How does she do it? wondered Will, this time placing his digestive biscuit he had hovered above his mug of tea down next to his laptop before answering the phone to the number that came up on his phone screen as Celeste's.

"Celeste! How are you?"

"I'm fine, thanks, Will." She was keen to get on with the subject on her mind. "Is there anyone in the office with you? Can you talk?"

Cue serious conversation, Will concluded.

"This is going to be another one of those just me-and-you chats, Will. Not to go beyond the two of us aside from the main message I would like you to go back to the board with. Understood?"

Yes, I think I do. Maybe being a tad rude and patronising there, my dear Celeste. "Of course. Fire away."

"I'm afraid that the content of the marked-up term sheet that your board sent back to us did not go down at all well over here."

Will had guessed that would be the outcome when the Granta Pain board had discussed their response to the offer from Myers-Stratton, but his voice was a lone one at the emergency board meeting and the consensus was to at least try to ramp up the valuation. *I just knew those tossers would fuck it up. How is it that they can now find the money to put into a deal and get a piece of the action when there was no money to directly fund Granta Pain before the offer? Shysters.*

"I did argue your case, that the valuation did not fully reflect the potential upside of Granta Pain, but I just couldn't get any traction." Which was a lie. Celeste did nothing of the sort. She hated making these 'little white lies' to business associates, but such amendments to the truth were meant to help fashion a working relationship where the potential partner felt that she was on their side. Which would come across as clearly ludicrous to anyone with a modicum of business experience, but Will was not such a person. "Myers-Stratton feel that they are going out on a limb offering what is in the term sheet we sent to you, and I think I can say with some degree of confidence, having discussed this internally, that if Granta Pain don't sign the term sheet as is by the end of next week then, I'm afraid, the offer will be withdrawn."

The fuckers! screamed Will inside his head, trying to come up with the best description of his investors. *Incompetent. Stupid. Greedy. Yes. Greed is the driver here.* Why should he be surprised?

Celeste was expecting Will to say something but in the absence of a reply she decided to fill the airspace. "I know you want this deal to happen, and I hope that you also know that I want this deal to happen." Time for the ego boost switch to be thrown. For copious smoke to be blown up asses. "You are just the sort of innovative scientist we want to work with. Granta Pain have a terrifically exciting asset that would fit so well within our portfolio, and we believe that the skill sets of our two companies are complimentary, making us ideally placed to get this drug into the clinic. A drug that will transform patient care. An efficacious, non-addictive treatment for chronic pain that clinicians have been crying out for, for decades."

"That's so kind of you to say and means so much coming from someone of your experience. But what can I do that would make any difference at all?"

"It needed saying, Will, and I meant every word. What can you do? I'm trying to head off any likely VC between your board and our in-licensing team. I can't see it going well, as it won't take much for us to walk away, which means that your board would have to perform a humiliating climbdown in front of us for the deal to happen. Can their egos take such a climbdown? I don't know them so I don't know, but why take the risk?" Celeste paused.

"Well, I do know them, and I think you have probably called it right. I'm guessing that they will try to find something to change on the term sheet just to save face and that will likely get them nowhere."

"Hence my concern. So, where am I with this? A suggestion for you to consider but one I would urge you to follow through with. Call a meeting with your board. Say that you and I have had this conversation in confidence and then pretend that you are betraying that confidence in order for your board to reconsider their position and save the deal. All a bit Machiavellian but it might provide them with at least the illusion that they have some sort of control, but you know what, Will, I just don't know. It's the best I can come up with to keep this deal alive. What do you think?"

Will carefully considered his options. They both knew he had none other than the one Celeste was trying to sell him. "Listen, I do appreciate you trying to help on this, I really do. Will my board swallow this? Will they listen to me for a change? Their fucking CEO, for fuck's sake. I can only try, and I will try, Celeste. What else can I do?"

"Difficult times, Will, and I appreciate you hearing me out on this. There's a lot at stake and, in my opinion, it's worth going that extra mile even if it's just so that you can reassure yourself that you have tried everything if the deal falls through." Celeste paused to collect her thoughts in trying to fashion a strong finish to her argument. "You now have a good understanding of what Myers-Stratton's position is on this deal and I truly hope you can get that across to your own board and make this deal happen. So sorry to put you into this position. You're a scientist and not a corrupt businessman. At least not yet! But I have every confidence that you can pull this off, Will. They would be fools not to listen to you. This deal's just gotta happen."

"I understand. I can only do my best. I will try to get a board meeting sorted out and we will see what happens from there."

"That's great, Will. I will keep my fingers crossed on this side of the water and do please call me if I can be of any help. Night or day. Good luck, Will."

"Thanks, Celeste. Speak to you soon."

Celeste always felt uncomfortable manipulating people, and this was how she was feeling when she ended the call with Will. Nevertheless, this was her business. An often-difficult balance trying to match the expectations of her company and the company she was dealing with. Trying to maintain a good working relationship even when there were contrasting cultures and differing priorities. But with Will it was more than that. There was the personal angle to also consider. Celeste was struggling to understand how and where Will fitted into her life. If at all. Clearly not at all if the deal fell through, but if the acquisition did take place, then she was likely to be involved with Granta Pain in some fashion moving forward based on past precedent with other companies. That could range anywhere from just supporting the transition through the change of ownership through to a seat on the new board. Any likely scenario would provide an opportunity for them to develop both their professional and personal relationships. But did Celeste want a personal relationship? Right now, after only just leaving Charles? How would that appear to her parents and work colleagues? A personal relationship with someone in the same company? Not impossible but, at the very least, difficult. That's precisely what she was struggling to understand. What did she want?

CELEBRATION

Li was muttering quiet little nothings under her breath as she was gradually clearing up the mess her son and his friends had left in the kitchen the previous night. She was keen to shift the worst of the mess before Nev turned up for breakfast so as to avoid any potential differences of opinion arising between father and son. Li was fortunate that Nev had other things on his mind that late-October morning as he strode purposely into the kitchen, taking his usual seat at the breakfast table.

Without looking over to her husband, Li announced, "Big day coming up for the big man."

"And as it is indeed a big day, perhaps the big man can for once enjoy a big breakfast if that's OK with Dr Li Chamberlain GP FRS Bar, the world-renowned health guru. Please, anything other than that bloody muesli."

"Hot, buttered toast it will be for my dearest husband. Would that be two slices or ten?"

Nev chose to ignore such a stupid choice. "As I said last night, I'll be bussing it to the Milton Science Park this morning for that second interview with Biopharmaco but the excuse I have used to Jeavons for not getting into work until this afternoon is that I am meeting them on Granta Pain business. All sorted. Bish, bash, bosh. Thank you very much indeed."

"Do you think they will offer you the job?" asked Li, having sat down at the dinner table, satisfied that her husband was sufficiently distracted so as to not take issue with their son's messy habits.

"Not today, I doubt. According to Ron, this morning will be all about seeing if their top brass shares his opinion that I have the skills and experience for the job and that I am not a complete headbanger."

"Touch and go then, Nev."

Nev once again chose to ignore her attempted humour. "Then back to work for a couple of hours before coming home to get spruced up for tonight's celebrations. Dinner out on the town with all drinks paid for. What's there not to like?"

Li decided to shift towards serious-and-concerned mode. "I know exactly what you are going to say back to me but be careful, Nev. You and the drink don't always get on and you don't want to find yourself airing any of your more outspoken views in front of Jeavons and the other staff tonight. The trouble you would likely land yourself in is just not worth any satisfaction you might get from telling everyone what you really think. Remember what happened at SRL when you were out the door straight after their Christmas party? It's not as if you have anything in writing yet from Biopharmaco."

Nev smiled. "But that was a bloody top-hole Christmas party. Almost worth getting sacked for."

"Exactly my point, Nev. Don't be a clown. You're certainly a lot older now and so you should also be a lot wiser, and another thing: now that Granta Pain has been bought out by Myers-Shotton or whatever they are called, isn't it worth staying on to see how that works out? Better the devil you know and all that sort of thing. Might even get a new position and a pay rise. Who knows?"

"Myers-Stratton. Strat. Ton. Thought about it and usually I would hang around in these sort of circumstances," replied Nev, peering over to the toaster as a hint to his wife, "but I just don't trust the bastards. I know Jeavons is a bastard, and I bet you those Yanks are out of the same mould and probably worse, but it obviously makes sense for me to keep shtum about Biopharmaco for as long as I can just to see if there is any redundancy money I can pick up on the sly. You never know, they might offer voluntary redundancy. Wouldn't it be nice to have a bit of spare cash for a change? What was that about ten rounds of toast?"

"Oh yeah. Sorry, Nev," apologised Li, standing up at the table and making her way over to their temperamental and occasionally dangerous toaster from many years gone by. A wedding present.

"And another thing. Why has that lazy git of a son left it to his mother again to clean up all his mess? That's the last time we allow his mates to come round here. I can tell you that much for free."

*

Will was in a pensive mood as he walked from his apartment to the Anchor for the 7pm celebration dinner and drinks. He had plenty to be pensive about so why not walk rather than shortening the journey and time to think by taking a bus. Biking had earlier been ruled out as he was a self-confessed poor cyclist and much worse still after a few drinks. He was likely to have more than just a few drinks that evening. And why not? It is not every day that one gets to celebrate the sale of their own company.

This was the time to smell the roses. That was the saying his father, Ed, often used and how he ended the phone call Will had with his parents several nights ago. Will was sure that his parents were even happier than he was himself at the news that his company had been bought. Their son. A brilliant scientist and a successful, soon-to-be wealthy businessman. The deeply troubled little boy they took under their care all those years ago may not be the prime minister Ed playfully prophesised he would be, but Will had truly made the very most of his many hard-won abilities.

"Are you courting yet, son? Thinking of settling down?" asked Lindsey.

"Not yet, Mum. Give me chance, for God's sake. I'm only thirty-eight!"

Will had found the best way to put his mother off the scent was with humour, although he did worry that they had convinced themselves that their son was one of those dirty homosexuals. If only they knew.

The usual pangs of guilt stalked Will after the short phone call. When was the last time he bothered to go up to the old house in Birmingham to see them? He honestly couldn't remember, outside of the few hours he used to spend there almost every Christmastime. The empty promise that he made at the end of this call, just like those he made after every call, that he would be up to see them soon was not something that Will nor his parents really took any notice of. The annoying thing for Will, and which made him feel even worse, was that they never showed any disappointment in only very rarely seeing the son that they were so very proud of. The son who they talked of so much to their friends and neighbours. The brilliant scientist who was their very own son. *Not acceptable, Will. Not even close. But how the bloody hell am I going to find time to go up and see them with all this important stuff going on right now?* How many times had he used that same tired, old excuse? Ed would be eighty in just a couple of years and Lindsey was not far behind. There was no guarantee that there would be a next time and what could be more important than family? But Will didn't quite see it that way. He just preferred the guilt.

The walk took longer than Will had anticipated, and the party had already started around the bar by the time he passed through the door of the Anchor. A shout of 'Will' rose up from a few of those at the bar. The first to speak to him was Nev.

"Thank God you've arrived, boss. Not a minute too late. We've taken the liberty of getting in the first round and told them you would pay when you got here. Cheers, boss!"

"Cheers, Nev. I don't suppose you got one for me?" was a question Nev didn't answer, as he was already making his way to the tables Grace had reserved for the celebration dinner.

Rather a good turnout, thought Will as he settled down at one of the tables with a pint that he ended up having to buy himself. *Our lot. A few of the lecturers who could still bother to talk to me. Most of the departmental admin team including the lovely Amy. What a pity that she is not up for it tonight, but I suppose husbands do have to take priority from time to time. And what a great pity none of the board could make it along. Bunch of useless tossers, although it would have been nice to see if we could have teased Hirami out of her shell. I don't know about the rest of this lot, but I am going to have a fucking good night out!*

Will had perched himself at one end of the long dinner table and waited for everyone to take their seats before standing up.

"Don't worry," he began as the excitable chatter died down, "I'm not going to bore you for any longer than is absolutely necessary." Will ignored the undercurrent of sniggering. "All I ask of you this evening, and by the way many thanks for finding time to come along to this celebration, is to raise your glasses to recognise the unique and world-class research carried out by the Granta Pain Therapeutics team. Without them and their dedication," Will's arms were swept out in front of him, "we would not be here this evening to celebrate the start of the next exciting phase of our company. Our very own little company. I am so much looking forward to continuing our rollercoaster of a ride to the success I know will be ours. The toast is to you, my friends. The scientists."

A genuine cheer rang out and all raised their glasses. Will was pretty sure he saw a tear rolling down the cheek of a beaming Grace and Nev whispering some deluded conspiracy theory into the ear of one of the admin staff sitting next to him.

A free bar almost guarantees an enjoyable and memorable night out for the British and that night was no different. *At least the board approved the celebratory dinner, but I wonder if they would have agreed to do so if they had known beforehand what the bill would end up being,* thought Will as he tapped in the PIN to the company card, approving an eye-watering sum.

Almost all had stayed until the end, including Amy, who came up to Will just as he had thanked the bar staff for their patience and good humour in tolerating a pretty raucous group.

"Will. Hope you don't mind me asking, but could you walk Grace back to the train station so that she can get on the last train to Saffron Walden? She has had rather a lot to drink, and I wouldn't want to leave her walking on her own in town in such a state. The others who were catching a train have already gone. I believe you have an apartment near the station, or at least that's what I remember someone telling me." Amy believed that she was delivering the last sentence with a wicked smile but it more resembled someone who was suffering from a stroke. Grace was not the only one who had enjoyed themselves that evening. Amy gestured to whisper into Will's ear. "What I would give to fuck you tonight."

"Not a problem," coughed Will. "I'll go and find her and offer to take her back. Thanks for letting me know and I'll see if I can find time to help you out with your very understandable request when we get back into work. Sound good to you?"

Amy flashed another wicked smile, turned and walked off to join a hysterically laughing group of her colleagues trying their very best to put on their coats. Will stood up on his toes to look over the heads of those in front of him and locate Grace when Nev suddenly invaded Will's space.

"Fucking fantastic night out, boss. So far, that is." Nev glanced behind him at a group who were hurriedly seeing off their drinks. "Me and the boys are planning to make a proper night of it. Fancy joining us? I can guarantee that you will both enjoy it and regret it!"

"Sounds too good to turn down but I've promised to take Grace back to the station and I'm travelling tomorrow morning," he lied. "But you boys have a good time," shouted Will to the group standing behind Nev, who to a man shouted something unintelligible back.

"Yes. Poor old Grace. Or should I say, poor young Grace. I didn't even know the girl drank and perhaps she won't be doing so again anytime soon after tonight. What an absolute fucking state. You will have your hands full walking that one anywhere tonight. The very best of British with that, boss," ended Nev, turning to embrace one of the group who were 'planning to make a proper night of it'.

Will was tending to agree with Nev's appreciation of the situation he had found himself in, wondering just what he had volunteered to do as he slowly made his way through the departing party-goers to see Grace slumped in a corner of the bar with a fully coated Amy sitting next to her, seemingly trying to hold a conversation. Amy saw Will walking towards them and patted the bench next to where she was sitting. As Will sat down, he could feel Amy's hand touching his ass.

"We've managed to get a couple of cokes down her and I think she's starting to slowly come round."

"You mean she was even worse than this?" asked Will, trying to imagine just what 'worse' must have looked like.

"Oh, I think so. Quite a bit worse, I would say," answered Amy, slowly moving her hand from where it had been resting. "She threw up a couple of times in the ladies' and I think that might have helped sober her up a bit. Which is why I don't think she is a great candidate for a taxi all the way back to Saffron Walden. Hopefully she will sober up even more on the walk to the station for you to put her on the train."

"You think so?" asked Will, who clearly wasn't thinking so.

"You'll be fine, Will. Trust me." She smiled in reply. Amy bent over as she stood up to leave. "After all, you really do know how to look after a woman, don't you, Will?" With that teasing closing comment, Amy strolled over to the pub door after waving back to her secret lover and stumbled badly out over the step to the obvious delight of her colleagues who thought the mishap hilarious.

"Great. Absolutely fucking great," muttered Will to himself as he considered how this was all going to work. But somehow it did. At least to start with. After a few tricky moments helping Grace to put on her coat and guide her out through the pub door whilst trying not to put his hands where they shouldn't be, the unlikely couple made their rather laboured way towards the train station. Will passed at least two taxi ranks but, as Amy had said earlier, no taxi driver was going to entertain a couple who were struggling to stay upright on the pavements. By the time they had arrived at the station, Grace had, to a certain extent, recovered the power of speech.

"You wait here, Grace," advised Will as they stood at the station entrance, "and I'll find out the time of your train and the platform." He did so not really sure whether he should take the risk of putting her on a train anyway. She was far from sober. In the end, the decision was made for him.

"Bad news, I'm afraid," announced Will as he walked out of the station entrance and up to his patient, who was using a wall for reassuring vertical support. "Your last train left over twenty minutes ago. We took a long time getting here. You won't be going home tonight by train."

"What happens next?" asked Grace to no one in particular. "I'll just get a taxi."

"I don't think so, Grace. You're just too pissed."

"I'll be alright. I'll be alright. *Taxi!*" she shouted across the station concourse. "*Taxi!* Over here." She waved to a taxi driver who was clearly ignoring her.

"Not going to happen, Grace."

"So, Dr Jeavons, what is going to happen?"

"You'll have to crash out at my apartment just down the road and catch a train in the morning when you sober up."

"Staying overnight in your apartment?" She laughed. "A man of your reputation?" She laughed even more.

"So it would appear, Grace, unless you have a cunning plan to argue otherwise. Is there anyone at your home we need to contact? Parents? Housemates?"

"Parents? How old do you think I am? You could ring my flatmate Jo, but she'll be long asleep by now. It's cool. No one to ring. But no funny business from you, Dr Jeavons, I'm still a pure-white virgin." Another burst of hysterical laughter followed.

"Nothing will happen other than us both having a good night's sleep in our own bedrooms. Let's go home. My home."

Will always bounded up the three flights of stairs to his apartment but thought it wise that night to take the lift. By the time he had guided Grace through into his short hallway, his guest had become silent once again. She was ready for sleep. Will took her into the spare bedroom and got her to sit up on the bed.

"Why don't you lie down and get some sleep. Keep your clothes on and just lie on top of the duvet for tonight. I'll get you a glass of water." By the time Will had arrived back with a small tumbler filled with water, Grace had already done what had been asked of her. To finish the job, he laid her on her front with her head to one side and a strategically placed plastic wastepaper bin next to the bed should she feel the need to use it.

Thank fuck for that, thought Will, pleased that he had done all that he could and should. *Hardly the best end to the night but, all in all, it wasn't a bad old do.* With that thought in mind, Will made his way to his own bedroom, looking forward to finishing the night with some refreshing sleep. But it wasn't to be. At least not completely.

The first sense that arrived the next day was a general awareness that dawn was almost thinking of getting going through the drawn curtains. But there was something else going on. Will sensed that there was someone walking around the foot of his bed. That feeling was compounded when that someone pulled back the duvet on the other side of the bed and climbed in next to him. He was about to turn round to find out what was happening but was prevented from doing so by a naked Grace folding one arm around his back followed by her leg. Nevertheless, he forcibly pushed her back so that he now faced her.

"What the fuck! Grace! What are you doing here?"

"What am I doing here? I thought that would be quite obvious to a man of your reputation," she teased, flashing her victim a smile in the gradually lightening darkness.

He sat up to look down on her young, tight breasts and narrow hips.

"No, no, no. This is not happening. Go back to your room and stay there."

"What a naughty girl I must be. Back to her room she must go!"

"Not playing around here, Grace. I'm serious. Get out of this bed."

"What's wrong with me? Don't you like what you see?" she asked, pulling down the duvet to reveal the whole of her naked body.

"As I said, this is not going to happen. You're ten years younger than me and you are one of my reports. Now how do you think our new American owners would react if they found out about this?"

"Why would they ever find out? It's not as if I'm looking for a long-term relationship and marriage. I just want to fuck you. Just this once. Just this morning. Just to see if what I've been hearing about you is all true. I've absolutely no intention of telling anyone about what I'm going to do with you right now and even if I did go running off to our new American friends, as you call them, then who do you think they are going to believe? Some drippy, wet-behind-the-ears, pissed-up floozy or the man they probably can't afford to lose? And anyway. Would they really care? I don't think so." She then climbed onto Will, pushing him down so that she could straddle him. "And, actually, I'm only nine years younger than you."

*

The morning heralded a feeling of disgust and self-loathing for Will. He could hear the sound of the shower running as he sat up in bed to slowly recall the events of an early Saturday morning. He decided to stay in bed to see what Grace did next, which sounded like her walking into the spare bedroom to presumably change back into the clothes she wore the night before.

Minutes later, Grace opened the door to Will's bedroom and poked her head around the door with a smile. "I'll be off now then. Maybe see you on Monday?"

"Hold on, Grace. Do you want a coffee or some breakfast before you go?"

"No, that's fine. I'd better get going. I've arranged to see someone in Stevenage."

"Wait a minute," Will called, dragging the duvet around him as he stood up. "But what about last night? I mean, this morning?"

"A bit of fun, wasn't it, but don't you worry. Our little secret. A nice ending to a good night out, don't you think? Nothing more than that. And your reputation remains intact!"

"Are you sure you don't want some breakfast?"

"You are sweet. I'll let myself out."

Will I ever learn? Will my brain ever be able to overrule my prick? But it's hardly like I took advantage of her. She took advantage of me. Took advantage of my weakness. The weakness of being a man.

A vivid recall of that night and the morning that followed stayed with Will into the following week. The thought of the possible consequences kept him company for even longer. Like all such nights, he had very much enjoyed the experience, but he was certainly not accustomed to having to worry about any consequences. He had assumed he would be getting knowing looks whenever he bumped into Grace at work. There were none. Not even as much as a wink or a secretive smile. Will was even half expecting that she would want to meet up with him again despite what she had told him. But she didn't. Nevertheless, that didn't stop Will imagining the worst. That he would soon become a blackmail victim and all that he had worked for and dreamed of would be lost in a heartbeat. *Great timing on her behalf,* thought Will as Myers-Stratton were moving in to acquire his company. *All because of a fuck I wasn't even looking for! Maybe it was all destined to end this way and payback from Him up there for the man I have become.*

But what would she want from him for the price of her silence? Money? Promotion at work? Her apparent indifference to what had happened and the uncertainty of what, if anything, might take place next were actually worse than being propositioned again or even just teased. At least he knew how to walk away from a relationship with good grace and a genuine appreciation and concern for the feelings of the woman. Had he underestimated that little, young girl or was he becoming paranoid? Is this really something he needed to worry about? A real threat to his career? A rational person would discount Myers-Stratton walking away from a potentially lucrative deal just because their key employee-to-be had rolled under the covers with one of his reports, although it would not have been a good look for Will, not least in front of Celeste. But Will was struggling to be rational, preferring instead to drift into panic mode.

Maybe I will just let sleeping dogs lie, at least for the time being, as what upside could there be in doing anything about it, whether that is confronting Grace or even telling Celeste? After all, it's not like either of us are married, for fuck's sake. The problem is that I just can't work her out. Yes, another bloody one. Surely Grace is not the sort of person who is up for one-night stands. Not that sweet little girl. If that is really the case, then why the bloody hell did she do it if it was not to blackmail me. Fuck! We didn't use a condom.

THE DATA

"Jeavons is not going to like this," muttered Nev over the breakfast table whilst moving his perennially unappetising muesli around his bowl. In his other hand ,he was holding some loose sheets of A4 paper that he had just printed out.

Li suddenly stood to attention after bending over to pick up a spoon she had dropped. "But I thought you were not going to tell him about the job offer you had from Biopharmaco. You were going to wait to see if Granta Pain were going to offer you some sort of redundancy deal. Or am I going a bit mad here?"

Nev could see the concern in his wife's eyes as she sat down opposite him clutching the spoon she had recovered. He held up his printout. "This?" he pronounced. "This is nothing to do with the job offer, which is safely stashed away upstairs waiting for my signature. And don't you go worrying your little head off, dear, I have no intention of telling Jeavons that I've got another job, or at least not until I have to, and hopefully not at all if they make me redundant. This document is likely to be much more worrying to Jeavons and his new American friends than any lost sleep they might have over Neville Chamberlain finding another job. It's the preliminary data we got back last night from Biopharmaco on the GTP107 tox and safety pharmacology. Pretty good on the whole, I would say, and matches the data that has already been publicly disclosed apart from one teeny, tiny, wee problem. Without going into details to my non-scientist wife, there is one potentially alarming result that suggests that the drug could cause serious cardiovascular toxicity. I can hear our Dr Jeavons swearing and throwing all sorts of things across the room when he opens the Excel spreadsheet, which he could well have done yesterday evening when it was posted."

"Is it serious? Could it mean that the drug's no good and won't work?"

"Yes. I would say it's potentially a *very* serious finding. A showstopper, even. I can't see the very safety-conscious Americans allowing GTP107 to be tested in any more patients at the very least until they can understand the finding."

Li scrunched up her face. "Could the Americans just walk away from Granta Pain?"

"Very possibly, my dear, but not until after many lawsuits have been filed to try and claw some of their money back. It could get very nasty very quickly for our Dr Jeavons. It will be very interesting indeed to hear what he's got to say when I go and see him about the data after

I get into work." Nev placed the paper down next to his bowl of muesli with the slightest of self-satisfied smiles. "Very interesting indeed."

The prospect of his boss having to face up to Granta Pain going to the wall was far more compelling than any unlikely invite Nev might have to remain as an employee. Such was his personality.

*

"Not clear-cut at all, I would say, Nev. Not an issue and nothing to be overly concerned about, my friend."

Will was hunched over his laptop and Nev was behind him peering over his shoulder at the spreadsheets and graphs he had poured over just the night before. If only his office had enough room for standing in some degree of comfort.

"What do you mean, not clear-cut? Biopharmaco have not only given the actual number with error limits but have also written in plain English, POSITIVE. Doesn't that worry you, Will? Because it certainly worries the fuck out of me."

"Of course it does, as would any tox finding, but we have to put this into perspective. The drug would have to reach very high exposures for this result to be relevant. Agreed?" He didn't get a response from Nev but wasn't really expecting one. "Only then would there be a slight risk to a very small proportion of the population of the drug causing an irregular heartbeat, which might lead to a stroke. How does that risk stack up against the benefit patients would have from a non-addictive therapy for chronic pain? All those people we could save from dying from an opioid overdose. Many thousands of people compared against a mere handful of people who might, just might, be affected by this potential side effect. As always, Nev, this is a risk-benefit argument." Will looked over his shoulder up to his fellow scientist, hoping to hear that Nev agreed with his conclusions.

"But it's not for us, not for you and me, to make these calls. We just generate the appropriate data and throw it over the fence for the development and the clinical people to make the call. We are just not qualified to make that sort of judgement."

"And you know what they will say, don't you, Nev? The drug is too risky to take into humans. Terminate the programme. Make us all redundant. Close down Granta Pain."

"That's as maybe, Will. But the final decision on the drug is well above all our pay grades."

"So the world will never get the opportunity to finally be able to treat chronic pain without the risk of causing addiction. Thousands upon thousands of people all across the world will continue to be killed from opioid abuse. All because of a potential tiny risk to a small cohort of the population. Don't forget, this drug has already been in over two hundred patients without any evidence that it increases cardiovascular-mediated adverse effects."

"What are you suggesting we do then? Pretend that we never saw this data?"

"It is not a regulatory requirement for this test to be carried out. We didn't have to ask Biopharmaco to do this test, did we?"

"Whoa. Hold on a minute there," shouted Nev, now standing bolt upright. "It was Biopharmaco who suggested that we run this test and not me. It was you who signed off the invoice approving this. Not me."

"Calm down, Nev. You're not being blamed for anything. As you said, I signed off on this and I will take full responsibility."

"Fine," answered Nev, who had relaxed his stance. "As long as we are both clear on that."

"In fact, you don't need to have any further involvement with this. I want you to step back and allow me to deal with these data and working with Biopharmaco moving forward. I will be the point person in dealing with Ron. This could get tricky with the Americans, and I am doing you the favour of you not being associated with these data and any decisions made. As far as you and I are concerned, you never saw these data. Is that clear, Nev? Let me deal with it from now on."

"What are we going to do with these findings?"

"You don't have to do anything. Remember, you never saw the data. You are not implicated. You just passed it onto me to deal with. What am I going to do with these findings? I don't know, Nev. I really don't know."

*

Will's response to the worrying data and the important, potentially career-defining decisions he must now make was typical. To go for a long walk. His usual lunchtime walk was through the busy shopping malls and markets of Cambridge. Past the grand facades of the colleges. Up the winding, cobbled streets. Browsing amongst the second-hand bookshops. Even add in some people-watching. But not today. Today, Will needed time to be alone. Away from people and in open spaces. He was a member of the botanical gardens and that was going to be his sanctuary this lunchtime. There would be others making the most of a fresh and bright day but not many at this time of the year. Spring was Will's favourite time to visit the gardens but here was a chance to think amongst the autumn colours that were beginning to be lost to the coming winter. A chance to consider his options.

If he had been in Nev's position, then he would have argued exactly the same. Listen to the data. Follow the data. Respect the data. Keep to the science. Act rationally. But he wasn't in such a fortunate position. Will was the CEO of a company that could succeed or fail on the fine margins of how these data were interpreted. His career and future prospects in the industry would pivot on whatever he did or did not do in the days that followed. Even more important, his decision might negatively impact the millions of patients currently having to deal with being addicted to drugs that might eventually kill them if GPT107 never made it to market. Worse still could be that he was responsible for a drug that actually killed people.

Will decided to sit down on an empty bench next to a large, ornate fountain to consider the options he had formulated as he walked up through the avenue of towering ancient pine and yew trees. Both options seemed as frightening as the other. The easy option would be to disclose everything to Myers-Stratton and to do it now. No future worries about adverse drug effects to concern Will even if it did mean that the drug and his company would likely be no more. It would take time, but he believed in himself enough to think that he would overcome such a career setback. How long? No investor would likely trust him for at least five years was his best guess. The likely price of Will taking this seemingly easy option.

Every time he circled around the options confronting him, he just couldn't escape the imagined presence of his mother amongst the bushes surrounding the fountain he was engrossed in. If only life was as reliable and predictable as the water tumbling from the fountain he was staring at so intently. With her ethereal presence came a reminder of what he had been striving for. The thought of being able to make the deaths caused by opioid abuse no more than a shocking part of medical history. How could he ever consider giving up on such an opportunity to save the lives of so many, even at the cost of those who might die from drug side effects? Many faced with such a moral dilemma would consider how they would feel if it was someone dear to them who died from an already-known drug side effect as the price for others to benefit. A thought process Will struggled with, as there was no one in his life other than his adoptive parents that he cared about.

By the time he had walked past the last soaring pine tree on his way out of the gardens, he had convinced himself of the option he must now take.

*

It was early morning on a late-October day and so only the faintest of autumn sunlight was struggling to break through

Will's bedroom curtains. A restless night had followed a day filled with impossible, life-defining decisions to be considered. A night that visited upon Will the latest rerun of the events leading up to his mother's death, ending with him waking up standing over his mother's lifeless body and feeling so desperately alone. But worse was to follow that night. His subconscious was visited by the ghost of his mother, who appeared on the chair in the corner of the bedroom.

"Hello, my dear, dear son. Do you still remember me? Do you still think about the mother that gave you life?"

Will struggled to focus his eyes on whatever was in his room and sat up in the bed to help him visualise the intrusion.

She smiled at him. A smile he had never forgotten and would always recognise. "No pyjamas, Will? But I suppose you are no longer that sweet and handsome eleven-year-old boy I remember you as. I've just popped in to see my little boy."

"It can't be. No. You're not my mum. Who the fuck are you? How did you get in here? If you don't leave now, I will call the police." Will reached for his phone on the bedside drawer but there was no phone and there was no drawer. This was a dream he didn't know he was in.

"But you really do know it's me, don't you, Will? How could anyone else be me? Think about it, Will. I'm your mum. Always have been, always will be. Do you recognise the clothes I'm wearing? The same clothes I was wearing when you last saw me lying on my bed. Who else could remember that last night we spent together. That terrible, terrible night in Wandsworth when I made you do those

167

awful things in the chemist's. I know for sure that you never told anyone about the little details of that night, such as the angry bus driver and me switching the door sign to closed. So, who else could I be other than your mum?"

A sudden chill swept down the top of Will's back. He was petrified at the apparition that looked and sounded so much like the mother he loved. "It's not possible. This is just a dream. You're not real." He wanted to go back to sleep to prove he was right but was too frightened to close his eyes. Ghosts don't exist. All scientists knew that. The vision of his mother lying motionless brought a tight knot to his throat.

"I've been watching over you for all these years; seeing you grow up with those kind foster parents, but you should always remember that I will always be your real mum. I was so very proud when you passed all those hard exams and got into university. The first one in our family who has ever gone to university. Did you know that, Will? The first. And then you become a university lecturer. You are such a clever little boy. My son Will. A university lecturer. Who would ever have believed it? And now, even better. You have your very own company. I just know you are going to be so rich and so famous and so happy. I just know you will." The apparition smiled and clutched her hands together tightly just as his mother always did.

"Thank you, Mum, that means so much to me. Perhaps it would mean a bit more to me if you were actually alive but hey ho, beggars can't be choosers. Why is it that you have suddenly turned up this morning? Where have you been for the past thirty-odd years?"

"Like every day of your life, I am here this morning just as I was with you yesterday. I was there when you had those difficult discussions with your work colleague. I was with you when you walked through the gardens. When you sat down next to the fountain. I could see what you were thinking. The reason I am here this morning is to help you through this difficult part of your life. To help you make this so important of decisions."

"Please forgive me, Mum. Mum? Is that what I should call you? But what do you know about science? About drug discovery?"

"Of course I'm not a scientist, Will, and we both know that I haven't got a clue about all that exciting research that you are doing in your labs. However, I am a human being. Like many of us, I have also been a patient. I do understand something about medicines, and given all the drugs I took, then I think it is probably fair to say that I probably know more about drugs than most people. So maybe I'm allowed an opinion. It seems to me that it is you scientists that make all these risk-benefit decisions, and no one asks the patient what side effects and risks they are prepared to put up with for a drug that cures them. The point I'm trying to *make*? A very simple one, my boy, and perhaps one you would do well to listen to. If I had been lucky enough to be able to take a non-addictive painkiller like the one that you are working on, then the person talking to you now from the other side of your bedroom would actually be real. Your mother would still be alive. As would so many, many thousands of other victims from all over the world who would not have died during the opioid pandemic if only they had also been offered that same non-addictive painkiller. That benefit versus the tiny heart risk that you are so worried about. What do you youngsters say? It's a no-brainer to any patient who suffers from a symptom that haunts their every waking hour. Pain that affects not only their lives but also those who care for them. All those that love them and worry about them. Pain that is so bad that they are willing to risk overdosing and death just to get some relief. So, my boy. For the sakes of all the millions of people who suffer every day from excruciating pain that never goes away, please, please don't throw away your marvellous discovery because of a risk that may never be realised."

*

A very rushed morning followed, including missing breakfast, which he hated doing, and he was going to be even later for work than he usually was. It was only a little later when he found himself unable to get across the traffic lights and onto Lensfield Road because of the road being dug up one more time that he thought through what had happened only hours before. The unconscious argument he had with himself as to what he should do next. Will's imaginary ghostly mother was merely articulating and reinforcing what he himself had already considered was the best course of action. The best path through the moral and personal dilemma he had found himself in. Ignore and so don't disclose the aberrant data. Take the risk. Give sufferers of debilitating chronic pain a real option. Save the drug. Save his conscience.

THE SANCTITY OF SCIENTIFIC DATA

*T*he *inescapable premise underpinning the so-called scientific method is the veracity of the data that is used in support of a hypothesis. If the experimental data is flawed in some way or not found to be reproducible, then one should question whether the hypothesis has been fully validated. Even when the experimental data is robust and reproducible, it is far from unusual for scientists to disagree on the interpretation of the data. The conclusions, if you like. You see, much to the annoyance of us all but especially to us scientists, science isn't really an exact science. All part of the gig, I suppose, but what is not acceptable is the fabrication of data or even omitting data because it does not fit in with a preconceived hypothesis. It was the latter very big no-no that Will was guilty of.*

Will was fully aware that if the drug was even close to as efficacious as he hoped it would be, he would be responsible for patients dying. Millions of patients on the drug would inevitably lead to at least tens of patients dying from the cardiovascular toxicity flagged up by the data that Will had buried. Not an unreasonable judgement call for him to make, even if it wasn't his to make. Such judgement calls are the responsibility of faceless committees populated by scientists and clinicians able to hide behind collective decision-making so that it can always be considered as somebody else's fault if something goes wrong.

So. A ballsy decision by Will to take given the demons that will almost certainly haunt him for the rest of his life knowing that he and only he would be responsible for the deaths of patients who took the drug believing it was safe. Rather him than me carrying such a burden on just his own shoulders. Rather him than me having to worry about the consequences of being found out, which could even lead to a prison term but at the very least would signal the end of his career in science. But you've got to hand it to the man, whatever is your point of view and however wrong you think he is. Will was prepared to risk all to push forward in his crusade to find a non-addictive treatment for chronic pain. Unfortunately, risking all also included risking the lives of patients. He was the not-so-proud owner of a very personal moral dilemma.

THE SIGNING

"I know the deal has been signed and we are now full steam ahead – how exciting! – but I was thinking of maybe dropping by your labs and doing a sort of mock signing, which will help with the publicity," was Celeste's opening gambit.

"Great idea but how would this work? As you might have guessed, I really don't have much experience in this sort of thing."

"Myers-Stratton has its own press office and so I will ask them to look into how they can rev up the local Boston press and maybe some UK nationals, although that might be too much of a stretch. Perhaps, Will, you could contact your local Cambridge press. They must be very used to publicising biotech deals."

Will tried to imagine just where he would start in trying to contact the local press. *Surely someone in the university could help me with that. Good publicity for the university as well as for Granta Pain.*

"Sure. I'll see if I can sort something out, Celeste."

"But here comes the catch! Could you sort this for next week. Ideally next Wednesday. The 17th November, according to my calendar. Terribly short notice, I know, and I do apologise. But I am in Germany at the start of the week, and I thought I would drop by on my way back to Boston. Could you possibly squeeze me in next week, Will?"

Will pretended to look through his calendar and paused for added effect. "Should be OK at the moment and of course you will be my top priority should anything crop up in the meantime." *Which it won't.*

"That's great, and it's not as if we don't have a lot to talk about. Perhaps I can leave it to you and my PA to sort out details, as I will be travelling from tomorrow. I will ask Kate to get in touch with you before the end of the week. Does that all work for you?"

"Of course. Very much looking forward to meeting up again."

"Me too. Could I also ask you to make sure all your staff are available on that Wednesday? I would like to have one-to-one meetings with them."

Faint alarm bells were ringing in Will's head. *Being interviewed for their own jobs? I suppose I shouldn't be surprised but I'm going to have to try to find a way to manage the guys panicking when I let them know.* "Not a problem. Will get onto it. What about local hotels and travel? Do you want me to arrange anything for you?"

"Thanks, but no need. Kate is very good at arranging my itineraries. Local transport in Cambridge? I didn't think that such a thing existed other than by bike or punt! Maybe a horse or two?"

"Very good, Celeste," Will joked, "but you can always choose to be ripped off by a local taxi driver should you so wish."

"Maybe one thing you can arrange, if you don't mind. Book a table for two somewhere in town for dinner on Wednesday evening. Somewhere nice but, as I mentioned on an earlier call, not too nice, if you get my drift! OK. Last thing before I go. The team here are keen for you to come over to Boston ASAP to talk about your proposal, deliverables, budgets and work plans as well as us discussing the make-up of the new board. So, another little job I have handed over to Kate is to organise everyone's diaries. Poor girl! Including your diary, of course. I would suggest that you consider this meeting your top priority. Allow at least two full days in Boston if not longer." Celeste paused and Will heard someone talking in the background. "Fine. In a minute, Kate. Listen, Will, better sign off now but I think we have covered everything. Very much looking forward to catching up with you next week. See you soon enough."

"Safe journey and take care."

*

With so little to do at work while he waited for further instruction and hopefully approval from Myers-Stratton on the next steps he had proposed, Will had spent much of the previous week obsessing about the toxicity finding. Part of his problem was that this was not an area in which he had much expertise and so there was a great deal of background to learn. Will spent hours scanning through scientific databases he had begged and borrowed from his university colleagues, to which he even added more than a few Google searches. The conclusion he had arrived at was that it was difficult to arrive at a conclusion. Too much contradictory data and differing opinions from the so-called experts in the field. After exhausting all the possible sensible search queries plus several searches that were far from sensible, Will had pretty much arrived at where he had started. Yes, the finding was a concern, but it was a judgement call as to whether it would predict what happened in humans. Will was reassured that regulatory authorities like the FDA did not insist that the results from this particular toxicity assay be included in any drug submissions, presumably because it was not reliable enough to predict an adverse event in a patient. But, even after becoming a blagging expert in this new area for him, Will's problems had pretty much remained the same. The toxicity assay had been run, it had provided an adverse finding and the judgement call was not for Will to make, even though that's exactly what he was going to do. Ignore the data and hope that it didn't translate to humans and lead to serious side effects. But if it did, hope that any investigations by the regulatory authorities would not uncover Will's big secret. Unfortunately for him, a secret that Nev was also aware of and another potential blackmail threat for Will to deal with, but all in good time. Blackmailers flourished in Will's paranoid world.

*

"Hi, Will. It's Celeste. I'm just outside the front door of your building."

"Great! With you in a few seconds."

He threw on a jacket he had perched on the back of his office chair which he had brought to work for the occasion of Celeste's visit. He had considered also bringing along a tie but that thought didn't dwell on the mind for long. Will believed that he had pushed the boat out by wearing a pair of socks and real leather shoes. The tie-less scientist bounded down the wide sets of stairs and opened the front door to the building. Celeste was dressed exactly the way Will had expected. Smart business suit. Immaculate hair and make-up. Briefcase. He toyed with the idea of a friendly hug but decided otherwise. *Too familiar.* He offered his hand to his American guest.

"Celeste! How nice to see you." She shook his hand.

"No welcoming hug for your future work colleague? I am surprised," she teased.

Just can't fucking win, thought Will as he smiled and signed in the visitor. "How did you get here from the University Arms? Don't tell me you walked all that way through the dangerous streets of Cambridge City."

"But of course not. I went with the option of being ripped off by one of your friendly cab drivers. A very chatty gentleman indeed."

As they approached the landing leading to the Granta Pain labs, Will asked if Celeste wanted coffee before starting out on what was a very full itinerary.

"Thanks, but no. Let's crack on with the one-to-ones as I am going to have to finish up on them before meeting your contact at the local newspaper over lunch."

"That's fine. What's not so fine, however, is that I'm afraid you will have to use my office for the interviews. I was too late in booking the meeting room upstairs. Too short notice. On the plus side, we have managed to provide seating for two people. You will be sitting on stools!"

"That's OK. I have put up with worse," she lied. "But where will you go?"

"Don't worry about me. Perhaps you would be kind enough to ask your last victim to come and find me when you have finished, and then we can go to lunch with the newspaper guy."

"I trust you didn't use that word when you told them about the interviews."

"Just my little joke, Celeste. But I should give you a heads-up on the reactions I had when I did tell them. All rabbit-in-the headlights petrified. I guess they are all still pretty young and inexperienced."

"But what about Nev? I can't imagine him being petrified."

"Ah, yes. He wasn't. You might well have your hands full with him."

"I was expecting as much. Perhaps you could send him up first. See you for lunch."

After taking Celeste up to his office, he closed the door behind him and walked down the corridor and into the Granta Pain lab. Nev was at his bench swearing at a blocked micro pipette.

"You're up first, Nev," called Will from just inside the door. "And behave yourself, young man. We should all show the company in its best light."

"Of course, boss," answered Nev, throwing his lab coat at the clothes hanger next to the door and missing badly. As he bent down to retrieve the lab coat, he smiled back at his boss. "I've got my cardboard box ready for when she's finished with me," added Nev, pointing to the box underneath his workbench.

Will looked to avoid taking the bait. "As I said to you all last week, this is not an interview for your job. Celeste just wants to meet the team, which I think is more than reasonable, don't you think, Nev?"

"Of course, boss," replied Nev, looking over to the others in the lab who had been watching the conversation intently. "Just saying. That's all I'm doing. Just saying."

*

"What was it like, Nev? What was she like?" Grace was, not surprisingly, the first to start interrogating Nev as he sat down with his coffee. "You're up next, Antonio. Smash it, my son." Antonio stood up sharply and almost ran to the door of the tearoom. No one present that morning thought he looked as if he was going to smash anything.

"What was it like?" He picked up his mug and immediately replaced it on the low table. Still too hot. "She's a smooth one, I'll give her that. Knows all the right long words to say. The bullshit. The patter. Lots of 'we's' and lots of 'teams' and 'cultures' and 'diversity' and 'world beating' this, that and the other. I rather got the feeling that we are very different people, but I don't think that opinion would shock anyone."

Grace again. "Did she say anything about headcount?"

"Not a dickybird, but in fairness to the woman, I didn't ask. No point. Anyway, you won't get any straight answers out of these corporate types. They've already made their minds up and there is absolutely fuck all we can do about it."

Not even Grace could think of anything to say or ask as all focused on the drinks in front of them and their jobs that might no longer be.

*

"I've booked a table at a small Italian place around the corner, close enough even for Americans to be able to walk to," joked Will as he opened the main doors to the building for Celeste to walk out into the cold November afternoon.

"Well, we'll just have to see about that, won't we," replied Celeste, pulling her coat tightly around her.

"Sam Chalmers from the *Cambridge Evening News* is due to meet us there at around one, so we have time to chat over a few things first." Will let his companion walk ahead of him as he struggled to zip up his overcoat. *With all that has been going on, I completely forgot what an absolutely cracking ass that woman has got.*

Both were happy to find the restaurant warm and that they had been seated near the back to enjoy even more warmth.

"So, Celeste, how did the interviews go?"

"Pretty straightforward, I suppose. Lots of nerves, perhaps not surprisingly, but I think there were some good conversations, and I now have a much better understanding of the strengths and weaknesses of the team."

Very business speak. Very Celeste. Very worrying, thought Will as he nodded through her comments.

"As I think I said when I was last here, Grace was easily the standout person. Still a bit nervous but she came across as having a strong interest in the project and enthusiasm for the work she has been assigned. Also, a nice personality. On the other side of the spectrum is Nev."

Will looked down at the table and the menus in front of him. "Yes. Our Nev."

"Well 'our' Nev was a real handful. Very outspoken and critical of you in particular. Evasive of several of my questions. I know you Brits like to think of yourselves as eccentrics, but I got the feeling that he's had enough of Granta Pain. That he wanted to be made redundant. A very bizarre interview. Almost felt like an exit interview."

"I think we can both agree that he's a maverick but his experience as a scientist has been invaluable to the company. He's been a great mentor to the young team, and I would go as far as to say that we wouldn't be where we are now without Nev's expertise."

They both picked up a small, laminated lunch menu. "I think I'll just have a salad if it's alright with you, Will. Keep some room for dinner tonight." Celeste clearly did not want to talk any further about that strange man, Nev.

A stranger to them both stood uncomfortably close to their table. "Dr William Jeavons? Hi, I'm Sam Chalmers from the *Cambridge Evening News*."

Will stood up to shake the hand of the reporter. "Please, it's just Will and this is Celeste Simmonds from Myers-Stratton."

With introductions made and lunches ordered, Celeste launched into a very impressive description of the two companies, the science and their ambitions. The poor, young reporter hadn't fully appreciated what his editor had teed up for him as he furiously attempted to write down what he hoped were the main points of Celeste's excitable monologue. All Will had to do was sit back and smile at the clear mismatch. *What a pro*, admired Will.

"Anything you want to add to that, Will?" asked Sam, desperately hoping that there wasn't. He had hardly touched his rapidly cooling pizza slice.

Will smiled at the question. "No, I don't think so. My esteemed colleague has pretty much said it all. And maybe even a bit more." He winked at Celeste.

"How about a few photos? Back at the labs, perhaps?"

"Yeah, OK I suppose. OK with you, Celeste?" enquired Will. She nodded in the affirmative.

The smiling couple were pictured at various places around the lab and the university building, some even with them wearing lab coats, which did not go down well with Nev.

"Can you believe that? Can you fucking believe that!" whispered Nev through gritted teeth to Antonio. "When was the last time that woman did any lab work? Absolutely ridiculous. We should be the ones in that photograph."

The hours remaining that afternoon were spent in Will's office going through his proposed next steps through into the New Year. His ego struggled from time to time as Celeste picked apart some of Will's more ambitious objectives, defending her criticism by saying that she knew how the scientists back at Myers-Stratton would respond and so she was really just trying to help him. He had never taken well to criticism and was pricklier than Celeste had expected.

It had just passed 5pm and Celeste looked up at the clock on the wall to their side as a polite way of suggesting game over. Will took the hint.

"Yes. Getting late and I was going to pick you up at the hotel to take you to dinner at 7pm, if I remember the plan correctly."

"Looking forward to it. Where are we going to?"

"My little secret. Another must-do Cambridge experience. That much I can say."

"Sounds exciting." Celeste stood up, brushed herself down, and stepped forward towards Will's office door, opening it out into the corridor in the same motion.

"One last thing before you go."

She pulled her stool back and sat down again.

"You told me how the interviews went, but will you be making any decisions on headcount on the basis of those meetings?"

"This was something we were going to discuss when you come over to Boston, but I guess I could let you know our current thinking on this as long as you keep what I say strictly confidential." She leaned over and gently closed the office door that she had only just opened.

"Goes without saying, Celeste."

"The focus for Granta Pain for the next two to three years will be getting GPT107 through to an efficacy read out in the clinic. Will the drug have a significant effect on chronic pain and will it be non-addictive. If the drug does not work as we are hoping it will, then that will almost certainly be the end of our interest in the asset and Granta

Pain. I know that sounds very brutal, but I'm afraid it's the nature of our business, Will, and our competitors would behave similarly."

Will nodded with the pretence that he was also familiar with the nature of 'our' business.

"On that basis, we need every cent to go towards moving the drug forward through the clinic."

Get to the grisly point to all this fluffy preamble, my dear.

"What does that mean?" She paused before delivering the line they both knew was coming. "What that means is that I'm afraid we will have to cut your headcount."

Will was not going to make it any easier for her, so he remained silent.

"All of your headcount apart from you, naturally."

He had been expecting to have to make a few of his staff redundant but definitely not all of them. Will was genuinely shocked, and Celeste could see that in his face.

"All of them? But when? How quickly?"

"As soon as their notice period ends after we let them know sometime next week."

"All of them?" he repeated. "And just before Christmas?"

"I am genuinely sorry, Will. I have personally gone through this sort of thing far too many times before and so I know how you must be feeling right now, but I'm afraid that it is the correct decision given the circumstances. We are prepared to take a risk and go into the clinic without a back-up drug and so we no longer need the staff to work on developing such a contingency."

"But what about working on fully understanding and definitively proving just how GPT107 works? If you sack all the team, then you have lost the expertise needed to do that."

"As a scientist myself, I perfectly understand your rationale, Will, of course I do, but we consider such blue-sky work as a 'nice to have' rather than an essential piece of research to be funded."

She could see that this news had completely thrown Will, who was now busy staring at what little floor was visible in his office. Celeste needed to throw him a bone.

"I've shared with you our current and highly confidential position on this sensitive matter. You're coming over to see us in Boston, why don't you present a counter proposal? A robust and convincing justification for holding onto the staff if you believe it would help our business moving forward."

"I could do that, yes, but is this just playing games and I would end up wasting my time? And yours."

"No. I'm being genuine here. However, perhaps some words of advice for you to consider. I do think you would be wasting everyone's time by trying to argue that all the staff should be kept on. Also, I personally would push back if you wanted to keep Nev as an employee following on from what I said earlier. Most important of all, the headcount must be directly linked and responsible for key company objectives and deliverables. Make sense to you, Will?"

"Sure, sure. I'll give it some thought and maybe present something in Boston."

"I'm sorry that we have ended the working day on rather a sour note, but I hope you understand our business priorities. We shouldn't let this undermine our good working relationship. You and me. At least, what I think is a good working relationship."

"We're fine, Celeste," commented Will, who was beginning to regain his composure, "and even finer still when we enjoy dinner out tonight. Have I got a treat for you?" Will couldn't supress a wicked smile.

"Now you really are starting to get me worried," whispered Celeste as she stood up and once again opened the office door. "Very worried indeed!"

As Will waved off Celeste, who herself was waving from a taxi that she insisted on Will ordering, he turned back into the building and made his way back to the office to lock up and leave for home to get ready for dinner.

Not good. I really needed to keep on Nev and Grace. Sure because they are the best two I have but also because I'm worried to fuck that they could blackmail me. Nev over me burying the Biopharmaco data and Grace because I was stupid and weak enough to shag her. But hang on a moment. If Nev is toast, I could just tell him that I've changed my mind, and I will disclose the data to Myers-Stratton just as he thinks I should. He will never find out that I haven't. Sorted! Brilliant! And to be honest, the man has been getting on my tits recently, so I think the lovely Celeste has probably done me a huge favour. Grace? Not so easy. Maybe she's the one I need to keep on as an employee. Certainly a lot nicer to look at in the mornings than that pig-ugly Mancunian.

*

It was a reenergised Will who was smiling at his dinner guest across the reception area as he walked into the

University Arms. He now had a plan, and everything might just work out fine for him after all. Time would tell.

Will made a very obvious point of hugging his guest before she even had a chance to say hello.

"Is that what is considered a hug back in Boston?" asked Will, relinquishing his surprised victim.

"Close enough, I would say." She smiled her approval. "Have I come suitably dressed for this treat you promised me? A Cambridge experience everyone must have?"

Celeste had certainly dressed for the part. That ageless black dress that Will was sure he had seen her wear before, covered with a long woollen coat she would soon need to fasten up tightly before stepping out into the winter evening. Unfortunately, unbeknownst to her, the part she had dressed for was not the part she would be playing that night.

"The place I'm taking you to, Celeste, has no dress code. You can come along looking a million dollars like your good self or ten dollars like me." Will was being a little harsh on himself, as he had at least kept hold of the jacket, shoes and socks he had worn earlier in the day even if he had rather undermined his efforts by wearing jeans.

It was the jeans that made Celeste rather nervous. "Are you sure I'm not overdressed for this treat of yours?"

"You're just fine, Celeste. In fact, better than that, you look great. Trust me!"

"No cab, I see," observed Celeste, wrapping her coat around her as they walked out onto Regent Street.

"No need. We have the very shortest of walks and I promise you, it is well worth the effort."

"In this weather? What do you Brits say? Brass monkey weather or something like that?"

"Maybe a tad chilly but you must have much worse in Boston this time of year."

"So people tell me, Will, but I never venture out in such weather."

"OK, let's make a deal. If you start to freeze up on the walk there, we will stop one of your taxi friends and get them to tell you that it's not worth their effort to drive such a short distance."

"Let's get it over with then," barked Celeste, hooking her arm under his.

The walk to Mill Road took longer than she was hoping for but less time than Will had allowed for, such that they arrived slightly earlier at the restaurant than the time Will had booked the table for.

He stopped Celeste just outside the restaurant door for them both to take in the view.

"And here we have it, Celeste. The premium eatery in the whole of Cambridgeshire where people flock to from miles around. The one and only, the very famous, Curry Queen!"

"If I'm being honest, Will, I'm struggling here to not be underwhelmed. Just not picking up on the superior ambience," she joked. "I really do hope it's better from the inside."

"We'll have the best of times. Trust me," promised Will as he guided Celeste into the restaurant.

And the best of times they both had once Celeste had stopped worrying about being 'ridiculously overdressed'. A deliberate ploy on Will's part not only because he just loved women dressed up to the nines but also because he felt that she would fall in with the joke. Given time, maybe.

Their conversation was immediately friendly and flowed easily. As the evening wore on with Celeste thoroughly enjoying the experience of several tastes she had not encountered before, the topic of conversation gradually veered from work to their personal lives. All this was oiled by the various Indian beers that Will insisted she should at least try. It was not long before Celeste felt the need to update Will on her car crash of a marriage when he asked her about home.

"Even worse than when we spoke about it back in the summer. Much worse. My marriage, that is, of course, but I don't want to bore you with all that."

"Not boring at all. Talk about what you want to talk about. I know I always do."

"OK. Perhaps I should be right up front with you."

Will was now not so sure that he should have granted the concession. "Are you sure? You know you don't have to be."

"That night we went to that Italian restaurant in Boston, remember? The real reason I rushed off leaving early was to get back home to catch Charles with his latest bit of pussy I thought he was entertaining that night. Sorry. I do so hate that word. I don't know why I used it. What do you Brits call it? Skirt. His latest bit of skirt. Oh, Charles is… was… my husband, if I hadn't told you before. Anyway. I needed something… I don't know… Struggling for the word, here, must be the Indian booze… Something definitive, I suppose. Final proof, at least to my father, as to what a little shit my husband was, and that divorce is the only sensible option."

Will was genuinely shocked at her candour. *Why is she*

telling me all this? It's like she has gone from 0–60 mph in a heartbeat. It's not as if she's drunk that much.

"But it didn't turn out like that. If there was some floozy he had hidden up in the house then I couldn't find her, although that didn't mean there wasn't someone there. We have a big house. That wasn't the real shock, though. The real surprise was that we, I don't know… made up that night. Decided to give our marriage another go. A final chance." She paused, using the need to pick up her drink of India's finest as an excuse to gather her thoughts. She hated talking about something that she felt so ashamed of. A failed marriage caused by her choosing a failure of a man. But there was just something about this man she was with that brought out this strange feeling of wanting to drag out this pain that she had inside in her. Lancing a boil. Someone to share her raw feelings with. A confidante. Not that it really made any sense to her as to why all these closely guarded secrets were now being spilled to someone she barely knew.

Will could sense that this was not the end of the story. "I'm picking up that there might be a 'but' here."

"There is. But the biggest shock was really that I went along with it all. That I believed he was true to his word and really wanted to try and make our marriage work. That he would be faithful to me. Well, that particular honeymoon barely lasted two weeks. He went out one evening and forgot to take his phone with him. An unheard-of event. Which was a pity because he missed a text from Naomi, who was wondering why he was so late getting to their hotel. Young Naomi who, I must say, has a fantastic body, decided it would help in rushing him along to send a few snaps of her in various poses unfettered by as much as a stitch of clothing."

"Oh, that's just terrible, Celeste. So sorry to hear what you have been put through." After the experiences of his own life, Will was genuinely sorry for all the painful emotions that Celeste was now going through herself.

"I will spare you the details of what followed other than to say that I have instructed my lawyers to file for divorce. Doesn't that sentence sound so good?"

"Has he moved out?"

"After all that has happened, you would have thought so, wouldn't you? But it is me who has moved out. Living in a hotel with my parents storing all my stuff. They offered to put me up, but I couldn't bear the ignominy of going back home to live with my parents. I'll start looking for an apartment when things calm down a bit at work."

"Really? Sounds a little unusual. Shouldn't he be the one who moves out?"

"His argument is that he doesn't want a divorce so why should he have to move out. So stressful. And I'm not going to stay there if he isn't going to move out. I just can't stand the sight of the man anymore. I want him out of my life. For good."

Will shook his head in disbelief, which he hoped would also convey some understanding of the position Celeste had found herself in.

"Sorry to burden you with all this. You didn't really need to know. So why have I told you?" Celeste asked herself. She looked around the busy curry house full of mostly young people whose excited chatter and laughter seemed to her full of the energy and hope of the long and full lives they still had in front of them. Unlike herself. "I have told you so that you are now aware of my status. Status? Such a horrible word. Maybe I should cut to the chase here." Celeste moved her drink to the side and leaned forward over the table. She placed her hand on his. "I do have feelings for you, Will, ever since that night of the conference dinner, and I'm saying this because, unless I'm very wrong, I think you also have feelings for me."

Will straightened in his chair and was about to say something before being stopped by Celeste, who gently placed her finger on his lips. *That was so sexy*, thought Will to himself.

"Please let me finish, Will. None of this is easy for me to say, although the drink helps. God willing, or more likely, good lawyers willing, I will soon no longer have a husband. I think you probably understand what I am saying." Celeste held up her hand to prevent Will interrupting. "But this is just me, my feelings, my position. For all I know, you might well be dating the future Mrs Jeavons."

Will smiled at the notion. "If there is a future Mrs Jeavons out there somewhere in this quaint city of mine," Will raised his hands up and around in support of the point he was going make, "then I have yet to meet them. It's maybe that she does not exist or perhaps it's just because I've not yet met enough women."

It was now Celeste's turn to smile. "Not met enough women? I very much doubt that from what I've heard on the grapevine. Quite the lady killer, aren't we?"

"Guilty as charged, my dear."

"I concur wholeheartedly with the jury's verdict.

Might the guilty party be interested in meeting his next potential victim for cocktails at the University Arms bar later this evening?"

"I might just about be able to squeeze you in between all my other victims. Do you have any preference for the poison you would like me to bring along?"

"Why don't you surprise me."

"Oh, I think I can manage that."

*

"Haven't we been here before?" asked Will as Celeste settled down in the chair opposite to where he was sitting with his glass of Irish whiskey on the rocks. "Dinner. Cocktails. A nightcap in your hotel room. How will tonight end? Any different from the last time we were here? Am I hoping for a moment that will never happen?"

"I don't think so. Maybe that moment will happen. We'll just have to see, won't we. I may be in the process of getting a divorce and you allegedly may not be seeing anyone, but we have still our careers to consider. You may not be reporting to me in the new structure of the company, I can promise you that little concession of information, but we will be working together. So not a good look if people find out we are in a relationship. At least for a good while yet."

"Oh, so we're in a relationship now, are we? Betrothed to each other for the rest of our lives," teased Will.

Celeste continued with the theme. "You don't really fancy me then? Maybe it's because I'm too intelligent. Too cultured for you. From high society."

"No. None of those. I don't fancy you anymore because you're no longer married."

That was the cue for shared laughter and Celeste calling for a toast. "To no longer being married. Cheers."

A slight awkwardness came across Celeste as they were both aware that the next likely move was to disappear under the covers.

"Can I be serious for a moment. Yes, I do want a relationship and not just a one-night stand and a quick shag as you Brits call it. I'm a businesswoman who travels a great deal and so one-night stands have always been on the table. Never been interested. And if all you're interested in is just tonight, then I would prefer you to be honest and leave now."

"If you've met so many and turned them all down, then why me?"

"Why you? Sometimes it's difficult to translate feelings into words. But why you? People see on the outside this brilliant scientist full of self-confidence. A beautiful man full of bravado. A man who everyone knows is going to be successful and wealthy. And yes, I see these things too, but I also see something else. I see an enigma. I see a fragile persona desperate for approval. The self-confidence is really just a veneer serving to hide your vulnerability. You keep people at arm's length because you are too frightened that they might find out all about you. Work out who the real Will is. You are the sort of man who's looking for reasons to leave someone almost as soon as you've met them because you are frightened that they might leave you first and just reinforce your worst fear. That no one wants to be with you. That there is no one who really cares about you. What woman wouldn't want such a wonderfully complicated man? A challenge."

This was not the time for humour. He wasn't prepared for such an accurate character assignation wrapped up as a compliment. "Looks like you know me better than I know myself." He struggled to find what words to say next. "I'm willing to give this a try beyond just tonight but neither of us can say with any certainty that we will fall in love, get married, live the rest of our lives together, be the one each of us is looking for."

"Of course. I'm not a lovestruck teenager and neither am I a fool. There are no guarantees that we will even be friends. The distance between us certainly doesn't help. Or maybe it will be depending on what sort of relationship we end up with."

"This is all very deep and all very sudden, Celeste. Can't we just enjoy what's left of tonight and see what happens after that? You have my word that I am not looking to take advantage of you, especially with what's going on in your marriage."

"I know, I know, Will. I don't need your word for anything. I trust you and yes, this is all very heavy. For which I apologise. I just see you as someone I can confide in. A soulmate? I'm not interested in marriage or even taking a lover. I'm just looking for someone I've never had before in my life. Yes, a soulmate. Someone I can share the good times and the bad. Someone who will listen when needed. Someone who will write letters to me when I am away. Someone who truly wants to be with me more than anyone else. Look, I know I've had too much to drink, and my marriage is breaking up and my feelings are all shot but I really do mean what I have just said. Don't you think it is so terribly sad and empty that I am nearly fifty years old and have never known a true soulmate? I'm just so lonely, Will. So terribly lonely."

A sudden and shocking emptiness crept under Will's skin. Celeste could have just been talking about him. He has never had that person with whom he could share his darkest worries and greatest hopes. There had never been anyone he had known other than his parents who would phone him up just to ask him how he was. Never anyone who worried about him when he was sick. Would anyone apart from his parents really care if he just disappeared off the face of the Earth? But the worst thing of all? It was all his own fault. All because he pushed women away whenever there was a chance that they might get too close. That they might want to know too much about Will Jeavons. He may not be nearly fifty but how many more years did he want to continue such an empty existence? How many more years of loneliness?

The smallest of tears were forming at the edges of Celeste's eyes as he gently pulled her up from her chair and embraced her entirely. He then laid her down in the bed and made silent love to her before they both fell into a deep sleep, which lasted through until dawn.

*

He'd enjoyed better sex. He'd laid down next to more beautiful women. He'd certainly had more fun in bed. But there was something very different about that night. Will couldn't get near what that something different was as he

196

recalled the events of the past day during his walk back through Parkers Piece and back to his apartment. A cold November morning that was soon to become a working-from-home one. *The least I deserve.* The closest he could get to answering his question was the word 'natural', which kept springing up in his mind. Their being together just seemed so natural. The way their conversation flowed so effortlessly over dinner. Their shared humour, their common interests, but what felt most natural of all was how Celeste shared her deepest feelings with him. In the early morning, he woke to find her facing away from him sobbing silently for a reason or reasons which Celeste couldn't or wouldn't say. Maybe there were still some secrets yet to be shared. But were they soulmates? Will had not yet unlocked the box of stars in his mind he dare not open. Feelings that would take no more than a moment to say but feelings so deep that they might take a lifetime to share. *Maybe that time has finally arrived. A time to let somebody love me. But could that really be true?*

HELLO AGAIN, BOSTON!

Never before had he so looked forward to flying. Maybe it was more about where he was flying to and who he was going to meet rather than the relentless waiting around in that Wetherspoons he was currently suffering in that lovely Heathrow Terminal 5. Although Will would soon be earning more money than he would know what to do with, there was still no little satisfaction in getting good value for his hard-earned cash. Not that he realised that morning, but it would not be long before he was enjoying free meals and drinks in the BA members' lounge. Such can be the benefits of corporate life.

He had been cradling his strong mug of coffee, watching the clock above the bar go slower and slower, but his real focus was on his latest 'girlfriend'. Celeste was the person who was front and foremost in his mind; such had been the case ever since that wonderful night in Cambridge the week just passed. All came as a welcome respite from his gnawing worries about the tox data. A good part of this latest obsession was due in no small part to the whole affair being utterly confusing to him. *Just what the fuck is going on inside my tiny little head? And in hers?* Never before had a woman thrown him so quickly and so completely and he just couldn't understand why.

During the slow progression to the front of the queue waiting to board the plane, it took a rather too frantic search through his rucksack to eventually find the documents he needed to get on the plane and those needed for when he got off. After his slight panic, three things came to mind. Be a better traveller. Buy a new rucksack. Remember what Celeste wrote in her most recent email – *whatever you do when you get here, don't hug or kiss me in public.* He would never do the latter anyway, even if they were married, but he was surprised that hugs were, all of a sudden, now banned. *Hey ho.* Will was not overly concerned. There were still two nights to look forward to and be enjoyed, although a venue for the sleepovers was still to be decided. He needed something to look forward to, as he was dreading the grilling he was likely to receive over his proposal over the next few days.

*

"Jesus, my man. How the devil are you, sir? Good to see you again," was how Will greeted his driver for the day.

"Still clinging to the wreckage, Dr Jeavons."

"It's Will you are talking to. Not Dr Jeavons. No need for any formalities with me."

"If that's what you would prefer. Just come back off a course where they told me I should avoid being overfamiliar."

"I won't tell if you don't. Now let's get to the InterContinental, my man."

It was the InterContinental restaurant that was to be the venue for that evening's dinner for two with Celeste. *A sensible and very Celeste choice*, thought Will, given the busy and very important two days that were to follow. What he had not considered was that when they had finished dinner, Celeste was not even going to come up to his hotel room, let alone stay the night.

"I'm doing us both a favour here, Will, especially you. You're looking tired enough now and so imagine what sort of state you would be in after a busy and sleepless night."

He was understandably disappointed, and it was showing. "Don't you think I've been in this position before? Spending the night with someone and then working the next day. It's not as if I'm playing football for England tomorrow, for God's sake."

"Wasn't difficult for me to predict that this call wouldn't go down with you too well. Tomorrow is your most important day so far. You will be meeting many people for the first time. The onus is upon you to demonstrate that you can lead Granta Pain through the next key stages because if there is any doubt that you're not up to the job, you will be replaced in a heartbeat. Trust me, I know these people. To a person, you will find them all very pleasant and personable, but they can be ruthless when they want to be. The company comes first. What impression do you think you, and me for that matter, will make after a sleepless night? Am I making myself clear, Will? There will be plenty of other times in the future when we can spend the night together. Just not tonight."

"What about tomorrow night?"

Celeste laughed. "You really are an incorrigible rogue, aren't you, my love."

"Like I've said before. Guilty as charged. But you didn't answer my question."

"Why don't we see how tomorrow goes and how much we have left to cover on Friday morning? And that is not meant to sound like a promise because it isn't."

"You're a real hard bastard behind that hard exterior, aren't you?"

"You'd better believe it. Guilty as charged."

"How about a nightcap up in my room and a little hug before you go home. That's all I am asking for."

"A nightcap in a hotel room with a man of your history? Perhaps I will take a raincheck on that offer. See you bright and early in the morning, Will. You make sure you get a good night's sleep."

Celeste pulled out her chair, stood up and made her way out to the hotel lobby to pick up her coat and order a cab.

I might well have said this before, but that woman has a truly magnificent ass. I wonder how long it will be until I get to see it again all upfront and personal!

*

Will was nervous enough about presenting to his new employer before he had even left Cambridge. Celeste

201

merely served to ratchet up his apprehension a few more notches still, with her insistence that he should rest up. He had worried too much. After the introductions around the table had been completed, including meeting for the first time several people with important-sounding jobs, it was mainly to the CEO, Declan O'Connor, to whom he addressed his presentation. The juices immediately started flowing and he was playing the part he always enjoyed playing the most. Being the centre of attention. He wondered why he had felt nervous at all. After all, he had been there, done that so many times before, even if to very different audiences than he was facing today.

His pitch finished, Will looked down towards the foot of the table to where Celeste was sitting. She was smiling. *Job done*, thought Will. But not quite. The next hour was spent by several of the present dignitaries pretty much demolishing Will's proposal and arriving at a consensus on a radically different plan, which had much more detail on the later clinical phases. An area that Will was far from familiar with so perhaps he should really have expected as much. The only concessions that Will was able to get approval for was to keep Grace and employ Hirami as a consultant financial officer to handle local budget issues. With those appointments came a relatively modest budget to support further scientific research on how the drug worked through using the university and external service providers. Fodder for future scientific publications and publicity as well as a nice excuse to allow both Grace and Will to keep on top of the science. A pleasant surprise was that Will was asked to find office space in Cambridge to move into now that there was no longer going to be any need to rent lab space. *A proper office. At last. My first time not working in a lab since I left school. That will be strange.*

Lunch was at the alcohol-free company cafeteria, which Will found a huge jump up from anything back home. Conversation with the third-generation, extremely tall Irishman CEO was something enjoyed by them both. Celeste, who was sitting next to Will, was almost beaming with pride. Or so Will thought.

If anything, the afternoon meetings were even more demanding, and Will's concentration levels were not helped by the jet lag starting to kick in. He just about managed to stay conscious through the final meeting of the day with the new project team assigned to support him. Some very experienced and capable people with the essential skills Will was clearly lacking. If nothing else, this meeting and the people around the table served as yet another reminder of just how amateur Granta Pain Therapeutics were. A painful lesson for Will's ego. It was clear from the discussions that the team were already well informed and were aware of the publicly disclosed data on GPT107 as well as having caught up with the new Biopharmaco screens that Will had sent over to them. They were happy to conclude that there were no clear red flags with the new data, which didn't really surprise Will, as he had already removed the only red flag. That tox data, which remained buried back in Cambridge. The team proposed some final studies to be carried out as well as contacting the original manufacturer of the drug. An action point for Myers-Stratton to follow up as Will had continued to be ignored by them. Demanding timelines were set for drug manufacture, meetings with the FDA to approve the clinical development plan, a short bioequivalence Phase 1 study with the new drug formulation and the all-important Phase 2 efficacy study in patients suffering from chronic pain.

Will was exhausted after the long day of back-to-back meetings and all he could do was flop down on his hotel bed as soon as he arrived back in his room. That was until he was suddenly woken by the harsh ringing of the hotel phone.

"Finally! What are you doing? You're supposed to be down here in the lobby for me to take you to the restaurant. We're going to be very late unless you can get down here in ten minutes flat."

He was conscious, but only just. "Who is this? Oh it's you, Celeste." He looked at his watch. "Fuck! Down with you in a couple of minutes," he almost shouted as he threw the phone back on the receiver.

And he was almost true to his word. Celeste timed it at five minutes.

She was impressed. "How did you get ready so quickly?"

"In my line of work, it pays to be able to put your clothes back on pretty damn sharpish, I can tell you."

She decided to ignore his latest attempt at misogynistic humour.

When Will and Celeste arrived at the restaurant, nearly all that evening's dinner guests were seated at a large dinner table near a window apart from, luckily for them both, Declan, who was even later to arrive. In normal circumstances, Will would have spent no little time admiring the lavishly furnished French restaurant with a small serving of people watching thrown in to pass judgement on the sort of people who dined at the place he had been taken. That night, however, was all about work. Continuing his crusade to try and impress the natives. Thus far, Will reckoned he hadn't done so bad. *Rather well in fact, I would say. So don't go fucking it up tonight, Will. Stay off the booze and no flirting with Celeste.* And it was between Celeste and the freshly arrived Irishman that Will found himself as the waiter appeared to take the drinks order.

"Just mineral water for me, please," was Will's request. "The jet lag has turned me teetotal," was his excuse for abstinence to an open-mouthed CEO.

"You may not well be Irish, my friend, but surely you Brits are close enough to us to allow yourself at least one glass of champagne to toast the deal and the future success of Granta Pain Therapeutics, jet lag or not," suggested Declan.

"Maybe just this once." Will thought it sensible to agree with the host. *And why not?*

And a great deal of smiling and no little laughter was very much a theme of the evening, with Will playing his usual role of raconteur of all things Cambridge and its university. Before the end of the evening Declan had already marked up some probable dates early next year on his phone to meet Will *in situ* and see for himself some of the sights Will had been describing.

"Been to the land of the Brits many times but never to Cambridge. Oxford a few times, but never Cambridge," admitted Declan.

"Maybe a word in your ear before you travel, Declan. Probably best not to mention that you have ever been to the 'other place' when you get to Cambridge. The locals can get a bit tetchy about that sort of thing. Having an Oxford stamp on your passport and all that." Will was happy that this attempt at humour was well received, as had been the case throughout dinner. *Whoever said our cousins across the pond don't understand our sense of humour?*

"What a star!" announced Celeste to her passenger as she pulled out from the restaurant car park. "A real smooth operator. I think I know Declan pretty well and I reckon he genuinely likes you. Not that he has to, but it all helps."

"All part of the training, my dear. Years of entertaining to try and earn the next buck. Isn't that also your forte?"

"Believe me, you are in a different league. Like I said, you seemed to get on very well with Declan."

"Which, I hope, was the case for everyone I have met over here in Boston. Declan came over as a very chatty and personable character, albeit with one caveat."

Celeste's smile turned to a frown. "Don't tell me there was a problem. Please, anyone but Declan."

"Nothing personal against Declan but I'm just deeply suspicious of tall people. They can't be trusted. Mark my words."

Celeste laughed. "If only I had your impeccable judge of character."

"What can I say? Some of us have it but, sadly, some of us don't."

"Have you ever thought of going into business development?"

Not unlike Cambridge back home, Will found most places not far from anywhere else and so Celeste was soon on the street leading up to the InterContinental.

"What's it to be tonight, then? Business comes first? Continuing chastity for you and painful abstinence for me?"

"Well, you have been rather a good boy the last couple of days, and I have been told that good things come to those who wait."

Will stared ahead and afforded himself a gentle smile as Celeste drove down the ramp to the hotel car park.

*

Will was completely disorientated when he was suddenly woken up by the hotel room phone. He struggled to lean over to the other side of the bed to reach it.

"Good morning, Dr Jeavons. This is the morning call you requested. Have a nice day."

"Hold on. Hold on a minute. I didn't request a morning call. What time is it?"

"It's 7am on Friday 26th November, sir. 2021." The receptionist clearly felt that their guest needed further context. "Please let me check the details. Ah, yes. I have here in front of me that we received a request for an early morning call at 11.47pm last night through your hotel room phone. My sincere apologies if we have made some sort of mistake, sir."

"No, no. That's fine. Thanks for the call," ended Will before he slowly placed the phone back on to its receiver, trying to remember making the call and a surprising one at that since he always used the alarm on his phone.

And then random pictures of the night before started to appear in his mind. They had definitely made love, that much was clear, as Will tended to remember such things. The detail? That was lacking, which rather implied that it was all rather a low-key event. *Absolutely nothing wrong with that. Nothing at all. It's all about the place and the time.* After that so-called 'event', nothing at all. His memory had failed him. The rest was reasoned conjecture. He must have fallen asleep, not surprising after the stress of the last two days on top of the jet lag, and Celeste must have left to go back to her apartment but only after she had called reception to book a morning wake-up. *The sneaky vixen! Depriving me of a morning in bed with a lover.*

It was not until he roused himself to think of taking a shower that he noticed the long, scribbled note on the dressing table that she had left him.

I'm guessing that there is a rather annoyed Englishman who is reading this. You looked so sweet last night when I left you. Dead to the whole world, never mind me. There will be other times. Other mornings. But now, get off your sweet little ass and get ready for Jesus to pick you up at 8.30am sharp with all your luggage ready for flying home tonight. See you soon XXX.

The last morning was the most relaxed session of his stay in Boston. A chance to meet the new board, most of whom he had met before at earlier meetings or at dinner the previous evening. Nat Stevens was going to be the chair of the board and Will was delighted and not a little reassured that Celeste was a non-exec board member. The new CFO,

Lewis Adams, seemed like someone Will could work with as long as he had Hirami to help him out locally. All in all, some good appointments and a definite improvement over the last board, although he was a little concerned about just how independent the board was from Myers-Stratton. *It is all their money, I suppose.*

The working day ended with Celeste coming down to the company reception to say goodbye to Will as he arrived to pick up the luggage he had left there earlier in the morning.

"Thanks for coming to see us again. My turn next and hopefully sooner rather than later." She moved to shake his hand.

"What? No hugs or kisses for your soulmate?" whispered Will a little too loud for Celeste's comfort as he shook her hand.

She leant forward to answer him. "Why don't you shout that out again but maybe a bit louder."

"Calm down, my dear. Just having a bit of fun. No one can hear."

"You'd be surprised," answered Celeste, glancing over at the two women standing at reception. "Please try and act professionally for just a few more minutes."

"You know me. Always the professional."

"Jesus is waiting for you outside. Wishing you a safe journey, Dr Jeavons. Maybe I'll send an email to you when I get home."

"Well thank you, Ms Simmonds. Very much looking forward to receiving that. See you soon, I hope."

Jesus kept Will entertained on the short drive to the airport about his passion for the Red Sox and a promise that he would take Will to a game and after-match entertainment. Just call him whenever he had the time.

"I might just do that, Jesus. Thank you for your kind offer. But only as long as you accompany me to a game of cricket should you ever find yourself in my neck of the woods. My understanding is that baseball was invented for those who could not understand cricket."

"Is that right, Will? Well maybe you can explain that to the guys who I meet up with at the ball games!"

The wait around the airport was as interminable as ever, but he had been to far worse airport terminals. Maybe time to write an email to Celeste before she sent one to him.

Short-changed again!

Left by myself again this morning. Am I picking up a pattern here? Is this what being a soulmate is all about? Struggling to see the positives at the moment if I'm being honest. Humour aside, I absolutely adored those few hours you granted me even if they were only a few hours. I wonder if or when I will be granted any more.

The email reply was almost immediate even though Celeste was still at work.

Poor, poor Dr Jeavons!

What I did might have seemed a bit cruel but all for your own good. And mine too. Not the time and not the place but what about a time and a place? Christmas in Cambridge sounds nice to me if you will have me. Do they have Christmas decorations in the Curry Queen? Not that I need any excuses but good reasons to justify the trip would be to do some office viewings with you – nice – although less nice will be announcing the redundancies, which I can help you with. Make sure you book the big meeting room this time. Wouldn't want to carry out those interviews in your tiny little office. How about w/c 13th December? You never know, perhaps Dr Jeavons won't feel so short-changed next time. We'll just have to see, won't we.

The stress and excitement of the last few days meant that the now confirmed redundancies had completely slipped Will's mind. *Fuck! Shocking even if all rather predictable. Those poor bastards, and I am far from blame free.*

*

The flight had long since settled into its cruising altitude and the cabin crew were hurriedly clearing away dinner so that they could get their passengers to sleep as soon as possible. As Will struggled to balance the empty food containers, bottle of water and glass of wine, he wondered if Myers-Stratton flew business or even first class rather than the premium economy seat Will was occupying on this particular flight. *Surely the likes of Celeste wouldn't have to put up sitting next to the sort of fat git, computer-game-playing man-child I will be having to put up with all fucking night.*

With the lights having been dimmed and Will trying

to cover himself with the thin blanket he had unwrapped, all that remained was for him to do the easiest thing that had been expected of him for the past few days. Fall asleep. But that wasn't happening. He wanted to fall asleep thinking about Celeste but instead his mind drifted to those meetings of the previous day. The more he thought about some of the conversations, the more he believed that he was being played. The proposal he had prepared and presented was clearly viewed by Myers-Stratton as no more than his rather transparent attempt at window dressing the Granta Pain assets. Will was slowly coming to the conclusion that all the key decisions had been made long before the meeting had taken place. Even the few concessions Will had thought he had bargained hard for had almost certainly been pre-agreed. They had already decided to throw him those bones. However, most apparent of all was that Will had essentially been made redundant. He just didn't have either the experience nor expertise to contribute to the upcoming clinical trials. He would really just be an observer at the project teams even though he was the appointed chair. So why have they kept him on with such an attractive salary? Why didn't they just close down Granta Pain and manage the drug out of Boston?

Money and publicity, concluded Will. *Yeah, of course. How could I be so fucking ignorant and sycophantic? I, and more importantly my links to the University of Cambridge, would be very handy in any future publicity. Nice dinners out in the colleges when they come to visit. Bit of shopping in the old town for the wives. What's there not to like? But money is the real driver here, just like it always is. Making full use out of the UK government research tax credits? Why the fuck not? And maybe even more lucrative than that, would they get any tax relief on the products they sell in the UK now that they have got a UK-based subsidiary? Another nice little earner. Even if GPT107 is a failure, they are probably still quids in. A genuine shot to nothing with a huge potential upside. Does all that make me a fool for accepting the job offer? I don't think so. Where else would I get this sort of salary in the UK with my lack of real industrial experience? Not many places that I'm aware of, that's for sure. Why not hang around for a couple of years, take the money and wait for the clinical trials to read out. If they are successful, I will literally be financially secure for life after cashing in my share options. Being associated with a non-addictive painkiller will also make me hot property and I could probably get my pick of jobs either in industry or academia. So maybe I might just hang around for a few years and see what happens regardless of me being played big time. And of course I'm being used big time. But isn't that the definition of being employed? Being used. I wonder if Celeste knows anything about this? About Granta Pain just being a big fucking tax dodge. Best not to ask, as how would any answer she could possibly give actually change anything? And probably an answer that I would rather not want to hear.*

CHRISTMAS 2021

"Another big day then, Nev," announced Li as she sashayed around the school bag their son had dumped on the kitchen floor the night before.

"Yeah. I think they call it closure in the sort of circles I never seem to get invited to join. A piece of paper or two that will include the word termination somewhere and a place for me to sign my last ever Granta Pain document. The bit I'm struggling to call will be how big the all-important number will be. I'm hoping for the best but assuming I'm going to be very fucking disappointed."

Li sat down opposite her husband whilst combining listening to his monologue with opening the morning's mail. "You're saying all this, but you still don't know for certain that you will be made redundant."

"Two things, my dear. I will be made redundant, and I don't give a flying fart anyway as I'll be starting at

Biopharmaco in the New Year. Jeavons and the lovely Celeste can just go and fuck themselves."

She raised her eyes slightly at her husband's latest breach of the recent 'no swearing at the dinner table' treaty. "I don't suppose you have picked up on any changes of behaviour from Will? Has he been treating you any differently?"

"Hardly seen him at all this last month. None of us have. Fuck knows what he's been up to. But, you know, actually thinking about it again, there was a bit of a strange episode last week. One of the rare times he was actually on site and he called into the lab asking me to see him in his office later in the morning. Nothing terribly unusual about that but all he got me in his office for was to tell me that he had changed his mind about not disclosing that worrying Biopharmaco tox data. So now he's going to give Myers-Stratton the full dataset, dodgy tox result and all, as he should have fucking done in the first place instead of dicking me about. Man's a charlatan. Why did he think it was so important to tell a soon to be ex-employee something that the soon to be ex-employee will have no further interest in what-so-fucking-ever? Very strange."

"Doesn't sound all that big a deal to me, Nev," replied Li, who had decided that none of that morning's mail was worth keeping.

"But it is, Li. It is. He was adamant that the toxicity finding should not be disclosed to Myers-Stratton, as they might just bin the compound, but now he is all of a sudden agreeing with what I said he must do."

"Perhaps he's thought about it a bit deeper and sees that it is the right thing to do."

"And it is the right thing to do. You can't just go round hiding data and the man knows that, but he looked a long way away from agreeing with my point of view when we discussed it back the other week. Not often you see Jeavons that angry like he was that day." Which was more than a slight exaggeration of the truth.

"Anyway. I guess you can say that he got there in the end. Made the right decision and all that. He agreed with you. But isn't your compound now at risk of being pulled?"

"Not my compound, dear, not anymore, so I don't really give a fuck." Nev stood up from the table and pushed his chair back. "And on that bombshell, Neville Chamberlain took to the road for what may be, given a fair wind, his very last day at Granta Pain Therapeutics. Wish this hero and his trusty steed God's speed, my love, as they once again enter the valley of the shadow of death. And you can give what's left of that disgusting muesli shite to the birds. Or to our delightful son of ours if he ever wakes up."

*

The first that Will knew of Celeste's late arrival from Munich was a text.

I need you tonight.

Which was all that Will needed to invite himself to a sleepover in the University Arms. Unfortunately for him, the invite was not extended to a slap-up breakfast at the hotel.

"Like I keep saying, Will. I would rather not draw attention to us being seen together socially unless it is a very obvious work engagement. Tonight's Christmas shopping apart. Some things are worth taking a risk on," she teased. "It's only been a few months since I left Charles, and he is hell-bent on making the divorce as messy as he possibly can. Not a good look in front of my parents or my work colleagues to be seen galivanting off with a new partner this early after leaving Charles and so close to tying up the deal. Being seen together for a hotel breakfast? Not a good idea."

Will raised himself up onto an elbow to face his lover, who was still resting on her back in the hotel bed. "I get your drift. But hang on a minute there. Just because we are having breakfast together doesn't necessarily mean that we spent the night together. Why don't I just leave the hotel, come back in and then meet you for breakfast? One of those power executive breakfasts or whatever you people call them. What can possibly go wrong with that plan?"

"Fair enough, I suppose, but it must be a proper working breakfast. As you say, a high-level executive breakfast or brunch unless we get a move on. We can work on preparation for interviewing the staff. Believe me, it won't be nice, and you need to be prepared to handle the sort of reactions that can be very upsetting for all parties."

Will decided to spring into action by rolling out of the bed and making his way to the en-suite bathroom. He shouted back at her en route. "And that's where your big problem is, Ms Simmonds. All work and no play."

She sat up in the bed and called after him. "You don't count last night as play?"

217

He leaned his head out of the bathroom. "It's a start, I suppose, but no more than that, my little American goody two shoes."

*

Will had managed to book out the departmental meeting room for the whole morning. "Right. You sit there. I will sit over here, and the interviewee will be between us. Yes. That should work. As we'd agreed, I will manage the meeting as the Myers-Stratton representative, and you should be very careful of not saying anything inappropriate. If in doubt, either don't say anything or refer the question to me."

"As I said. More than happy for you to manage this as I literally have no experience at all in this sort of thing. Thank God. Not looking forward to this at all. These are my guys we are sacking. Without them, you and I wouldn't be sitting here today. I don't know who will be the most upset. Me or them." All of which was at least a slight exaggeration. Will clearly had some empathy for the staff he had employed, but he was also comfortable with throwing them under the bus if his own job was ever threatened.

"Please, Will. No emotion. Just doesn't help. Show empathy but don't burst out crying."

"I can't see me bursting into tears but I'm definitely not looking forward to this," repeated Will.

"I understand, of course I understand. Time for a last run-through of what we decided over breakfast were the main points we must get across."

"We decided? I think you mean you decided, but don't

get me wrong, Celeste, I'm so grateful for you coming over and helping me with this nightmare."

"We're not paying you to be a blagging HR representative. We're paying you way more than you deserve to be a top scientist," she teased.

Will's response was a weak smile, as there was a small part of him that actually felt a little guilty about how much they were paying him given how little he was likely to be doing. *Not my problem. Absolutely no need to feel guilty. Take it when it's given, Will, because it may never happen again.*

"Last time, then. The main points we have to cover. Why there is no role for them moving forward in the slimmed-down company. Basically, the company will now just focus on clinical development, which is not a skill set any of them have. Terms of the redundancy agreement and how we arrived at the numbers and timelines. Offer of the rest of the week off if they prefer to go home. You agreeing with them what work you want them to clear up before they go on garden leave for the rest of their notice period. Grace? We can briefly map out the main responsibilities of her new role, but you need to go into detail with her on that sometime next week. Not urgent. All clear?" finished Celeste.

"At least for the moment. But what about the order of the interviews?"

"I was thinking about in order of increasing difficulty, perhaps? Maybe Grace, Antonio, Nirmala and Nev."

"Makes sense. Leaving Nev to set off the fireworks at the end of the party."

"Indeed, Will. Indeed."

It was just before noon when Nev walked out of the

meeting room and down to the lab to pick up his coat and rucksack. He then left the building and cycled over to the Panton Arms for a prearranged boozy lunch with his colleagues. It was there that he found Antonio and Nirmala already sitting on a sofa in the far corner of the bar. Both were red-faced when Nev sat down with them, and it was obvious that Nirmala had been crying.

"What a complete shit show," commented Nev. "You two? You two deserved much better. Grafted from start to finish and all you end up with is a month's notice pay on top of a piss-poor redundancy package. As predictable as it was fucking scandalous." Nev paused his invective to take the first taste of the beer he had bought himself. "And that Grace. What a bitch."

"I think it's a bit unfair of you to say that, Nev," remarked Nirmala, wiping her weeping nose with a well-used handkerchief. "She's a nice girl. I've got a lot of time for her. You can't go blaming her for being offered a job."

"Yeah I agree with you, Nirmala. I've always got on with Grace. Maybe a little bit too ambitious for my taste but I got on with her. I guess the only thing that confuses me was why she was offered the job instead of you, Nev. After all, you are much more experienced than Grace and you've known Will for a lot longer."

"They didn't tell me about Grace being offered a job at my interview and I only found out later when I asked her if she was coming down the pub to help drown our sorrows. But it turns out she didn't have any sorrows to drown so we won't be seeing her anytime soon. And doesn't that tell you something about the girl? Couldn't be arsed to come here and show a little bit of sympathy for you two."

"Are you going to ask them why they picked Grace over you?" asked Antonio.

"No fucking point. They're not going to change their mind, and they would never tell my why anyway. At least they wouldn't tell me the real reason why, which we all know is because I tell it how it is. Warts and all. Go with what the science tells us. Grace is a wannabe political animal. Like you pointed out, Antonio. She's very ambitious. A yes-man much more to the liking of the Yanks rather than a stroppy northerner." Nev takes another drink. "And you know what? She is very welcome to it because I've got another job lined up. Biopharmaco. I can put a good word in for you two if you would like me to."

"Already? Well, congratulations then, Nev," Nirmala commented, looking even more surprised than Antonio.

"Yeah. Well done, Nev, congratulations," added Antonio, raising his glass towards Nev. "You didn't hang about."

"Well I did warn you all months ago not to trust Jeavons. And I guess that I was right all along."

*

Will and Celeste were relaxing over coffees, carrying out a debrief on the interviews that had taken place earlier in the morning. "I think that couldn't have gone much better. Perhaps these sorts of things are less traumatic with you emotionally anal Brits. Even Nev was a bit of a pussy cat. Could have got a bit sticky when he pushed back on the settlement figure, but he seemed pretty resigned about it all when we explained that the terms represented Myers-

Stratton typical termination agreements, and we are probably more generous than most of our competitors. The problem for them all is that they have not had many years of service given the age of the company, so the final payouts are not exactly huge. But nothing more we can do about that."

"Yes, I was a little surprised by our Nev. I thought he would kick off at some point, but he was very reasonable. I reckon it was because Ms Simmonds was present and he wouldn't dare, so well done, you. In fact, well done you all round, as I simply couldn't have done this without you. I must come up with something to show my gratitude. Any thoughts?"

"Absolutely. As I said earlier, you can take me Christmas shopping after work! As friends, of course, so keep your hands off."

"Christmas shopping? I rather had in mind something decidedly less festive but perhaps that can wait until after the shops have closed."

"That all depends on what Santa gets me!"

*

After Celeste had left to go back to the hotel to prepare for the late-night Christmas shopping in Cambridge, Will turned to cleaning up the mess the last few days' neglect had left in the office. He had almost finished a very poor attempt at his task when he saw Grace hovering at his door. The only Granta Pain employee who was still in the building.

"Have you got a minute, Will?"

"Not really, as I need to leave early today, but maybe thirty seconds." Perhaps it was best not to tell her that he was taking Celeste Christmas shopping.

"I just wanted to say how really grateful I am to be kept on at Granta Pain. I have been so worried over the last week convincing myself that I would be made redundant. Really looking forward to the new role that you and Celeste explained to me earlier today. My dream job. Science and business. Fantastic. But if there's one last question I can ask. Why me instead of Nev? He's far more experienced than me and you have worked with him for a good long time."

He looked beyond Grace out into the corridor to see if there was anyone near his office but thought better than sharing anything she might then tell her colleagues.

"All you need to know, Grace, is that both Celeste and I believe that you are the standout person for this job, and we hope you will accept the offer and sign the contract we hope to get out to you soon."

"Which of course I will and thanks again for offering me the opportunity. I won't let you down, Will."

"I'm pretty sure you won't." Will smiled encouragingly or at least that's what he hoped was the case.

Grace made her way to leave the office but paused and turned her head to face towards Will. "And that night at your apartment? Our little secret. Don't you worry. You can trust me."

That grabbed his attention by the throat. *Why is she telling me this now? She's never brought it up before.*

"To be honest, Grace. I have never given it a second thought." *The wrong thing to say.* "I mean, it was a great night and all that and I really enjoyed your company, but I

have never thought of telling anybody else. Why would I?"
An even more wrong thing to say! Stop fucking about, man.

Grace didn't reply. Just a little smile played around her lips before she turned and walked back out into the corridor.

She's got the job and pay rise to follow, what more does she fucking want from me? A guarantee that I won't sack her in the future? I've no intention of doing so and she's more likely to leave for another job than me sacking her. But, I suppose, she could play on my paranoia to demand future promotions and pay rises. Perhaps I'm imagining something that isn't really there. I do fucking hope so. Anyway, even if I am not being paranoid and it really is a card she is prepared to play sometime in the future, it will be old news soon enough. Be patient. Play the long game. Just another bloody secret I will have to keep from everyone. Including Celeste.

*

"Not exactly Macy's in New York and maybe that's exactly why it all looks so traditional and so beautiful," suggested Celeste as Will led her down through Trinity Street and onto the Market Square.

"It is a nice place to live, and Christmas is a good time to be in Cambridge if it were only that it didn't last so long, but I suppose that's the same everywhere these days, including Macy's."

"Maybe especially Macy's, you could say."

The couple who still weren't a couple were stopped on the pavement by a man holding out his hand in front of them.

"Will? It is you, isn't it, under that very fake fur hat?

Yes it is. How are you, my good friend?" asked Giles, vigorously shaking Will's hand.

"Good God! Giles. I thought you'd died or, worse still, gone to Oxford or something like that. And how are you? How many years has it been?"

"Must be ten if it's a day. And you're right. I did choose Oxford over death, but I left the university over five years ago and have already gone through a few failed biotech start-ups. You know how it is. But, of course. You don't. Been doing pretty well for yourself, at least from what I have read and heard. But sorry, how ignorant of me. The very unfortunate Mrs Jeavons, I presume," presumed Giles, making to shake Celeste's hand. "As Will is far too ignorant to introduce me, I guess I will have to do it myself."

Celeste shook hands but waited for Will to make the correction. "No need, Giles. May I introduce Dr Giles Radlett. An old rogue I first met in those early days at the University of Cambridge when there were not nearly as many Christmas lights as there are these days. And maybe I should introduce you, Giles, to Celeste Simmonds from Myers-Stratton, who is over here on business following the sale of Granta Pain, which you may have seen in the press."

"I'm so terribly sorry, Celeste. This man is even older than me so I just thought he would be married by now and you just look like the sort of woman I would expect him to be married to." His face reddened. "Maybe it's best for us all that I should just shut up now. I am really sorry, Celeste."

"Since when did you think it was a good idea to start

thinking again? It was never really your strong point," joked Will.

"Hands up. All insults duly deserved. But great news on Granta Pain. Very well done, old man. Exciting times."

"Early days and still a bit mad at the moment but yes, exciting times and no little thanks to the sterling efforts of my imagined wife."

"Very drole, Will. Listen. I'm around abouts the next couple of days staying at the in-laws. Yes, some of us do get married and even have kids. If you fancy a catch-up and a few drinks, then here's my mobile number." Giles dug a grubby business card from out of his wallet and passed it onto his old friend.

"Maybe tomorrow night? I'll give you a call."

"Looking forward to it. Nice to meet you and my apologies again, Celeste."

"Don't worry. No offence taken. Nice to meet you, Giles," replied Celeste in an attempt to cushion his awkwardness.

The friends shook hands warmly and Giles turned around towards Rose Crescent. The still-unmarried couple headed down through Sidney Street.

"Daft old bugger," observed Will. "A nice man. Used to be a close friend but our careers took us to different places, I guess. He means well."

"Funny, though, wasn't it. Maybe we do look good together as a couple."

"Of course we do, dear, even if we have to pretend otherwise," teased Will. He was far from desperate for them to be considered as a couple and more than happy with the status quo, which was consistent with his usual modus operandi. Even back from when he was a teenager, Will hated the saying 'going steady'.

Celeste picked up on the unspoken theme. "I know you're being patient with me, and I do appreciate it. Anyway, given your reputation, I'm pretty sure you are comfortable enough with the way things are now. You wouldn't want to go frightening off some Cambridge totty, isn't that what you English say, by having this bit of scrag end hanging on your arm, would you?"

"I don't think either of us expect me to dignify that comment with a response. I'll assume you are trying to be amusing, although it does sort of point out your current state of mind, don't you think? Your perfectly understandable lack of confidence after what Charles did to you. Things will get better. You'll see. How many more times do I have to tell you what a breathtaking woman you are?"

She smiled. "Maybe one more time, Will. One more time."

They carried on walking down Sidney Street, becoming increasing oblivious of the gaudy Christmas lights around them, focusing instead on each other.

Celeste mused over his seemingly casual observation. "Is it that obvious that I am lacking confidence? I am sorry. It's horrible living out of a hotel room. It just does your head in. Once I find a nice apartment, things will settle down for me and I can plan for what will be the next part of my life. Everything's just all too much up in the air at the moment. Too many uncertainties to worry about. Big holes in my life to make good."

"You know what I think you need right now, Celeste?

A bit of human warmth and emotion. A sweet kiss and a close embrace."

"When we get back to the hotel, Will. All in good time."

"I don't think we need to wait until then."

He hooked his arm under hers and guided her towards a dark alleyway off the side of Sidney Street.

"Where are you taking me?"

"No people and no cameras down here. No one to see two lovers embracing."

After walking further down the alleyway, he stopped and turned Celeste around so that her back was against a cold, dark wall. She was nervous and looked up to the entrance to the alleyway to see if any late-night Christmas shoppers could see down to where they were standing. They couldn't because the alleyway curved to the left.

"Is this wise?" asked Celeste. "People of our age kissing in a back alley?"

"At what age are you supposed to not enjoy the touch of another?"

He cradled her neck and brought her forward to embrace his lips. She reciprocated by putting her arms around him to clutch Will tightly. He then started to unfasten her coat.

"No, Will. Not here. It's just too risky. What if someone sees us?"

"What if they do?"

He stepped inside her open coat and clutched her waist. He quickly pulled up her skirt and reached though between her legs. She was already wet.

Celeste brought her arms down to her sides. "No, Will,

I don't think we should do this." She gasped as Will forced his hand further between her legs.

"If you say stop then I'll stop right now. Do you want me to stop?"

Her answer was to fumble around the front of his trousers and pull down his zip. She then pulled him onto her and raised her leg slightly. There was a loud intake of breath as he entered her. He was aware of her constantly looking to the front of the alleyway as he pushed himself deeper into her. He was also aware that she was becoming agitated and pulling him onto her faster and faster. This would not take long. Her breaths were getting shorter and her groans louder until she almost shouted 'now' as she released all her tension with a guttural sound, which he had never heard her make before. She released her grip on him as she slowly returned to normal breathing.

"I think perhaps maybe I need a drink," whispered Celeste as she hurriedly adjusted her clothes before fastening up her coat.

"There's a coffee shop just around the corner I can take you to," answered Will, who had adjusted his own clothes similarly.

"No, Will. I mean a proper drink. That was truly shocking. Is there something wrong with me? Did I get turned on by having sex in such a public space? This is not me, Will. Not me at all. As exciting as it was, please promise me that we won't do that again."

"I promise, even if it is a rather reluctant promise, but if there is something wrong with you then I have yet to find out what it is. You just got caught up in the moment. A moment where you let yourself go completely. Maybe that's just not something you are used to but there's really nothing more natural. Maybe for a few minutes you were actually able to banish all those demons you are carrying around with you."

The rest of the evening and long after when the shops had closed was spent trawling around Will's favourite pubs and bars. There were more than just a few. Over the many drinks there was laughter and even the odd tear as the couple, who were not a couple, shared what was left to tell about their lives and future hopes. One tricky question Will had to field was precisely how many other ladies he had similarly entertained down that dark alley.

"No I never. Never done that sort of thing before," was an answer Celeste just wasn't willing to countenance.

It was a good night. In fact, it was a wonderful night.

Both were too exhausted to even suggest a nightcap when they finally arrived back at her hotel, with Celeste and Will falling into bed in the early hours. Even Will lacked the energy and sobriety that night to consider anything more energetic than taking off his clothes. Anything more energetic would have to wait until the morning.

RISKS

*L*uke has always been an avid sportsman. And I'm not just talking about an armchair sportsman, although both God and this family are keenly aware of that particular affliction. His being an active sportsman was actually one of things that first attracted me all those years ago to the boy who became a man. I even chased him around here, there and everywhere watching him playing football; often standing in the cold, rain and sometimes even snow. I can't remember it ever being a warm day, although common sense would suggest there must have been at least a few. Looking back at all those 'wasted' Saturday afternoons, I must really have been smitten with the boy. Or something like that. A game I had no interest in, although the result was all important because if the game had been lost... oh dear. Bad moods. The silent 'leave me alone, for Christ's sake' treatment and 'I'm going out for a run' excuses to leave the house. But let's face it, girls, who doesn't like a nice six-pack!

Then, just like the rest of us, he suddenly got old. Couldn't keep up with the youngsters anymore on the football pitch, but there was no way I was going to put up with him moping around the house all weekend. He had to find another hobby. Or else! Cue his next obsession. Long-distance running. Which was fine for a while until his knees finally gave up on him after pounding up and down the streets of Cambridge every day of the week. Contrary to the sensible advice of the GP who said any more running would put him at risk of making things worse, Luke just strapped them up and went running anyway. What an idiot! And what an idiot I was to let him do it, although I don't remember having too much of a say on the decision at the time. And then came a time when the pain got so bad that even with the strapping he just had to stop altogether. Unfortunately, stopping running didn't mean him being able to also come off all the pain meds he had been taking for years and years, even back when he was playing football. Time to see the GP about the chronic knee pain as well as the abdominal pain he was also suffering from.

The GPs he ended up seeing were all friendly enough and tried to be helpful but without really managing to change anything apart from giving Luke a PPI to help him with his stomach pain, which was caused by taking all those painkillers. He did try a few different types of painkiller, but they were all much of a muchness and there were rarely any pain-free days that the poor man enjoyed. Putting on weight certainly didn't help, but that was almost inevitable given that the only exercise he got was from walking and swimming, the latter of which he hated with a passion.

The end of the road arrived when he tried to pick up our

three-year-old nephew after he had fallen down on the lawn playing football. I could hear his cry of pain from where I was sitting in the lounge. He spent the next two days in bed, only leaving to crawl to the bathroom. Something had to be done. He couldn't carry on like this. The man was still in his forties – just! – for God's sake.

Luke was fortunate that the medical insurance I had with my company also covered spouses. So it was off to a rheumatologist we went, explaining that the pain he was suffering impacted many aspects of his and our family life. It was me who had to drive him to the consultation. At least she seemed far better informed than the GPs we saw, which I guess should be the case.

A few weeks later, his X-ray results came back, along with the wholly unsurprising diagnosis of moderate to severe osteoarthritis in both knees. More of a surprise was that he also had mild to moderate osteoarthritis in his right hip. There's football for you! All very well to get a diagnosis but what next? Surgery was one option the consultant went through at the follow-up appointment but there was no guarantee that the surgery would be successful, and I could see Luke wincing at the thought of being laid up in bed for a few months. If I am being honest, that thought didn't really appeal all that much to me either. I have never been a patient nursemaid. Drugs? The consultant had agreed that Luke had essentially tried every reasonable option. Opioids were sometimes used as a last resort, but the consultant said that she would not be comfortable in recommending them to Luke. The serious side effects from taking opioids chronically were, in her opinion, not worth the marginal benefit in pain relief Luke might get over taking even paracetamol. That seemed like a very sensible decision to me, given all the recent publicity on the so-called opioid epidemic, which is truly frightening.

"Have you ever thought of enrolling in a clinical trial, Luke?" asked the consultant.

Luke looked over at me and then back to the consultant. "Well no, not really. I don't really know much about these sorts of things. Are there trials for OA pain? I suppose there must be," said Luke, pretty much to himself, "but would I be eligible for a clinical trial?" Luke looked both confused and enthusiastic.

"Very much depends on the entry criteria of any particular trial but there is one ongoing trial I am involved with here in Cambridge at Addenbrookes which I think you would have a very good chance of being accepted onto based on your X-rays, your pain scores and your general good health."

The consultant paused and reached for a folder from one of her draws, pulling out the topmost document. "This is a drug and a trial design we are very interested in because of its unique mechanism of action. The hope is that it will be a non-addictive pain medication potent enough to treat even severe chronic pain. The pinnacle for pain management, if you like. There is also some evidence to suggest that it can improve the underlying disease in OA, although that is a secondary endpoint and a bit of a stretch goal in my opinion, but we will see for ourselves soon enough. I'm sure this is all a bit too much for you to take in right now, but I've got your email, Luke, and I will send you more details on the trial as well as the surgical options we have already discussed, although you didn't sound so keen on undergoing surgery."

"That's great, Dr Grant, thanks for seeing me again."

"My pleasure," answered the consultant, standing up to shake our hands. "I do hope we can find a way of helping you."

"One last question before we leave," I asked as Luke was nearing the door. "Which option of those we have talked about today would you recommend for Luke?"

"If you, Luke, are not so keen on surgery then I would recommend that you at least consider enrolling on the trial we are running here, given that you have already exhausted the sensible drug choices. And if you are interested in going down the drug trial route, then I really should also send you a list of ongoing clinical trials relevant to your condition that are taking place elsewhere in the UK. But ours is the best one!" added Dr Grant only half in jest. "Looking forward to hearing back from you, Luke, but probably better sooner rather than later if you want to get onto our trial, as places are filling up quickly. No pressure from me, naturally, just letting you know what the situation is here. Take care. See you soon."

I couldn't remember when last I'd seen Luke so talkative. Non-stop all the way back to the house. We talked more about the possibility of him enrolling on a clinical trial when we got back, and although I didn't try to dash his hopes, I did try to put it all in perspective, including the elephant in the room of him ending up in the placebo arm. A long way to go with no guarantee of a positive outcome plus the potential for serious side effects. But I remember him still being in high spirits when we went to bed. If only we had good news like that every night!

Where did that leave us? Well, it left muggins with lots of homework to do, finding out about the drug in question and the design of the clinical trial that had been approved. I did some digging and some very interesting information was pretty close to the surface. The drug they were going to investigate had been around for nearly twenty years and already been tested in a few hundred patients without any serious side effects. A very big tick in my book. The proposed mechanism of action of the drug was interesting and unique as far as I could find. Another big tick. The company who was sponsoring the trial was based in Cambridge but owned by an American company. The CEO of the company, Granta Pain Therapeutics, was a well-known scientist around the Cambridge scene. I had been to a few of Will Jeavons' talks on the science supporting their drug, GPT107, and he presented some persuasive evidence in support of their drug, but I was not a big fan of him, the man. He came across as a bit of an arrogant pig, but I really didn't care what the man was like as long as the drug did what it said on the tin. My overall take was that it was at least worth trying because Luke's OA was only likely to get worse if he was not willing to consider the surgery option. He was too young to be in this amount of pain and face the rest of his life in agony.

The drug was hypothesised to work in a very different way to the drugs Luke had been taking. It seemed safe based on the clinical trials that had already been carried out. Unlike opioids, the drug should not be addictive. And the icing on the cake was that the trial was taking place almost within walking distance from where we lived. We joked that maybe one day Luke would actually be able to walk home from the hospital.

The decision had been made and all there was to do was for Luke to complete the pages and pages of paperwork and *sit back and wait to see if he would be accepted onto the trial. I still remember now Luke ringing me at work saying that he had himself had a phone call from his consultant informing him of the date of his first screening appointment. I could feel his excitement down the phone. It was almost like hearing that your child had passed that all-important exam. I tried to argue for some perspective, but Luke was having none of it. As far as he was concerned, he was going to be pain-free within a matter of months.*

Happy days.

TIME PASSES

The next two years passed by quicker than Will could ever have believed. They had been the best years of his life. He was living a good life. A great life. Maybe a little larger around the waist than he would like but Celeste always reassured him that he actually looked better and needed to put on some weight.

"But what about all this white hair that spurting out all over my head?" he worried, pointing to a few hairs that had appeared below his left ear.

"And you expect me to dignify that question with an answer?" responded Celeste with a phrase they often used and who secretly relied upon dyeing her hair to hide a much more serious outbreak of white matter, which was blamed on an acrimonious and, in Celeste's view, unnecessarily expensive divorce that was thankfully now all in the past.

With her share of what was left of the divorce proceeds, Celeste was able to buy a small but sumptuous house in one of the more upmarket suburbs of Boston. Her treat was that it came with enough land to justify employing an almost full-time gardener. Still very much a step down from the marital home, but why would a single woman without any children need any more than four bedrooms? In reality, Celeste only needed two. One for her and one to eject Will to whenever he had one of his 'snoring nights'.

Will had also been active in the property market, moving out of his apartment to a modest detached house just off the exclusive and eye-wateringly expensive Hills Road address. The three-bedroomed house he could now afford with his US-brokered salary was a big step up from his apartment but came with the very smallest of gardens. *And anyway. What the fuck would I ever do with a garden?* A big factor in Will choosing this particular house was that it was reasonably modern and came almost completely furnished. He was no DIY fanatic. Not all top scientists are capable of putting up a shelf or two.

His living space was not the only thing that had changed since Granta Pain Therapeutics was bought. In fact, Will's working life was what had changed most over the last two years. The remaining lease on the university labs had been paid off by Myers-Stratton and both he and Grace moved to the office space Celeste had picked out for the company near the city's railway station. A suitably executive-styled modern building which was part of a new development, attracting some big names to the city such as Microsoft and Apple. Their second-floor offices, a reception area together with three small offices and a meeting room, even boasted of a hotel literally just over the road. The now-preferred accommodation for whenever Celeste could conjure up an excuse to visit Granta Pain but, more importantly, to visit Will. She still felt the need to keep up the pretence that they were not a couple, which all came as good news to the hotel cleaning staff, as they rarely had any cleaning to do with Celeste usually spending her nights at Will's new house.

As he had predicted, it took some time for Will to adjust from a lab-focused environment to being stuck in an office all day long. However, he soon enough found some excuses for not having to go into the office. Will always enjoyed lecturing – *keeping the ego fully nourished, my boy* – and was genuinely delighted when, with the help of some more of Myers-Stratton money, he received an invite to present an optional module for those studying pharmacology at the university on the Molecular Pharmacology of CNS Acting Drugs. On top of that, he became more active on the conference circuit, presenting Granta Pain's research to a worldwide audience. It was an activity Myers-Stratton was happy to fund as it was good background promotion for the hopefully positive results coming out of the clinical trials on GPT107 due in the early summer of 2024.

Will's true work-related responsibilities were limited. Attending and writing up the minutes of project team meetings and board meetings, neither of which he had much input. Pushing along some basic ongoing science with external service providers with the intention of publishing the results just as the clinical trial read out, although this was really Grace's new role, together with supporting Will in developing a back-up compound strategy. A full-time job for Grace, although that was far from the case for Will, who was by far the least employed of all those on the Granta Pain payroll. *But pretty little figureheads don't need to work, do they? Fuck knows they get enough out of me hosting visits from Myers-Stratton top people and their spouses. I have never eaten so many college dinners in my life and even Cambridge can get boring after the tenth punt chauffeuring of the summer!*

Of the two confusing women currently in his life, Grace was probably the winner by a short head. Will had been in the adjoining office to Grace for a little over two years with only the occasional visit from Hirami, service providers and Myers-Stratton people to disturb the peace. It was difficult to believe that night of a few years ago back in his apartment when she just couldn't keep her hands off him had ever happened. Of late, the most that Will got out of his only work colleague was no more than a polite smile. Not that Will was interested in her sexually after his fears of blackmail, but how can someone turn so completely? On the rare occasion that he managed to get Grace talking about her home life, there was never any mention of boyfriends or even women lovers. Will's conclusion was that she was still a blackmail threat waiting to play her card when she was ready. *But she had better get on with it before that particular window closes.*

And then there was that other difficult woman. Few would be surprised to learn that their first love letter was written by Celeste and sent when she was alone in a Chicago hotel room no more than a week after 'that night' in the University Arms. Not that it was about love, more about longing, and not that it was a letter, as it was an email, but they were always referred to as letters by the soulmates. Letters that continued at least on a weekly basis but often

241

more regularly than that, especially when they were away from each other or were travelling. It was not that the letters were full of heartfelt romanticism. They were often just filled with the events of the day or what they had been doing on the weekend. What was important, although more so for Celeste than Will, was that there was someone out there to talk to. Someone who cared. A person each of them could rely upon. The only person they could trust with their worries and their secrets. A soulmate. Celeste enjoyed and looked forward to the opportunities they had to have sex, but it was never a priority for her and their differing appetites were sometimes a minor source of conflict, but they were always quickly resolved. They meant too much to each other to risk drifting apart.

Their long-distance relationship was kept alive through both striving to meet up as often possible. Both had a valid business reason to visit each other, which they managed to do almost every month, although there were times when they were apart for longer. A large part of the problem was their need to keep the relationship a secret from work colleagues and, for Celeste, her family. That all changed when Celeste was promoted in early 2024 to become a vice president of the company with the title of Head of Strategy for In-licensing, reporting directly to the CEO, which was still Declan. A new role that had essentially been created for her and one that still involved working with the Granta Pain project and with Will, although she could no longer justify travelling so regularly to Cambridge. A solution had to be found. At least in Celeste's opinion.

The couple were watching the people traffic walking through Kings Parade on a busy winter's morning, enjoying the warmth of hot-chocolate drinks served up in the Copper Kettle.

"I think the time has come," suggested Celeste, and by doing so, waking Will up from his thousand-yard stare.

"Oh. We need to go back to the office. Sorry, didn't realise the time."

"No. Not that. It's not even 1pm yet. I'm talking about another time. Time for us to go public about our relationship." Celeste immediately peered into his eyes to see how he would react to this suggestion.

Humour. Always a good way of buying time to think. "But we've only being seeing each other for two and a half years. What's the rush?" The ball was knocked back into Celeste's side of the court.

"Do you deliberately go out of your way to make difficult subjects even more difficult? And please don't feel that you have to answer that question. I think what you meant to ask was why now."

"But of course, my dear. Why now?"

"Main reason is that horrible divorce is now history. I am officially single and free to do what I want. The sanctity of marriage has always been very important to my father. Important to me is that I don't do anything to upset him while I was still married. My mother? God knows what she thinks about it, that is if she thinks about it at all. I'm now finally settled in my new house. The new job will inevitably loosen the ties I have with Granta Pain, as Declan has asked me to step down from the board. 'Your job has been done,' he said to me and, 'a bloody good job too,' he added. So I can't be accused of showing bias to you as there is not even the faintest of reporting lines between us. That's the good news!"

"So, I'm guessing the bad news is that we have now lost the excuse for you to come over to Cambridge regularly. Correct?"

"I'm afraid so, Will. There will still be the odd visit, I imagine, but not nearly as often as has been the case over the last couple of years."

He was now expecting the killer question. Would he like to go over to Boston to live with her? It made more sense that he would be the one to move as most of his job could be done remotely and his most important meetings were the project team meetings with the Myers-Stratton scientists in Boston. *So what the fuck am I going to say when she drops that little beauty into the conversation? I don't want to live in Boston. I'm not yet ready to 'settle down', or whatever they call it.* But she didn't. The killer question was never asked. At least not on that day.

"So I was thinking, if you are happy to consider me as your partner in public, we could see one another at our leisure. Instead of having to find work excuses for us to meet, we can now meet whenever we like and for how long we choose to, staying at each other's houses rather than hotels. Provided you sort out your living room first, of course!"

Will tried very hard to not let his relief show. "Sounds like a plan to me. It would be nice to spend longer over in Boston rather than to fly in and out for a few meetings. A chance to get to see more of Boston and also the rest of the country."

"You don't mind me telling the family and Declan about us, then?"

"Why not? I never had an issue with that anyway," lied

Will. "But what will your parents make of me? Do they even know about me?"

"Of course they do, although obviously not as my lover. In fact, I often have to stop myself talking about you to them when I hear myself going on and on about that wonderful Jeavons fellow of Granta Pain. How nice it will be that I no longer need to do that. Meeting them for the first time? It'll be a cakewalk. Your outgoing personality and all those anecdotes you trot out to order will go down a storm with my father. My mother? Dr William Jeavons, University of Cambridge lecturer. I think you'll be absolutely fine. In fact, I think she might even make a pass at you, so be warned!"

Will had never even seen a photograph of her mother. *Surely too old. Even for me.*

"Very much looking forward to meeting them sometime soon."

"And what'll you do about this? Send a letter to the *Times* with the announcement like the English do?" she joked.

"Already thinking of the wording as we speak. I guess I will just let it happen naturally. The next time someone meets us when we are together, I will just say we are together. To tell one person in the Cambridge 'scene' is to tell everyone, believe me, but I think my parents deserve a phone call, even if it is just to tell them that I am no longer a homosexual. I think they'll be pleased."

Will felt, to a certain extent, that he had dodged a bullet in her not asking the killer question. *But if we stay together then us living together must surely only be a matter of time. It's already been two years and at our age that's a long time.*

I wonder if she wants us to shack up together now and is just too frightened of asking. If she did, I would say yes despite all my reservations and fears about all that 'settling down' sort of stuff. So why would I say yes and be the person I thought I would never be? Simple. I don't want to lose her.

And so, they formally became a couple. No longer worried about being seen together. Happy for people to know that they were a couple even if they were not yet living together. Their distant jobs would be a convenient excuse to present to those who asked about their living arrangements. All was well for the happy couple.

*

Will was genuinely more than happy to meet with her parents, although, despite what he had said to Celeste, still a little uncomfortable with everyone in Cambridge knowing that he was in a long-term relationship. It did take him a little outside his comfort zone, as he had never liked being labelled as being in a relationship, or not being in a relationship, or whatever the latest Facebook terminology was. It was going to be a new experience for Will and something he was prepared to do if it made Celeste happy. But what Celeste wouldn't have been happy with was if she had known that Will had been continuing with his one-night stands. He might now be the proud owner of a family house, but he was still a bachelor about town. Maybe nowhere near to the extent of his worst examples of hedonism but there were sporadic times when the temptation was just too much for him. When his appetite had to be satiated. Without exception, he always regretted letting Celeste down. Risking breaking that trust she had in him and, worse still, risk losing the only woman who he had really cared for and who had cared for him. Greed, selfishness, stupidity. Whatever it was, there were times when he just could not stop himself. *What a complete arsehole I am. An irreversible cad. I honestly think I need some sort of therapy. She deserves so much better than me.*

*

Any hope that Will had of keeping his relationship with Celeste low key was completely blown out of the water by the surprise fortieth birthday party she had arranged for her partner. Celeste relied upon an unsurprisingly reluctant Grace to organise a venue and round up the usual suspects as guests. If Will had suspected something, he certainly didn't betray his suspicions when he stepped through the doorway of the Cambridge Blue pub to celebrate his birthday with what he thought would be spent with just a few of his old mates. What a wonderfully, heartwarming surprise it was to see that Celeste had flown over from Boston especially for the occasion.

It was Celeste who was the first to go up to him as the cheers rung out. She planted a big, public kiss on her lover.

"Congratulations, my English darling. Now you truly know what it feels like to get old!"

A hugely enjoyable night out followed, which included seeing some friends he had not seen for years, but perhaps his biggest shock, and what made the night truly special, was that his parents had travelled down from Birmingham to see him. They were clearly a bit overwhelmed with the crowds and the noise and so their son made sure that they were sitting next to him throughout the night. Parents on one side, Celeste on the other, who he thanked many times for organising the party and looking after his parents, whom she had booked into a hotel at her own expense. In fact, the whole night out was at her expense.

"My pleasure. But Grace has been a big help in organising this because I couldn't do much from over in Boston. Make sure you thank her."

It was Will's house where Celeste stayed that Friday night and through to Sunday when she flew back home. No need for booking hotels in Cambridge anymore. A relaxing weekend which included the couple taking Will's parents out to lunch at the Hotel Du Vin. A place where Will had taken them when he first moved down to Cambridge. Special memories. And it was reliving memories that took up much of that Saturday morning waiting for Celeste to wake. Memories of the death of his sister and of his father leaving their house. Of his mother's love and then her death. Of the love and care of his new parents and how they guided him through those so important early years in school. Of the universities he was lucky enough to go to and how those experiences helped craft him into the man he was now. Of his company – the good times and the bad. Of his lover lying next to him. What would the next few years have in store for a man who had already led such a tumultuous life?

THE PATIENT

*W*hen Luke started talking about headaches, it could have been one of two things. He's just got a headache. "Take a couple of ibuprofen tablets and get over it." Or it could be that he is in the drug group and headaches were just a side effect. It was the latter that I was favouring and what I thought was a positive argument to put to Luke. Just to cheer him up!

He'd picked up his first month's worth of tablets from Addenbrookes Hospital in the first week of December, which was a nice Christmas present. Luke just knew that he would be in the drug cohort and not on placebo.

"I can just feel it in my water," he said on more than one occasion.

It was no use telling him otherwise, as he just wasn't prepared to listen, but getting a headache three days in a row made me think that he might just be right.

"I'd prefer the drug effect rather than the side effects," moaned Luke.

I urged patience, arguing that the drug is unlikely to have any positive effect for at least a couple of days and the headaches might just be caused by stress. Very understandable. But as the days slowly passed, I started to feel a little more uncomfortable, although it was not a worry I was going to share with Luke.

It was on the third night after starting on the drug when even Luke had become concerned.

"This headache's killing me. It's getting worse, not better."

I looked over at the clock. It was almost 3am. "You can't take any more ibuprofen until the morning. Just try and rest your head and sleep and maybe you should phone up in the morning that number the hospital gave you." But I was worried. He's not a particularly headachy person. Never had a migraine, as far as I was aware.

Looking back now at that night and early morning, I can't remember if either me or Luke had fallen asleep first. All I can remember is the sensation of the bed moving beside me. I turned round to see Luke fitting. This was a first time for me. I had never before seen one and had no idea what to do. For want of something to do, I pulled the duvet off the bed and stood by the bed to stop him falling onto the floor. It was horrible. So frightening. I felt so useless watching him suffer. I looked over to the clock to see how long this had been going on, but I hadn't looked at the clock when it started, although he must have been fitting for at least a couple of minutes. And then it stopped. I gently nudged him and called his name. This I did several times, but he just lay there. Eyes closed. But there at least was a pulse I could feel when I picked up his wrist.

The next few hours were the longest of my life. An ambulance arrived mercifully quickly after my frantic call, and although they couldn't make him regain consciousness, they also did pick up a pulse. I can remember speeding through the empty roads of an early December morning. The breaths of the stressed ambulance crew showing up in the cold morning air as they took Luke through the double doors of A & E at the very same hospital where he received the tablets that had presumably left him unconscious.

"I'm sorry. I'm afraid you will have to sit in the waiting area," whispered a nurse, directing me to the corner of a large room, which was already half full despite it being so early in the morning.

"Is he going to be alright? He's not going to die, is he?" A stupid question I couldn't stop myself from asking. The answer was equally predictable.

"We'll be doing everything we possibly can. He is in good hands. Someone will come out to see you when we find out more."

I still have nightmares of staring into space in that waiting room. Watching the clock edge from minute to minute, wondering when my name will be called. Is no news good news? Means that he's still alive? My dear Luke. My poor Luke. He doesn't deserve this. I don't deserve this. Why us? Whatever is happening to us?

This time it wasn't someone else's name the nurse was calling out.

"Lydia Goldberg."

I put my hand up like a schoolgirl and did as I was told just as a schoolgirl should do. I followed the nurse into the resuscitation area and was told to wait in a side room.

"Please take a seat. The doctor will be with you soon."

And she was.

"Mrs Lydia Goldberg?" asked a statuesque doctor with a hint of a German accent. She slowly walked over to where I was sitting. "I'm sorry to say but I'm afraid your husband is quite poorly."

My heart stopped. "Is he going to die?"

"We are doing our very best to make sure that will not be the case but the next day or two will be critical and we'll know more then. I'm sorry that I can't be more positive."

"So he might die!"

"Like I said, we are doing everything we can. We are still waiting for a few more blood tests to come back but it looks like your husband has had a stroke and is now in quite a deep coma."

"But he's not even in his fifties. How can he have a stroke at his age?"

"Strokes in men of your husband's age are unusual but I'm afraid they are not rare. Is there any family history of strokes?"

I honestly didn't know. "I don't think so. But the drugs. Of course, the drugs. He's just started taking a new drug as part of a clinical trial. Here in Addenbrookes. Could it be the drug that has given him a stroke?" I knew that was another impossible question for the doctor to answer but she did raise an eyebrow.

"Very unlikely, I would have said, but that will be followed up the clinical team on the trial."

I felt so very helpless and lost. "What happens next? Can I go and see Luke?"

"Of course. Let me check first, though. What happens next? You must be exhausted and so once you have seen your husband, I would suggest you go home and rest up.

Nothing you can do here to help. We will leave you with contact details so that you can keep up to date with how he is doing. Will there be anyone at home to keep you company?"

It was then that I thought about Sam all those thousands of miles away in America. What am I going to say to her? It was then when the tears arrived.

Luke looked just as he did when I saw him disappear into A & E apart from the tube sticking out of his mouth and a bank of instruments on the left-hand side of his bed. At that moment he looked as helpless and lost as did his wife. This was the moment, that our lives would be irredeemably changed forever. All because of a drug he never needed to take. A drug he had taken because of my advice.

THE RESULTS

Grace could almost taste the tension in the air that bright Monday morning in late May. The results from the Phase 2 clinical trial in OA patients were due on Wednesday but they were told that they might be released even earlier than that. Will was in the office before Grace, had arrived for work that morning. Practically unbroken ground since he had moved out to his new house, which was further out from the Granta Pain offices than his apartment. Unusually for her, she went out of her way to say hello by poking her head around Will's open office door but only received an eyes-down grunt as a reply. This was not a problem for Grace, as although their relationship since they had moved to the new offices had been cordial and professional, she didn't feel any compunction to talk to him about anything outside of work, unlike on those occasions when Hirami visited where both were happy to talk about their home and family lives. Grace could see that this both confused and annoyed Will.

Grace never really had any time for Will, who she considered a leering misogynist. Through her early years at Granta Pain, she had treated her boss with respect for the position he was in and his abilities as a scientist rather than the man he was. Grace actually liked to think of herself as being ruthlessly ambitious and so if that meant tolerating a man who she privately loathed, then so be it if she could then hang onto the coat-tails of a scientist who was quickly making a name for himself. All of which involved an expedient abuse of her own principles, as she often used her femininity to attract Will's attention and approval whenever needed. However, that false but convenient relationship all changed on that night and morning she spent in Will's apartment.

That Grace found herself waking up in Will's spare bedroom was merely a consequence of unforeseen events. Destiny. She didn't mean to get as drunk as she did at that celebration and often wondered if her drinks had been spiked, since Grace always liked to be in control. But who there that night would want to drug her into their bed? She couldn't imagine Will would do something so reckless, not least because his ego was big enough to fool himself that he didn't need drugs to charm women into his bed. Grace had come up with a few likely suspects, including Yasmin from the admin team, but whoever it might have been, it clearly didn't work. The second unforeseen event was missing the last train. A few minutes earlier and that night would have turned out very different. But it didn't and Grace woke up in the early hours of that morning just about sober enough to realise that she had been presented with an opportunity. A way of making sure that she would fully benefit from Will's progression through the industry regardless of her own abilities. A fast track to realise her own lofty ambitions with the minimum of effort on her part and a safeguard against the vagaries of employment in an industry renowned for redundancies. That she had to sacrifice her body for one night to a man who didn't deserve it was a price Grace was willing to make. And anyway, she thought, it might actually be enjoyable based on what she had heard about the man.

The unspoken threat of future potential blackmail if she didn't get what she wanted was hopefully made clear to Will when she thanked him for being offered the new job. That she was offered the job at all suggested, at least in Grace's mind, that Will was very aware of the threat, maybe even before she dropped that not-so-subtle hint. Myers-Stratton could easily have managed without employing anyone, including Will, and so Grace allowing herself to be used for his pleasure had already paid dividends. She guessed that Will had pushed for a role for in the new version of Granta Pain. But it didn't stop there. She hoped it would be the gift that kept on giving, to be opened up again whenever the right opportunity arose, but Grace was well aware that the advantage she had would gradually lose leverage over time and she was already looking for her next job.

As almost per protocol, Will decided to leave the office for a walk. It was barely 11am. He opened Grace's office door. "Just popping out for a walk, Grace. I just can't handle the stress. Will the results come today, tomorrow, whenever? Why can't they just tell us when? How hard can it be? It's like waiting to be called in a doctor's surgery when the time of your appointment bears no relationship to the time you will actually be seen. Anyway. Rant over. But, Grace, if, for some reason we get the call on the landline instead of my mobile, for Christ's sake please ring me! Back in about thirty minutes. Bye."

Grace had assumed it would be at least an hour before she saw him again, which was not a problem for her. She wasn't to be disappointed.

Will had gone to his favourite quiet corner in Nero's on Station Square. Comfy chairs and a certain degree of anonymity. Hot chocolate was his choice of drink that morning, swapping caffeine for a much-needed sugar kick. Much needed so as to maintain the energy surge that had come over him after the phone call he had taken from Declan, who had rung him from a ridiculously early Boston time. Will had walked up and down the length of the train station car park listening to what Declan had to say. It was good news. It was very good news.

"To finish up, Will. I must say that I am very surprised and maybe even a little bit shocked at just how good the clinical data read-out is. Easily met the primary endpoint of significantly reducing pain and was even close to being significant on the secondary of showing evidence of disease modification. Absolutely incredible. Unbelievable. Never seen anything like it. But the coup de grace, the fucking coup de grace, my friend, was that we didn't see any signs of abuse potential, although with the caveat that the trial wasn't long enough to power such an endpoint." Declan paused for breath and inspiration for his final words. "Nevertheless, we just weren't seeing any withdrawal symptoms when the patients went back

257

to their maintenance regimes. Absolutely fucking brilliant would be my take-home message from the top-line data I have seen so far. Obviously, still a long, long way to go and lots that can go wrong in Phase 3 studies but if these data hold out then this will transform the way we treat chronic pain and catapult Myers-Stratton up to where the big players are. I don't know about you, Will, but I'm going to have a drink even if it's just gone 7am. Cheers!"

Silence.

"Will. Are you still there?"

"Yes, sorry, still here but just trying to take it all in. What about side effects? Any serious adverse events?" asked Will, pinching his leg to ward off any bad news.

"There was one stand out case with a male patient having a stroke and he is now in a coma. In a UK site, if I recall correctly."

"Sounds pretty serious. Was he in the drug cohort? Could it be a drug-related effect?"

"He was on the drug and, quite correctly, this was looked into in some detail but the decision made was that it was not drug related as there were no red flag cardiovascular-related concerns in the preclinical profiling, as you well know, Will, and nothing like this was seen in either this or previous trials. The finding is obviously a concern, and we will be watching out for any similar incidents moving forward, but the decision made was to continue with the trial. Thank God! After all, it's not unusual for a middle-aged man to suffer a stroke, so hopefully it is a background finding, and it also appears that the patient did not disclose that there was a family history of strokes, although they are still looking into that.

If only he had been in the placebo cohort and then we wouldn't have this worry."

Despite the reassuring background detail that Declan had provided, Will had been spooked because of the secret he was still clinging onto. The red-flag cardiovascular data from Biopharmaco. Very spooked.

"Were there any other patients with adverse cardiovascular findings?" was a question that Will felt came out rather feebly.

"Don't worry, Will. Like all trials, this one would have been put on hold PDQ if there was any evidence of drug-related toxicity. There wasn't. At least not at this stage. I think there will be a VC later this week when the data will be presented in full and we will all have a chance to raise these sorts of questions. In the meantime, Will, I suggest you celebrate big time. You deserve it. Speak to you soon."

The hot chocolate was still too dangerously hot to drink. The news was overwhelmingly positive. It was beyond even his own wildest hopes but there remained this nagging worry that he was personally responsible for that poor man being in a coma. A man probably local to Will himself, as the only UK site was in Cambridge. But surely the fact that the man had a family history of strokes would trump any side effect arising from the drug. The problem was that it was impossible to know for certain and Will dare not ask anyone for advice as it would risk disclosing his secret. Will decided to make himself feel positive. *How many scientists live to see their own research have a positive effect in alleviating suffering? And here I am with the chance of joining that select group. I should be ecstatic, as it just doesn't get any better. This day, this morning, will likely change my life forever. So why do I feel this way?*

If he wasn't still obsessed with the gnawing, guilty secret he held onto deep within his soul then perhaps he would have been ecstatic. This despite repeatedly reminding himself that the benefit far outweighed the risk and even more so now after the positive trial results. Maybe if he had someone to share the wonderful news with other than the mug of hot chocolate he was holding. Of course, he would ring his parents to tell them of the good news later, but although they would be thrilled to hear the news, they wouldn't really understand the significance of what he was telling them. Not their fault. If only Celeste was sitting next to him that morning. Now that really would have been wonderful. A day, a night and a morning after with someone with whom he could really share his success. The only person who was capable of making him happy. A person who was thousands and thousands of miles away and who was likely to still be asleep. But not for long.

"Who's this? Do you know what time it is!"

"It's Will and yes, I do know what time it is, but you're never going to believe what I'm going to tell you now."

DISCLOSURE

*T*he Biopharmaco cafeteria had been awash with talk about the Granta Pain Therapeutics press release all week. There was genuine excitement not only because of the impact the drug might have on chronic pain but also because we had done a substantial part of the drug profiling. Some positive publicity for our company somewhere down the line.

I did my best to stay out of these discussions and managed to do just that until the coffee break on that Thursday morning, which happened to be six months to the day after Luke was rushed into hospital. What probably kicked me off suddenly bursting into tears in front of everyone on my table was the memory of the phone call from Sam just the night before when we cried together for what seemed like hours. Me from the guilt of encouraging him to go on the clinical trial and Sam from the guilt of not being able to travel over to see us as often as she would like.

"Lydia. Whatever is the matter, love?" asked Mia, wrapping her arm around my shoulder. "Is there anything we can help you with? Has Luke taken a turn for the worse?"

I appreciated her kindness but there wasn't anything she could help me with. Sympathy rarely helps, instead only serving to magnify one's grief. At least for me. It was just the injustice of it all that I was struggling to cope with. The unquestioned admiration everyone seemed to have for a company and its local CEO whose drug had put my man into a coma and how they seemed to be revelling in the huge publicity that followed. All completely understandable given the circumstances but it all just stuck in my throat. Did I tell them what I thought? That I believed the company they seemed to admire so much was going to test their drug out on thousands of patients despite life-threatening side effects such as happened to my Luke.

The Biopharmaco staff I personally knew were well aware of Luke falling into a coma after suffering a stroke, but up to that day no one knew that he was one of the patients on the GPT107 trial. Up to that point, I didn't want that conversation to happen. But that was now no longer the case. The gloves were off. I told them what I thought.

"But you don't know for sure that it was the drug that caused the stroke, otherwise they wouldn't have carried on with the trial," suggested Ken after I had told them that I believed the drug was responsible for Luke being in a coma. "Surely they would have just stopped the trial, wouldn't they?" he added, looking around the table for support or even contradiction of his view.

My colleagues were scientists who bought into the 'scientific method' and so I assumed that even if they had genuine sympathy for my predicament, which I'm sure at least some of them did, they would be aligned with Ken's view. Luke taking the drug was coincidental to him suffering the stroke because that's what the science would lead you to believe. But they could all afford to think that way, couldn't they? They weren't the woman who was married to Luke.

They're a kind and thoughtful lot, my work colleagues, and so I was not surprised with them tiptoeing around me for the rest of the day, but I was surprised when someone approached me in the corridor leading up to pharmacology.

"Sorry to trouble you and I hope you don't mind me doorstepping you in the corridor, but I couldn't help overhearing your sad story in the coffee room. My name's Neville Chamberlain and I work in pharmacology."

I had seen his face around Biopharmaco but I had never met him before. I decided to hear him out.

"Well, this is very difficult. Very awkward. Still not sure if I should be telling you this, but I used to work for Granta Pain Therapeutics."

"Which must have been very nice for you, Neville, but I'm not sure it is something I would like to talk to you about given the circumstances. If you know what I mean." I was doing my best to not get angry and storm off, but surely the man can't be as insensitive as he was coming across.

"No, no, no. You misunderstand." He looked furtively up and down the corridor. "I have some information on GPT107 that I think you should be aware of."

"What information?" was my rather abrupt reply.

He looked up and down the corridor once again. There was still only the two of us in the corridor. "I can't tell you here but if you want to find out more, and I can understand

263

if you don't, perhaps we can meet up after work somewhere in town. Maybe the Eagle in the front room, say at 7pm tonight?"

"I must say that this all sounds a bit strange to me, Neville, but I will be there to at least listen to what you have to say, even if it is against my better judgement. I'm afraid that I have no idea who you are and what your motive is and so perhaps you will understand why I am more than a little sceptical. Now, I must get on with my work, so if you will please excuse me."

My head was shot for the rest of the afternoon at work, running overtime trying to think what this Neville man might say to me and whether I should even bother turning up at all. I asked a few of my gang if they knew him but only Sean had worked with him on a project at Biopharmaco. He seemed to check out. Wasn't an obvious psycho or stalker but I made sure my neighbour was aware of where I was going that night and who I was going to meet.

*

I turned up deliberately early at the Eagle so that I could choose a crowded place to sit and see him arrive. He saw me and came up to the table I was sitting. He looked even more nervous than me. A good sign.

"I was thinking we could maybe sit somewhere a bit more private," were his first words.

"No. I'm OK here if you don't mind." Based on the way he was looking at all the pub goers sitting around us, it wasn't OK for him at all but I wasn't leaving him with much of a choice.

"Can I get you a drink?"

"A Coke would be fine, thanks."

He returned after a little while with my coke and a pint of something warm and dark-looking for him, but I was pretty sure he sneaked down his throat a quick shot of something or other when he was at the bar.

"Look, Lydia. Can I call you Lydia?"

I nodded yes.

"Look, Lydia. Like I said earlier today, this is all very difficult for me and I'm still not convinced I'm doing the right thing. I could get into very big trouble by telling you what I am about to say. I know it really doesn't mean anything in law, of course, but could I at least have your word that you will never tell anyone else that I am the source of the information I'm going to pass onto you."

"Yes, you have my word." The man was starting to get on my nerves.

"I was responsible for the preclinical profiling work that Biopharmaco was doing on Granta Pain's lead compound, GPT107. I saw all the data that was generated and passed it on directly to the CEO, Will Jeavons. All of the data looked good and there were no obvious toxicity concerns. With one exception. The drug failed badly in one of the cardiovascular toxicity assays. An assay that was designed to predict cardiovascular adverse events such as blood clots and subsequent strokes. Strokes like your husband seems to have suffered."

All my concerns about this strange man and this bizarre liaison vanished in a heartbeat. "So why was the drug allowed to progress through into clinical trials?"

"That's exactly why I wanted to meet you here tonight.

I am strongly of the opinion that Jeavons buried the data. That he never passed on this key red-flag data onto Myers-Stratton. They never saw it."

"How do you know that for sure?"

"I don't. But I can't imagine any major company taking a compound into humans with such a red-flag tox finding. Can you? The regulatory authorities just wouldn't swallow it. On top of that, Jeavons told me himself that he wouldn't pass on the cardiovascular tox finding to Myers-Stratton as it would kill the compound and the company. He later denied that he would do this, but I just can't believe the man. I know him too well."

"What was the assay? How bad was the data?"

"Look, Lydia, I've really gone out on a limb big, big time to tell you what I've said already. If any of this got out, that I have leaked confidential information, I'd probably end up in court and at the very least never work in the industry again. You do understand the risk I am taking even just disclosing this information to you, don't you, Lydia?"

"Of course I do and I'm very grateful that you have, but there's not much I can do about this unless I know what the assay was and its read-out."

"I'm afraid that's something you're going to have to do for yourself. I don't want to leave any trace of me searching for the data in the Biopharmaco databases."

I nodded slowly in response, trying to think just how I could get hold of the data.

Neville quickly finished his drink and looked around him. "I think it's best that we don't talk again. I've told you all that I'm prepared to say and it's now up to you if you want to chase this up, but I will say one last thing. You will *be doing us all a favour if you can nail that bastard Jeavons. Goodnight, Lydia. I wish you well and I hope your husband recovers."*

Neville Chamberlain. He is a good man.

*

It took the rest of the week and also through the weekend to consider and reconsider exactly what, if anything, I should do next. It was a two-hour WhatsApp call with Sam that finally helped me make up my mind. I was with Neville. I was going to nail that bastard Jeavons whatever it took. It was he who was to blame for all that had happened to Luke. If Jeavons had just done what he was supposed to have done and not made up his own rules, if he hadn't abused his position, if he hadn't buried that data, then Luke would be at home with me now. How nice it would be to hear about all his little aches and pains. How nice it would be to wake up with him next to me. I am not the guilty person for encouraging Luke to go on the trial. The guilty person is Jeavons, and he has to pay for his crimes.

WHEN WILL I BE FAMOUS?

The celebrations in Boston were long, tiring and memorable but the hangovers were likely to be fierce and prolonged. Quite understandably, Will was the centre of attention, a role he played with consummate ease and modest grace, making every effort to bring Celeste and Declan onto the centre stage whenever he could. A night and early morning of exaggerated anecdotes and even a few songs from the 'old country', which Declan did proud, and it was Declan who was at least planning to say the last words of the night before the guests departed to stumble into the fleet of taxis parked outside the InterContinental.

"My final toast of the night. Or is it the morning? Yes, yes I know," argued Declan at the howls of playful derision, "but this is my final, final toast. I would like you all to raise your almost empty glasses one last time to the young man, OK, maybe ex-young man, sitting beside me in celebration of his truly world-class research and the world-changing consequences it will almost surely bring. To Dr Will Jeavons. A scientist for our times."

Will stood up as Declan sat down and waited for the clamour to die down. "My good friend beside me is far too generous with his words but I must thank him for the sentiment. But perhaps you, Declan, will indulge me with allowing another final toast." Will allowed a few more cheers to die down. "Without the support of companies like Myers-Stratton, even the finest of scientific research would fall on barren ground and never benefit mankind. It is impossible for me to exaggerate just how grateful I am to Declan and to all of you here tonight for taking on an idea I first had many, many years ago and providing the fertile earth that has led to the clinical success we keep toasting again and again tonight. But before you all start throwing things at me in the hope that this Englishman will finally stop talking, I would like to dedicate the final toast to someone without whose considerable foresight I would not be here today. So please raise your very empty glasses to the most clever, most gracious and most beautiful person I have ever and will ever have the good fortune of meeting. I give you, Celeste Simmonds."

*

"Do you enjoy making people cry in public?"

"Not really something I have given much thought to, if I'm being honest," replied Will, struggling badly with trying to remove his remaining sock from an unpredictable foot.

"Here, let me do that," offered a dressing-gowned Celeste, walking round to the other side of the bed. "But it was ever so sweet of you to say such things about me. No one has ever said what you said tonight."

"Well, more fool them. For the record, I meant every word."

"I know you did, Will, no need for you to try to prove it," answered Celeste, kissing his newly naked ankle. "You are a terrible old charmer and maybe even a closet romantic."

"More than happy to be whatever you want me to be."

"What an offer! Tonight, I want you to be the man that makes love to me until I fall asleep."

"All I can promise you is that I will do my very best."

Will decided that he should reconsider in the morning just what day had been the best day of his life.

*

Scientists know when they have carried out good research. Their common complaint is that it is just not well enough understood for it be recognised by their peers in the way it should. Their fault. That was not a problem that Will encountered in the weeks and months following the Myers-Stratton press release on the clinical trial results of GPT107. Appreciative editorials on the data appeared in *Nature*, *Science*, *The Lancet* and many other scientific journals, although most ended with the obvious caveat that further clinical studies were needed to fully validate the early findings.

A paper outlining the unique mechanism of action of GPT107 with Will as the main author, although mostly written up by Grace, was quickly accepted for publication in *Nature* and an additional paper was in the pipeline covering the clinical data. Will was nominated for several scientific awards and received more requests than he could possibly accept to attend conferences all around the world. The clinical findings and the potential for the drug to change the way pain would be managed even made the national press in several countries. However, the real highlight for Will's parents was when their son appeared on the main BBC news explaining his work to a reporter whilst wearing a lab coat, standing beside a thoroughly cleaned lab bench in the university.

"I appreciate that it's bending the truth a tad, Dr Jeavons, but it's what the viewers expect to see when we cover science stories. Someone in a white coat standing next to instruments with flashing lights that go 'beep'."

"The things one has to suffer for one's art," was Will's reply.

Celeste playfully endeavoured to keep his feet on the ground by frequently reminding him that he was yet to feature on the front page of *Forbes* as Will had promised her on that memorable day on the banks of the River Cam all those years ago. She was worried about the effect all the back-slapping adulation might have on her lover and was a little fearful that Will would begin to try to live up to his publicity. But, much to her surprise, he was also mindful of his own behaviour and tried what he thought was his best to maintain some degree of modesty despite even appearing on a few network talk shows. He was an Englishman, after all. Nevertheless, it wasn't something he found easy. However, by far the biggest effect all the positive publicity and public adoration had on Will was to at least temporarily lock away his demons. No longer was he constantly struggling under the burden of guilt for burying that data, although there was still the odd bad day when the guilt would randomly return. The outstanding success of the clinical trial and the astonishing publicity that followed reassured him that he had made the right decision all along, even if that decision was not one for him to make. Thus far, the benefits far outweighed the risks just as he believed they always would.

BUILDING A CASE

*S*o. What was the plan going to be? How was I going to
make Jeavons pay for his ego-driven abuse of his position
of trust, his disdain for the principles of science and, worst
of all, putting patients at risk? Perhaps I should also add my
personal revenge to that list as a motive if I am being going
to be completely honest. Vengeance for what that fucking
bastard has done to my family.

First of all, I needed proof. I needed to see the raw
data myself. But that, maybe not so surprisingly, proved
to be impossible. Not that I was at all surprised, but it
turned out that I worked for a highly ethical company that
insisted on multiple sign-offs to access confidential data
from client projects I hadn't worked on, such as the Granta
Pain Therapeutics portfolio. I could have potentially asked
someone who had worked on the project to download the
data for me, but I wasn't prepared to put anyone's job at risk
other than my own. I was screwed.

"I thought I said we should not talk again," whispered Neville when I approached him as he was leaving the company dining room one miserable Wednesday afternoon.

"Just one last thing, Neville, and I promise this will be the last time we talk." He looked agitated. I had to make this quick. "As you might have probably guessed, it's impossible for me to get hold of that data. The security is just too tight. So, I'm left only with your word that this important data actually exists. I have no proof."

"Well, what the fuck do you expect me to say here, Lydia? That I just invented all this as some sort of joke? Or even that it is just some way of me getting back at Jeavons for being made redundant? Believe what you want. My conscience is clear. I've told you everything I know. Up to you now. You do what you want."

"But what can I do without any proof? You're clearly not willing to be a whistleblower and I'm not in a position to be one."

"I can't be a whistleblower as I'm just assuming Jeavons didn't disclose the data to Myers-Stratton based on what I know the man to be. For all I know, he might well have told them. I just don't know for certain. Why don't you confront Jeavons? One way or another, he has the proof. He's the only person who knows what happened. Go and talk to him. Goodbye, Lydia."

Of course. Confront Jeavons himself. Not that he is likely to confess to the crime, because that's what it is, but I will at least have the satisfaction of looking into his eyes when he lies to me. But not before first meeting with the drug pedlars who dealt out the poison to my Luke.

*

274

"Please sit down, Mrs Goldberg. As I wrote in my correspondence with you, I'm terribly sorry that we couldn't find an earlier date to meet but there would be nothing I could have told you until after the clinical trial data had been unblinded."

"I understand. I just want to find out as much as possible about how my husband has ended up where he is now."

"Of course. How is he now? I had a brief chat with the team last week and it sounds like he's showing some encouraging signs, including responding to some forms of stimuli." Dr Grant shuffled some papers in front of her. "Your husband has been in quite a deep coma for some ten months and so there is probably some way to go yet before we can hope to see any significant improvements. I hope the team have been both encouraging and realistic in the feedback they are providing."

"I couldn't praise them more highly, Dr Grant. They have been my rock through some very hard times."

"I really can't imagine what you have been going through this last year but there now seems to be some genuine light at the end of the tunnel. But let's move on to the main question you have posed." She picked out from a file of loose papers on her desk an email I sent to her several months ago, which she had printed out. "Was the drug responsible for causing Luke's stroke? The drug being GPT107, of course. Well, I can confirm that Luke was in the active drug cohort and not the placebo arm. I can also confirm that Luke's case was reviewed in considerable depth, and it was ruled that his stroke was not likely caused by GPT107."

"Very easy and convenient to say that but what evidence allowed 'them' to arrive at such a conclusion?" I had decided

275

that I had had enough of being the compliant carer. Time to get to the point and ask some uncomfortable questions.

"I do understand your concerns, Mrs Goldberg. It is typically very hard to definitively rule in or rule out a drug-induced side effect and so we have to go on an evidence-based balance of probability. The key factors that were considered in this case included the finding that Luke was the only one who has suffered a stroke in the almost five hundred patients that have thus far taken the drug. That by itself is not definitively conclusive, but added to that, there were no concerns with any toxicity findings from the preclinical data and also that there is a family history of strokes. Well, the entirety of those key factors led to the conclusion that Luke's stroke was likely not caused by GPT107."

"Family history? What family history?"

She once again fiddled with her pieces of paper before handing one to me. "Although Luke did not disclose this information to us, as you can see, Luke's father has had two strokes, although, of course, he is still alive. We only knew of this when we chased up Luke's parents after he had fallen into a coma."

I was truly shocked. I just never knew. Why didn't Luke tell me?

"If Luke had disclosed this family history, then he would not have been enrolled on the trial. However, it would seem that the fault is with his father, as he never told Luke about the strokes. Didn't want to worry his son at the time, according to a phone conversation one of the team had with him. You'd be surprised at just how often this sort of thing happens."

This news flattened me but I nevertheless decided to play

my last card. "From what you have said, I am assuming that you are not aware of an adverse cardiovascular tox finding in the preclinical data that is predictive of a potential stroke liability."

I have never seen anyone react so quickly. She sat up ramrod straight in her chair and stopped her infuriating obsession with holding pieces of paper. "What tox finding? What are you talking about? I've seen the data from the drug submission myself and there were no preclinical tox concerns."

"You haven't had access to all of the preclinical data. Some of it was not disclosed."

"How do you know this? Where is this undisclosed data? What is it?"

This was as far as I could go. All I could do was create some doubt in her mind but also being fully aware that it would more likely just blow up in my face.

"I was told by someone who has actually seen the data."

"I'm not going to patronise you. You're an intelligent woman, Mrs Goldberg, and an experienced scientist, and so you must surely be fully aware that I cannot do anything on mere hearsay. Preferably I need to see this alleged adverse data or, failing that, at least talk directly to the person who has seen it. Are either of those scenarios likely to happen?"

I had no answer. I had no real argument. I couldn't mention Jeavons' name without any evidence.

She paused and looked blankly into my face. "I'll take that as a no. This is understandably all very distressing to you, and it is natural to try to find someone or something to blame, but it is often the case that there is no one or nothing to blame. I'm afraid that this is just such an instance. Once again, I am terribly sorry for all that has happened to your family, but

I would respectively suggest that you focus your efforts on helping your husband to recover rather than trying to find reasons that simply don't exist."

*

I never really expected to make any progress with the consultant. She made exactly all the comments I would have expected her to make. She was a professional. She was a highly experienced clinician. But it would have been remiss of me to at least not have seen her and plant just the smallest seed of doubt in her mind. Yes, I was the disconsolate wife, but I was also a trained and rational scientist just as she was, and Grant knew that.

The real test to come was to meet with Jeavons. To confront Jeavons; tell him to his face that I knew what he had done. How he had nearly killed my husband. Despite what Grant had said, I was still convinced that Luke's stroke was not all down to random chance or even a family history. She was wrong. There is someone to blame and unless the buried data comes to light, there will likely be many other families who soon will also have someone to blame.

CHRISTMAS 2024

Will doubted that there were many children looking forward to Christmas more than he was that year of 2024. The end of a tumultuous year that had changed his life so completely. A year that saw him become the toast and, for some, the envy of the scientific establishment. A time when his scientific credibility had been established beyond all doubt. As his father would say, a time to step back and smell the roses, and that's exactly what Will intended to do in the weeks leading up to the Christmas and New Year break. This Christmas he would be smelling the roses in Boston. A wonderful end to a wonderful year.

With the main scientific conference season having ended several months before and the media interest moving onto the next miracle cure, Will finally had the time and space to focus on what he was paid so handsomely to do. Work for Myers-Stratton. The trial success meant that there was finally some 'real' work for him to do other than passing on emails and signing off documents. Myers-Stratton was now committing significant financial resources to finding a back-up compound to GPT107, and this involved both Will and Grace working closely with several European and US-based service providers as well as continuing their close relationship with the university AI team. Will's comfort zone and what he enjoyed most was finding new drugs. So he wasn't surprised to receive a cold call at the Granta Pain offices from a representative of Biopharmaco given that the two companies had worked together in the past.

Grace leaned her head around Will's office door. "There's a Lydia Goldberg from Biopharmaco downstairs at reception who wants to talk to you about some new services they will soon be going live with. Apparently. Would you like to meet her?"

Will looked up over his laptop and said exactly what Grace expected him to say. "Perhaps you would be kind enough to do the usual and check her out before wafting her in here, including getting her details as per our wonderful security and H and S regs. Thanks, Grace."

An immaculately dressed Lydia, in a business suit bought just for this occasion, passed Grace's sniff test despite her lying about why she was really at the Granta Pain offices that late-November morning.

"Ah, Lydia." Will walked round his desk to shake the guest's hand. "Nice to meet you. Please take a seat. What can I do for you? Ron and I go back many years. Would you like some tea or coffee?"

"No, that's fine but thanks for asking. Perhaps you will excuse me coming straight to the point. Although I do work for Biopharmaco, I have come here on personal business and I'm afraid I have just used their name to get in to see you. This is nothing to do with Biopharmaco."

"Oh," was the response from a visibly surprised Will. "I'm pretty sure this has not happened to me before. Should I not just ask you to leave right now?"

"Which no doubt you will, but not before I get a response from you as to why you did not disclose adverse preclinical cardiovascular tox data on GPT107 to the regulatory authorities. A decision which resulted in my husband suffering a stroke and still lying in a hospital bed nearly a year after taking your poison."

She looked intently into his face to gauge his response to what she had said. Unmistakeable fear and shock. His face had become ashen, and his head was twitching. It was all the proof that Lydia needed. He had buried that key adverse data just as Neville had told her.

This is her. This is the woman. The wife of that poor man. I'm fucked. Get a grip, man, get a grip. Find a way out of this.

"Look, I'm terribly sorry about what has happened to your husband. Terrible shock, terrible, and I am genuinely sorry, but I'm sure you are well aware that your husband's stroke was adjudged by a panel of independent clinicians to not be caused by the drug."

"You didn't answer my question. Why did you bury the tox data?"

"I'm afraid I have absolutely no idea what you are talking about, and I deeply resent your baseless accusation. All of the data that Granta Pain generated on GPT107 was passed onto Myers-Stratton and then shared with the regulatory authorities. On the basis of that data, the FDA and EMA approved the drug to be evaluated in the clinic. Could you please show me evidence of this data I am supposed to have hidden? Where is it, Mrs Goldberg?"

"You know full well that I can't access that data, just as we both know full well that you buried it. I will take your reluctance to admit your gross misconduct as you being comfortable with sacrificing more lives to fuel your own ego and personal wealth."

"And we both know full well that you have absolutely no proof to back up your wild and baseless accusations. It is natural for you to try to find someone to blame for what has happened to your husband, but perhaps you should look no further than your failure to disclose his family history."

That was one comment too far for Lydia, who suddenly stood up, pushing the desk between them into Will's chest.

"You fucking bastard. You fucking, lying bastard. You will pay for this, Jeavons, just you wait and see."

Will's office door was opened, and a concerned Grace looked in. "Is everything OK, Will? Do you need any help?"

He pushed back his desk and stood up. "No, that's fine. Thank you, Grace. Mrs Goldberg is leaving and perhaps you would be kind enough to escort her out of the building and make sure security never lets her onto the premises again."

As Lydia turned to walk out of his office, she paused by the doorway and pointed a finger at her nemesis. "You haven't heard the last of this, Jeavons, mark my words. If you don't go public with your disclosure and stop the clinical trial, then there will be consequences. Consequences for you and your company."

"Both Grace and I heard that threat, and if this meeting is not the end of the matter, then you will be hearing from at least the Myers-Stratton legal team, if not also the police. I will also bring up your wholly unprofessional behaviour with senior management at Biopharmaco and I can assure you that will result in you no longer working in this industry. Mark *my* words, Mrs Goldberg. I trust I will not be seeing or hearing from you again. Goodbye."

*

"Not like you to phone midweek, Will, everything OK? Not that I don't love hearing your voice, of course, and thanks for that ever so sweet letter you sent on Monday."

"Maybe yes, but hopefully no, Celeste, but I thought I should at least give you a heads-up of what happened at the office earlier today just in case something comes of it."

"Sounds to me that you are a bit worried."

"I suppose I am, maybe because it was all rather bizarre and certainly new to me."

Will spent the next half an hour recounting his version of the confrontation in his office. He had thought of nothing else all day and needed to share his concerns with someone else. However, he chose to omit the valid allegation that he had buried key data instead focusing on the need for his visitor to find someone to blame for her husband's stroke. *No need to spook and heap worry onto Celeste, which may then end up with Myers-Stratton looking back through the files of all the service providers, because she will be duty-bound to tell them if I know her. She may well be my lover and my only confidante but, unlike me, she has an arrow-like moral compass.*

"That must have at least been very unnerving, Will. Maybe a bit like being cornered by a stalker, or perhaps that's going a bit over the top. I don't recall anything like that ever happening at Myers-Stratton, but I have read about similar things happening at other companies. Senior executives even being physically attacked by relatives of patients who blame a drug for what has happened, whether true or not. People just need someone to blame and I'm sure that's what we've got here. You're the CEO. You are the one to blame and the one who should suffer as a consequence. Did she demand any money?"

"No, no. Nothing like that. At least not yet. As you say, I think she just wants someone to blame and that someone happens to be me. Maybe she even feels a bit guilty herself and needs to shift that guilt onto someone else. Who knows."

"Do you want me to chase this up with Declan? Get the legal guys involved; take her to court for harassment?"

"Not at this stage. Hopefully she feels she has made her point and is too frightened of losing her job to push it any further, as I personally know the Biopharmaco CEO and would be taking the matter up with him if she had another go at me. As I said at the start of this call, I just wanted to give you a heads-up so you would not be blindsided in the unlikely event that this escalates. She left a business card with Grace as per our protocol, so we have her details on file."

"Understood. And, Will?"

"Yes, I'm listening."

"Don't you go worrying about this because I know you will. Obviously not your fault this has happened, and it may just be a fallout from all the personal publicity you have been getting, which has made you a target."

"That's OK. Good point. Thanks for putting up with me babbling on."

"That's why I'm here."

"How could anyone ever feel worried after spending a few moments with you?"

But Will was worried. Very worried.

THE NIGHT BEFORE THE MORNING AFTER

I'd rather given up on and almost forgotten about what, I *guess, we no doubt both considered were the empty threats I made that November morning in the Granta Pain offices. What could I ever really do to seek justice and revenge? He had all the cards. If Jeavons was not going to admit to what was essentially criminal fraud, then this would just be a hopefully very painful secret he would have to carry around with him for the rest of his life if GPT107 went on to claim further victims related to the tox finding. A price, it would seem, that his ego was willing to pay, but the arrival of New Year 2025 changed all that.*

How nice it was to have Sam with me for nearly ten days over Christmas and the New Year. I can't remember the last time that happened. If it wasn't for Sam, not as much as a Christmas card would have been posted nor plastic tree erected. We even curled up together one night in our dressing gowns crying through some soppy old Christmas films. Not so wonderful was the crying over my husband's hospital bed on Boxing Day when he unexpectedly took a turn for the worse and we were told to prepare ourselves for him losing what little life he still had left in his body. Those few days after Christmas were the longest and the saddest days of my life. Even Sam, our ever-ebullient little Sam, struggled to stay positive. But Luke pulled through. I wasn't in a hurry to thank God for that because that Man has plenty to answer for. That was the good news that allowed me and Sam to finally get a good night's sleep, but the not so good news was that Luke's slow recovery had been set back almost to where it was over a year ago. We were absolutely devastated. Heartbroken. The mental anguish and physical pain were just too much to bear through those dark days before the New Year arrived.

My last words to my poor husband just before we left him on New Year's Day were whispered and out of earshot of Sam, who was talking to one of the doctors. It was a promise. Maybe even a pact.

"Please promise me you will get better, my darling. The world is missing you. If you can manage that little promise, I promise you no one else will suffer like we have because of the ego and greed of one man. We will have our day."

I started making good on that promise by furiously writing down wild ideas on a notepad travelling back from Heathrow on a train after waving off Sam for her to be thousands of miles away from us once again. But there were no tears shed on that cold, dark train for a daughter I would not be seeing again until the spring. There were just none *left. And I was far too engrossed in plotting our revenge. Or was it just my revenge?*

*

Honey traps were invented to snare sex-obsessed, unscrupulous egotists like Jeavons and so it was far from difficult to come up with a plan likely to fool the poor man. He wouldn't know what hit him.

Locate the prey: Dr William Jeavons was hosting the Granta Pain Therapeutics sponsored one-day winter symposium on pain held in Queen's College, which I registered for as Dr Helen Hughes. Always fancied being called a doctor. Set the trap: room booked in the large and anonymous Hilton Hotel. Find the kit: van rented with tailgate together with a wheelchair. Get hold of the drugs: fingers crossed alarm bells would not be ringing at work until the stock levels became negative, and even then, the small amounts I took were likely to be put down to weighing errors and spills. And, last but not least, prepare the bait. I bought the most petite little black dress and most expensive perfume I had ever owned. Cut my hair to the shortest I can ever remember having it, plus dyeing it blonde to boot – wow! Brand-new and very painful high heels fitting into black stockings held up by suspenders. I decided against buying a thong – over the top – but I hoped Jeavons would at least appreciate the care I took in buying my push-up bra. In fact, I even enjoyed the time I spent on myself. A long-overdue reminder of better times. And finally. Glasses off, brown-tinted contacts in. My bet was that my Luke would have struggled to recognise his brand-new wife. Trap successfully armed and ready.

Easily the worst part of the plan was having to sit and listen to far too many pain symposium lectures which could easily have been about car maintenance for all I cared, as my mind was completely focused on the plot that would be unfolding in the hours that followed, starting with the drinks reception in the evening. The reception was a rather benign affair with thankfully very sparse competition for a forty-plus-year-old trying her best to look ten years younger – and doing rather well, if I may be so modest.

I must say that I was indebted to Will for allowing me to butt into a conversation he was having with a bald man who was struggling to keep Will's attention. A dolled-up cougar on a mission versus a balding middle-aged man suffering from very obvious halitosis. No contest. You do have to credit the man, as he is good company, and it was Will who suggested I join him and a few of his colleagues in the Anchor after the symposium reception had run out of drinks. It was pretty straightforward from there to ask him to walk me up to the Hilton after the impromptu gathering had ended.

"Not a problem, Helen. My pleasure."

Not once did he confuse Helen with the harpy who was in his office barely two months before. At least, as far as I could tell.

"Thanks so much for showing this country bumpkin Bristol girl the way. Much better than carrying a phone out in front of me at this time of night."

"Bristol? I thought your accent sounded more local, maybe Midland, even. Whereabouts in Bristol do you live?"

Maybe I had been rumbled after all. I should have picked somewhere I knew.

"Over Clifton way. Not that I was born there, of course, but I would have thought that my Essex accent from being born in Braintree would have disappeared by now," was my latest lie.

"You know what they say," which I didn't, "once an Essex girl..."

"I do hope not. Anyway, you must let me thank you by buying you one last drink at the bar."

"That's very kind of you to offer but I really mustn't. My partner's flying in from the States on the weekend and I will get a terrible shellacking if I don't tidy the house up before she arrives."

Very useful information indeed, which was duly noted.

"Nonsense. One more drink won't do you any harm. The weekend's far away and the night is still young, and I never did get to ask you that question about the CNS penetration of GPT107, which perhaps you could answer for me."

"You got me. A work excuse for a drink. But just the one."

I caught him eyeing up my partly visible stocking tops as we sat at a low table off to the side of the bar, but to be fair to the man, where else could he look? I could see that he was dealing with his well-known demons and struggling to keep on topic.

"So the preclinical data looks quite variable, I would say."

"Perhaps more than we would have preferred to see but the bottom line," another glance at my legs, "the bottom line, of course, is that the clinical data trumps everything. Look, thanks for the drink and your company, but I really must get going."

Maybe his latest beau, this Celeste Symonds we have

seen him with in various press clippings, really does mean something to him and he no longer deserved the hard-earned reputation he is usually associated with. But a man should know his limits.

"OK, Will. Please sit back down a minute and hear me out. It sounds like we both have partners. I'm married. Neither of our partners are expecting us home tonight. Yours is over in the States and mine back home in Bristol. We are very unlikely to meet again. Why don't we just go up to my room and get to fully enjoy the evening? No strings attached. And at least it saves you walking home until the morning."

Well, you already know what happened next but do feel free to read that earlier chapter again as a reminder.

DELIVERANCE

I

Not only was I struggling to believe that this was me, this very ordinary woman, Lydia Goldberg, doing this, but I also couldn't believe I had got away with it. So far, that is. Still very early days. No one had come knocking at the door. No phone calls on the landline nor my mobile. The landline belonged to whoever owns the Airbnb rental I had booked and, of course, only Sam knows the number of my new mobile phone, which I bought just a few weeks ago, so perhaps not all that surprising that no one had rang me. My work mobile phone was left at home. I had kept to my Helen disguise since the night I had picked up my prey.

It was little Helen who, the morning after the night before, somehow managed to get a deadweight and heavily sedated Will into a wheelchair after I had partly dressed him, taken him via the lift directly to the hotel underground car park and pushed him up into the back of the rental van, which had a tail lift. From there it was an uneventful drive to Foxton, a small village not far but far enough out of Cambridge, and a detached old farmhouse rental property well outside the main residential area. My hardest task was getting the man out of the wheelchair and into the downstairs double bed. I left him with the dignity of being able to keep his underpants on but less dignified were the plastic ties around his legs and arms attaching him to the bedposts to make sure this little soldier was not going anywhere soon.

When we arrived at our new holiday home, I just had no idea what to expect from my guest. The first I heard from him was early Friday evening when I was preparing myself some food in the kitchen.

"Help! Someone help me!"

I rushed from the kitchen to see the poor helpless little dab pulling at the ties.

"You! It's you. What the fuck's going on? Where am I? Is this your house?"

"Lots of questions there. But one for you to answer first. Do you know who I really am?"

"Of course I do. You're that mad bitch I met last night."

"Not completely untrue but maybe try again."

"What the fuck? I don't know you. Stop playing games. OK, who are you?"

"Try Lydia. Mrs Lydia Goldberg. The wife of the man who almost died because he took your drug."

"Fuck! That chin. I knew there was something bugging me."

I decided to ignore the chin comment and put it on file for consideration at a less anxious and less flustered time.

"What the fuck indeed. My disguise seems to be even better than I thought. Well done, me. Perhaps I now no longer need to explain why you are tied up, or do I?"

"What you could explain, if you don't fucking mind, is just actually what you hope to gain from kidnapping me, other than you ending up spending some time in prison. Do you think you will get a ransom for me? Because I don't think so, my dear."

"And neither do I. All I want from you is your signature on a piece of paper. Above that signature, I have typed a declaration from you that you failed to disclose key data that would have led to the clinical trial on GPT107 to be at least postponed if not cancelled completely. That you committed fraud and are guilty of gross misconduct, etc., etc."

"Why would I sign that? It's just not true. You're fucking barking, you are. Mad."

"That's as may be but we both know what's true, and I'm afraid you will just have to stay tied up in this bed until you admit in writing what that truth actually is."

"How long do you think it will take people to find out I've gone missing and for the police to find me? Look, I completely understand that you are angry, but this is all just going to end up with you in jail and without a job, whether at Biopharmaco or anywhere else in the industry. Look, I'll do you favour. Let me go now and I'll say no more about it. This never happened."

"Not going to happen, Will. At least not until you sign on the dotted line."

He thrashed around in his ties in a pique of temper.

"And just how many months do you intend to keep me tied up here because I promise you now, I'm not going to sign anything that is not true."

"Oh, it doesn't take months. A couple of weeks at most from what I have read."

"Just what the fuck are you talking about? Doesn't take months to do what?"

"Get addicted to opioids. Doesn't take more than a few weeks to get addicted to opioids. Unless you know better, of course."

"You're unhinged. You need help."

"Don't go anywhere. Back in a minute with a few bits and pieces that might help explain things a little better."

Out of all the planning I had done for my special holiday – three weeks' holiday granted by HR under special circumstances – getting hold of and actually dosing the drugs represented the most complex of things I had to do and carried by far the highest risk. Would I be able to take the drugs out of work without being noticed? Would I get the dosing wrong? Would I mess up the injections?

I took a plastic tray from the kitchen, on top of which I had placed five syringes I had carefully filled, and it was this which I presented to Will.

"Voilà, Dr Jeavons," I jovially announced to Will, showing him my handiwork and trying to avoid him seeing just how nervous and frightened I really was. "What you will be enjoying for lunch and dinner for however long you choose to stay Chez Lydia. Full room service all on the house. No extra charge. However, I'm afraid this house does not do breakfasts. I do apologise."

He bent his head up and forward to see the five identical syringes. For the first time since he regained consciousness, he looked nervous.

"What's all this? Are you actually going to inject me?"

I then went through a thoroughly practised monologue, which included some humour in order to try to show the *victim that I was in control of the situation even if that was far from the reality. I tried to picture Luke alive but dead in that hospital bed as my inspiration to see this all through. "Maybe I need to add some context. There are five different drugs in these unmarked syringes and, you know what, in all the excitement I can't remember which one is which. Silly old me. My apologies for coming over all a bit Clint Eastwood there, but this is all so exciting, don't you think? Just couldn't resist. But I do know that four of them contain the nasty opioid usual suspects. Morphine, tramadol, oxycodone and, my personal favourite because of how addictive it is, fentanyl. I know. I can tell. You're wondering what the fifth syringe contains. What else could it be than everyone's favourite toxin, GPT107."*

"And you are going to inject me with all of these. Someone without any medical training. I'll die and you'll rot in jail."

"But au contraire. I'm only going to inject you with one of these at every mealtime and instead of food. Think of all that weight you will be losing. So which one of the five is it to be this lunchtime? Well, I'll let you choose your own poison, so to speak. Aren't I such a nice person? No medical training? You just wouldn't believe how many Covid injections I have done over the last few years. No one can say that I didn't do my bit of volunteering."

"And what exactly do you think will come out of this fuck-show of a circus other than my certain death and the rest of your useful life behind bars?"

"Oh, I don't think it will come to that. Without food, I reckon you will get addicted to one or more of these before the week is out, or maybe worse than that if you end up

taking GPT107, but, of course, you know much more about that than stupid old me. So, maybe you should be planning to sign your name on the dotted line way before that happens. Right now seems as good a time as any, don't you think?"

"You still don't get it, do you? I'm not going to sign a document that isn't truthful and even if I did, I would say that it was signed under duress."

"Of course you could claim that. But the whole thing will be out there in the press long before you get to deny everything. Myers-Stratton would be honour-bound to search for that buried data and the only things that will be buried after that will be your drug, your reputation and your career."

"So why didn't you just go to the press after you came to see me?"

"They wouldn't run a story without proof. But they would run a story about a kidnapping of a top scientist. Sure, I might end up in prison for a little while, but it will be worth every minute to see the ongoing clinical trial stopped and you personally vilified. I think the press might well be on my side and maybe forgive a little bit of kidnapping as justification for revealing the big lies of the pharma industry. What do you think, Will?"

I didn't expect an answer to that and there wasn't one.

"Perhaps we can crack on then if you would prefer to sign at another time. I ask again. Which one will it be?"

"You know what? Why doesn't the good lady choose?"

"Fine. I pick…" my hand hovered over the tray with my eyes closed before bringing my finger down onto one of the syringes, "that one. No. Changed my mind. That one. Right in the middle."

The first intramuscular injection in his arm was midazolam, and the plan was to go with low doses of this, diazepam and perhaps also a paralytic if he started moving around too much. They were all sedatives to a greater or lesser extent. I had no intention of getting him addicted or even killing him. But, of course, he didn't know that. The first injection was a difficult one because he was, perhaps not unsurprisingly, struggling to avoid me and my needle.

"Ow. That hurt. I thought you said you knew what you were doing."

"If you had stayed still it wouldn't have hurt, but maybe I'm a bit out of practice, I guess. I'll soon get the hang of it in the end over the next few weeks."

*

Saturday was going to be a long day for us both and I was expecting a few tricks from him now that he had got a bit more used to his new environment. Not that it was much of an environment. An airless small bedroom with the all-important metal-railed bed to which I could tie him up, an uncomfortable bedside wooden chair, a large dark-brown wardrobe, a tiny dressing table with mirror, and mustard-coloured curtains which I kept closed. Just in case. There was a small TV perched on the edge of the dressing table, which I kept on at low volume as much to distract me as him. I should have anticipated how boring the days would become and at least brought some books to try to distract me from the suffocating stress I had only myself to blame for. Thank God I brought my laptop.

I was surprised at just how much he slept through that second day. Perhaps I had overdosed on the midazolam and needed to dial back at least for a few injections. Saturday lunchtime was pretty much a rerun of the prior evening.

I opened the door and sat on the chair next to the bed with the usual choices for Will to make. Sign the document or another game of Russian roulette.

"Wakey, wakey, Will. Time for your medicine." It took quite a bit of me shaking his shoulder to rouse him. I offered him some water, which he drank avidly with my help in holding the tumbler to his mouth.

"What would sir like for lunch? A selection from my impressive selection of the most addictive drugs known to man, plus your very own nasty drug, of course, or a quick signature at the foot of this piece of paper and me driving you back home? Your choice."

"Do you really have the guts to kill me? Because that's where this is all going to end up, you know. That life-changing choice for us both. Would your husband want to see you languish in jail for twenty-plus years just to get revenge for an imagined injustice? Doesn't sound like a very good deal to me, Lydia."

"Oh, don't you go worrying about little old me. I've got you down as far too much of an unprincipled coward to not cave in at some point. It's you who is the one not getting their sums right. Choosing death over admitting fraud and losing your job. I think I know which one you'll choose. I'll give you two more days, three tops, before you cave in and sign this piece of paper."

All along, my gamble was that he wouldn't have the courage of his convictions and allow himself to become addicted or, less still, be killed. But perhaps I had got the man all wrong and he was prepared to make the ultimate sacrifice to make sure his drug made it into patients.

"Don't you think the police will be out looking for me when they find out that I'm missing? They'll find me."

"But just when? You don't live with a family who can raise the alarm. The police are hardly likely to prioritise their time looking for a forty-year-old man who has likely off galivanting around. So no. That's not something I'm really all that concerned about if I'm being honest. Frankly, Will, I think you're rather stuffed, don't you?"

That dawning realisation visibly deflated the poor man. I almost felt sorry for him.

"One signature and this will all be over even before it's started. Surely this is a no-brainer, even for a second-hand car salesman such as yourself."

"You really don't know me at all, do you? But, I guess, why should you? A few drinks. A very boring, asinine discussion on basic science and a quick shag. Hardly the basis of a deep and mutual understanding between a man and a woman. You might have me tied down to a bed and drip-fed me hard drugs but please don't presume you know me. Don't patronise me."

Perhaps this man will still surprise me yet.

II

"Sorry to phone you out of work hours, Grace, but I've let myself into Will's house. He's nowhere to be seen and not responding to phone calls, texts, emails or anything. He was supposed to have met me at the train station, but he was a no-show. A long shot, I know, but I don't suppose you know where he might be?"

"Sorry, Celeste, no idea. The last I saw him was when he left the Queen's College drinks reception on Thursday night with a few of his friends, leaving muggins to sort everything out with the caterers we had brought in for the symposium. At least, I assumed they were his friends."

"What was he like that day? Acting normally? Anything strange you picked up on his behaviour?"

"Not really, although it was a very busy day and so it's not that I saw much of him. He looked his normal self from what I saw."

"Thanks, Grace. Please do ring me on this number if you should come across him somewhere."

"I doubt it but sure, of course I will get in contact. Bye, Celeste."

She's a cold fish, thought Celeste as she double-checked through her media to see if Will had sent anything. Which he hadn't. With no longer the planned lunch, theatre and dinner appointments to attend, Celeste was rather at a loss at what to do with the rest of the day other than worry. Will had never completely missed arranged meetings with her before. Very late, perhaps, but never missed one. It was not his typical behaviour, and he always answered messages, of which Celeste had sent many since she arrived at Cambridge train station earlier that day. She toyed with the notion of going to the police but that would be ridiculous. Reporting that a middle-aged man had gone missing after a mere handful of hours after a no-show. But she would ring the hospital if she had not heard anything by the evening. Celeste spent the rest of the afternoon tidying up a desperately untidy house, not least as a distracting activity.

III

My captive was a bit less sleepy when I first saw him early on Sunday to give him his early morning drink of water and an opportunity to get rid of any excess fluids by pulling his pants down and holding a bowl under him. I was sure he was getting off with this procedure but perhaps that was just my malicious mind.

"Any change of mind this morning, Dr Jeavons?"

"The only thing I want changed is that fucking TV channel. There's only so many times you can watch the news and weather without going completely mad. Is this your idea of torture?"

I couldn't help but smile gently at his humour. As I might have said before, he is good company.

"Why don't I put the remote near to your hand and you can choose your own method of torture."

He turned the TV off. Then came a narrative he had clearly been thinking of very carefully in his more conscious moments of the night before.

"For argument's sake, just this once, let's pretend that I did hide under a rock or somewhere that data you are so convinced actually exists. Even if I did, I would never sign your little bit of paper. As you well know, the trial was a magnificent success. GPT107 was at least as potent as the opioid drug control group but did not show any abuse liability. Do you know what that means? It means that there will be many, many thousands of lives saved from opioid overdoses when GPT107 comes to market and becomes first-line use for chronic pain. So, the choice for me represents a bit of a moral dilemma, don't you think? Almost certainly *the defining moral dilemma of my life. Risk me dying or at least become addicted to one of your narcotics or sign on the dotted line, which would then result in the opioid epidemic continuing unabated with many more thousands of deaths in front of us. Now, which option would you choose if you were unfortunate enough to be me right at this moment?"*

It was a compelling argument for sure, but not without obvious flaws.

"A very brave and admirable stance to take, and I would hope that I would be equally brave if presented with the same choice, although I'm not sure that I would. I'm also not sure that the rest of the world would share your unbridled optimism for this new wonder drug if they had all the facts to hand. Which they clearly don't because you stopped that, didn't you, Dr Jeavons, in your role of acting like God? Maybe even worse still is that you are prepared to risk the lives of many hundreds of patients in clinical trials now ongoing that should never have started. Even you can't guarantee that GPT107 will get to market and, in the meantime, you are just putting so many lives at risk."

"With all due respect, yours is not the opinion of a trained clinician."

"With all due respect, neither is yours. It is you and only you who has not allowed the trained clinicians to do their job properly because of the data you have denied them. Need I point out that you also are not a trained clinician despite acting as if you are one?"

And so the arguments pinged back and forth until he, mercifully for us both, fell asleep.

IV

In the end, Celeste did not phone Addenbrookes Hospital until the Sunday morning. The person she spoke to when she eventually got through to the right phone extension actually recognised the name of the local celebrity she was trying to find, but there was no Dr Willian Giancarlo Jeavons staying in the hospital that weekend.

Sunday became a very long day for Celeste, where she even walked into a drizzly city centre to try to pass away some time, although she was seldom free from increasingly worrying thoughts of what might have happened to Will. She even bought some of Will's favourite Indian tea from the specialist tea shop he so enjoyed visiting. A brew for when he returned home safely but all that achieved were floods of tears that ended up dampening the paper bag as she left the shop.

Back in Will's house, Celeste even contemplated ringing her parents for advice and reassurance but why worry them over something they could do nothing about? She was distraught without her lover. Without her soulmate. An early, tearful night in Will's empty bed only brought back wonderful memories of times she might never experience again but it did also bring about a determination to take back control of the situation and do something positive. She must stop feeling sorry for herself.

*

The jet lag had arrived with a vengeance on that Monday morning, but Celeste was determined to work through that as she had done so many times before and get to work. Work that day was to find Will. First up would be to visit the Granta Pain offices.

"Thanks for buzzing me in, Grace, I really should sort out my own pass sometime. Anyway, could you spare a few minutes?"

"Sure. Why don't you come through? Would you like a tea or coffee?" Her second question was asked as she guided Celeste to her small office room. "Has Will turned up yet?"

Even such a seemingly innocuous question almost brought a tear to Celeste's eye. "No, not yet, and that's why I'm here this morning, and thanks for making time to see me. No drinks for me, please."

"Oh, that is a little worrying," added Grace, sitting down at her desk covered with immaculately collated files and desk tidies. There were no photos.

"I wonder if I could pick your brains. You said Will looked fine on the Thursday at the symposium, but what has he been like over the first few weeks in this New Year? Anything unusual that has happened? Any noticeable change in behaviour?"

It didn't take long for Grace to come up with some gossip. "Well, yes there was. On the Wednesday of last week. Let me just check that." Grace insisted on using a large desk diary just as her mother had always used. "Yes. Definitely Wednesday. Wednesday morning. I had a call from reception at the front desk. There was a gentleman calling himself Giancarlo Messina, apparently from Palermo in Sicily, wanting to see Will on a personal matter. I called Will over to see if he wanted the gentleman to come up to our offices and he just seemed to freeze when I mentioned the visitor's name. Didn't say anything for what seemed like ages. Anyway, he finally asked me to tell reception that he would meet the gentleman at Nero's on Station Square in twenty minutes. I didn't see him again as he texted me just before lunch that he would be working from home for the rest of the day, and he would see me bright and early the next morning at the symposium."

"Any idea who this man might have been?"

"No idea, I'm afraid. We only ask for details if they come up to the office. Giancarlo. Isn't that Will's middle name?"

"Yes. Probably just a coincidence, I imagine. Anything else unusual?"

"This is a pretty quiet place to work, Celeste. Not much action going on around here. I guess the last bit of excitement was before Christmas when that psycho woman came in shouting at Will and actually threatening him if I remember correctly, but I thought you knew all about that."

"Yes! Of Course. That Goldberg woman from Biopharmaco. Lydia Goldberg. You're right, Grace. She did threaten him, didn't she, and I can remember at the time that he was pretty concerned about it all. Worried that she might follow up on her threats. I bet you, Grace, that's our woman! She's got at least something to do with him going missing. Find Lydia and I reckon we'll find Will. We must find her before something happens to Will. Could you dig out her contact details, Grace? Please."

Grace was far from convinced of Celeste's rather dramatic theory, but she nevertheless did as she was told. Grace was pretty sure that Will had just gone walkabout.

V

This was not working out as I had planned. The Monday lunchtime dosing time had arrived and instead of him giving up and signing the document, which I had convinced myself this weak, selfish man would have done by now, he instead seemed to be becoming increasingly resolute in trying to hold his ground. To keep choosing the injections and so accept the addiction he assumed he was soon to suffer to achieve what he was convinced was the greater good. To me, it was far from the greater good. Nevertheless, could I continue to play the heartless bitch to a point where he might actually die from starvation if nothing else? It was only the thought of how his actions had almost killed Luke that kept me going, but how much longer could he or I hang on for?

I took pity on him. He was flitting in and out of consciousness, so he was just going to get saline this lunchtime, although, of course, he didn't know that.

"Any one. Any fucking syringe. Just get on with it and leave me alone."

He didn't even register his latest injection. I thought I would try a different angle. Maybe an opportunity to remind him what he would be missing unless he changed the path he was currently following.

"I thought I should tell you. Your phone has been constantly buzzing since Saturday." I held the phone up to him so that he could see both the name and the number of the person who was so keen to get hold of him. "Celeste. Your partner, from what I remember reading in the press. She must be worried sick about you, especially given that she is all those miles away. Don't forget, it's not just you and me in this equation."

I toyed with the idea of playing him one of Celeste's many voicemails, but I thought it better to keep that back for a later time if he was still unwilling to sign.

He started crying. Big globby tears that he couldn't wipe away. It was almost shocking to see him cry. This seemingly heartless man showing real emotion. I thought I would show some empathy, which might end up helping us both. I mopped up his tears with one of the flannels I kept on the dressing table. This man was continuing to surprise me.

"No," he sniffed. "She is in Cambridge. I was supposed to meet her on Saturday at the train station."

This set off another round of tears and a worry that fired off in my head that there maybe someone onto me sooner than I feared. I needed to move more quickly.

"Sign this paper and you can be with her again within the hour. I promise. I'll drive you to her myself."

This might be my chance. The moment he was going to cave in. But no. He turned his head and closed his eyes. I found it impossible not to admire his spirit. What was driving this fierce conviction? I shook him awake.

"I'm struggling to understand this behaviour. Why you are risking your life for people you will never know and are not responsible for in front of the people you love?"

"I told you that you simply don't know me. You don't know that I lost my mother to drug addiction. You don't know that I have a fifty per cent chance of dying from Huntington's disease, but now that you do then perhaps you can see why I am prepared to risk what's left of my life to save so many others. Maybe it really isn't that much I am risking at all to prevent people like my mother chancing everything through taking opioids. I came from nothing, and I am more than prepared to go back to nothing if that is what I have to do."

What could I ever say next that would change anything? The conviction of this dichotomy of a man was beyond anything I could ever alter, regardless of whatever I believed was the truly rational choice. He was immovable.

Now back in the kitchen littered with more than enough boxes of food and drinks to sustain me for the anticipated two-week siege, together with sufficient syringes and drugs to keep my victim sedated, it was now beginning to look like I was the one who would have to make a decision. Allow my redoubtable nemesis to be set free or me face the consequences of his death or at least his addiction. Surely this could not be. I was supposed to be the one in control of this situation. The one with the power to dictate the narrative. My thoughts drifted to what Luke might have thought, no doubt wondering just why and how I got myself into this mess and what I should do next.

That fearful introspection was interrupted by a new email that appeared on my laptop screen.

Re: The whereabouts of Will Jeavons
My name is Celeste Simmonds and I am Will's partner. Based on the argument that you had with Will in the Granta Pain Therapeutic's offices before Christmas and the threats you made to him, I have every reason to believe that you have kidnapped Will. If you don't respond to this email before the end of today, Monday, I will contact the police and pass on your name.

Fuck! How did she get hold of my email address? Of course!
I left my business card at their office. How fucking stupid of
me. But she's bluffing. She must be bluffing, as she would surely
have already gone to the police. She knows the police won't do
anything yet. Not this early. But what the fuck should I do now?

VI

Although a rather brutal nature programme was being
screened on Will's home TV, Celeste's full attention was
concentrated on the much smaller but blank screen of her
mobile phone she had been firmly attached to for almost
two hours, and which was perched on the armrest of a
chair. Will's favoured living room armchair. Her next meal
was long overdue, as had been the case for all the meals
she had mostly skipped over through what were turning
out to be the most traumatic moments of her life. What
little food she did manage to force herself to eat was of
the deep-fried, fast, type. Even her always-immaculate
personal hygiene was suffering. All those non-essentials
could wait. And then the reply came.

> *Re: Re The whereabouts of Will Jeavons*
> *I will pick you up at 10am on Tuesday outside*
> *the Clayton Hotel near the train station. If we are*
> *followed, I will stop and turn around and neither of*
> *us will be seeing your partner again.*

Celeste's heart was racing. He was alive. Her hunch was
correct, and he could be found. She had found Lydia. The

question of whether or not either of them would be found kept Celeste awake through the night until a redundant alarm broke out on her precious phone at 7am. The phone was fully charged as she had made sure was the case over the last three endless days. Would she be getting to see Will again in the next few hours? The only other email that Celeste was to send before she left the house to walk to the rendezvous was to Grace.

> *Re: Re: Re: The whereabouts of Will Jeavons*
> *Grace, I have copied you in the below email messages to and from Lydia Goldberg who, as we suspected, is the one who has kidnapped Will. At least it looks like we have found the woman, if not yet where she is keeping him. I have agreed to go with her and, please God, bring Will back home safely but, if you don't hear back from me by this time tomorrow then could you please contact the police and tell them all you know? Thank you, Grace.*

VII

I was continuing to ruminate over whether I had made the right call to reply to her email on the short drive back to my house, but my victim and I had clearly reached an impasse that I was struggling to see a way through. Something needed changing, as I was just not capable of carrying on with this cruel charade for much longer. I had to find a way out. The game needed a wildcard to change the repetitive narrative and unresolved moral dilemmas. My gamble was that Celeste could change his thinking. Show him what he was seemingly prepared to give up, regardless of how many more years he would live even if he really was the owner of the Huntington's mutation. Would anyone make up such a thing?

Why my house first? To pick up Luke's 0.22 air pistol just in case Celeste is stronger than she looks in her photos. Only an air gun and unlikely to kill anyone but painful enough to deter most people even in the unlikely event my guests work out it is not a proper firearm. Finally, a cast-off of yet another one of Luke's many abandoned hobbies finds a use.

I deliberately arrived at the hotel forecourt ten minutes late to see an elegantly dressed businesswoman standing outside the main hotel door. It must be her. She had clearly not come dressed for a fight. But she had not seen me. Perhaps Celeste was not expecting a short woman dressed in dungarees driving a van. Finally, it clicked, and she walked over to open the passenger door.

"Before you get in, switch off your mobile phone, leave it at reception and tell them that you will drop by to pick it up later."

Without saying a word, she turned away from the van, walked through the main doors and up to the reception desk. I got out of the van to watch her through the window to see if she was at least making a good impression of handing over her phone. The hotel porter was starting to get a bit jumpy of me staying too long on his precious forecourt and so I got back into the van to be closely followed by Celeste.

Her first question arrived before we had even left the hotel forecourt.

"What have you done to Will? Is he safe?"

I decided to rudely ignore her question so as to reinforce the unpredictable psycho image I had hopefully left with Grace what's-her-name when I visited their offices. It was not until we reached Trumpington Road that I answered the poor woman.

"Soon enough you will see for yourself that he is alive but only if no one is following us. If I do suspect someone is following us, and I have been police trained in surveillance," I lied, "then, as I wrote, I will take you back to the hotel and neither of us will see him again. Do you understand me?"

"You have my word that no one is following us. I have not gone to the police."

I dug out of the front of my dungarees a pair of black-out eye covers I had kept from a Biopharmaco trip to Chicago and handed them to Celeste.

"Wear these until I ask you to take them off."

More for show rather than effect, as I imagine the poor woman is no more familiar with Foxton that she is with Felixstowe, but the intention was to bring back my position of power and control over events, which had gradually slipped away over the last few days. I heard nothing more from the poor, blameless woman for the next nearly thirty minutes it took for me to drive to Foxton.

We had arrived at the 'safehouse'. Now for the tricky bit, but I think Celeste was sufficiently worried to do anything I asked of her. I opened the passenger door and guided my blindfolded captive carefully onto the gravel drive. I asked her to hold her hands behind her so as to allow me to tie them together with a plastic tie, which she did without comment. I then led her into the house and onto a chair in the kitchen. Based on the way that she negotiated the narrow hallway, it would seem that the blackout eye protectors were not quite as blackout as advertised. I sat down on the other *side of the kitchen table and reached over to take off the semi-transparent blindfold.*

"So where is he? Is he in this house?"

"All in good time. First, you and I need to discuss how we can help Will help himself."

I then went through the events of the last five days in enough detail to make sure she fully understood what he had done and why we were all here now in this house. She at least sounded sympathetic about what had happened to my family, but that is easy enough to fake. She repeatedly refused to believe that Will could ever had hidden key data from Myers-Stratton. If only I could have used Neville's name. There were tears of denial when I told her about my one-night stand with her partner, but I think they were more from self-pity and, in her eyes, he at least had the partial excuse that it was clear case of entrapment. She became understandably angry when I told her of the options I had presented to Will – opioid addiction or admitting that he had committed fraud. But the real tears flowed when I told her about his fears of having Huntington's disease. I related to Celeste the conversation Will had with me about meeting his estranged father just last week and finding out that he had Huntington's.

"But that can't be. That's just not true. He would have told me."

The tears were still flowing when I took her into the bedroom to sit down next to Will. The tears turned to guttural howls of anguish when she first saw her almost-naked lover tied to the bed. By this time, he was as pale as the white sheet he was lying on. I really did feel for the anguish and pain of a fellow, innocent woman.

"Will, Will, wake up. Please wake, my love," she called from a few feet away.

This was enough to slowly rouse him from his latest drug-induced slumber.

"Celeste? Is that you, Celeste?"

"Yes, yes, my love, it's me. I'm here now. You're safe and I'm going to take you home."

I felt the time had come to intervene. To provide a few words to the good for the crying couple, the vision of which made me desperate to want to consider any possible way of allowing me to get out of this cavernous hole I had dug for myself.

"How very touching to see just how much you mean to each other. I am so very jealous. You see, I have dreamed every night for more than a year of such an emotional reunion with my true love. The true love that you almost took away from me by allowing your poison to be given to my husband. Your stubborn resistance to admit the fraud has led to the suffering I can see now with my very own husband and with no doubt many more to follow the same fate. Is this what you really want to happen?"

"It is a real tragedy what has happened to your husband, but all this you are doing is not going to help him. You need real help. Professional psychological help, which I can guarantee that Myers-Stratton can provide for as long as is needed. Trying to pretend that Will buried some bit of data or another is not going to help your husband. All it will do is vilify a scientist whose only interest is the needs of patients. On top of that, you are denying future generations a drug that will transform the way we treat pain."

The wrong thing to say. Words straight out of a company press release. I almost expected her to ask her audience if

315

they had any questions. It looked as if my gamble had failed. The very last card I had to play had been trumped.

"Stop this. Enough," whispered Will across to where Celeste was sitting. "Fine for me to suffer. I deserve it. But not you, Celeste. You have done nothing wrong. You never could."

Once again, tears streamed down her face. Tears she could not wipe away.

"What do you mean, you deserve it? Deserve what? What could you have possibly done to deserve this?"

"Betraying your unquestioning trust. Betraying the only woman I have ever loved and the only woman that has ever loved me. The woman that completes me. That's what I have done to deserve this. I've screwed around. Just ask this woman. No matter how I justify my actions, and I still strongly believe I'm right, I did bury that data. But you know what, the only thing that really matters in this world to me is you and now even that has gone because why would you want to ever see me again after this? I just wish I was the man you believe I am."

"You really did hide that data, Will? She's right? It is true? How could you, Will? How could you? Whatever were you thinking?"

"Yes, I did, and you know what, I would make the same decision again because I truly believe it will result in many lives being saved. That's why I am prepared to carry on being injected by addictive opioids, as I don't want anyone to needlessly die like my mother did."

"What are you talking about? I met your mother a few months ago."

"She is not my real mother. My real mother died from a drug overdose in front of my own eyes when I was eleven.

This was a few years after my father left us to go back to Italy following the death of my younger sister from cancer. A useless father I didn't meet again for thirty years but who turned up in my life as if by magic just last week to tell me that he had Huntington's."

Powerful stuff from a man who must have been to some very dark places in his life, but maybe none so dark as the place he finds himself now. All Celeste could do was cry what few tears she had left. Maybe it was time for me to say something.

"I think everyone has said their piece. Truths have finally come out and maybe that will allow us to find a way out of all this. Now that you have admitted, Will, that you did bury that key data, perhaps you could now sign the document I have asked you to sign all week, and we can all go away and live the rest of our lives and forget that this ever happened?"

"Forget this ever happened?" shouted Celeste through her tears. "You have kidnapped a man. Tied him to a bed and injected addictive opioids into his bloodstream for five days. I might not be too familiar with British justice, but I think the dangerous stunt you have just pulled is worthy of many more years spent away from your husband than you are thinking. Will signs that and probably loses his job, but you go to jail. How does that work for you?"

I trotted out the same reasoning I had already touted to Will. "You're right. To a certain extent, I would say. But how do you think the worldwide press will react to my vigilante story? A woman seeking vengeance from the lies of Big Pharma and preventing a toxic drug from being given to countless other victims. I think I will get a good hearing and a lenient sentence, as wouldn't any other wife do just the same to protect their family if only they had the balls? But you know what,

317

I'm also not really picking up good vibes about that precious company of yours, Myers-Stratton. Would this ruin them? Surely no coming back from this very high-profile fraud. You two will never get a job in the industry again and I wouldn't bet against Will spending a little time inside, even if it is not in the same prison as me. So, how does that work for you?"

Even the crying had stopped. Complete silence and the stand-off continued.

Celeste was the first to break rank. Ever the businesswoman keen to find a working consensus.

"There will have to be a compromise. We obviously can't go on like this. What if Will and I agree to run again the assay you are talking about, and I have no idea what it is, and report the results to Myers-Stratton? If the data is as bad as seems to be the case, then the trial will have to be stopped until either the issue is resolved in some way, such as changing the patient exclusion criteria, or the drug is pulled. Will can pretend that he found out about the assay at some conference or another and an assay he thought would be useful data to have on GPT107. The data from the original test will forever remain buried. You get your confirmation on whether or not GPT107 causes strokes and likely a damages payout if it does. A sum of money that is likely to mean that you will never have to work ever again, although I realise that is no compensation whatsoever for what has happened to your husband. On our side, we promise not to bring charges against you for kidnapping and causing bodily harm."

I didn't appreciate the self-satisfied way she ended her proposal but maybe, just maybe, this was the best way we could all get ourselves out of this mess. I certainly had no counter suggestions to offer up.

I asked Will what he thought.

"Maybe it's all these fucking drugs you have been pumping into me, but I don't really care as long as Celeste doesn't lose out. None of this is down to her. Her only crime is to stay loyal to a lifelong feckless liar and one she is well shot of."

And that's pretty much how we left it. No more than an hour later, I watched them get into their taxi, and despite them having already told me several times just how sorry they were about what happened to Luke and hoping that he will recover soon, this time I actually believed them. My final words though the open taxi window.

"For the record, the only things that went into your bloodstream, Will, were tranquilisers."

I think he believed me.

*

The winners and the losers from this long, sorry and bitter tale? Depends on your point of view, of course. Your moral compass. The biggest loser is my family, my husband. To be followed either by those unfortunate enough to suffer a similar fate after taking GPT107 or all the many opioid addicts who won't be able to take the drug because of what I have done. Time will tell. It's not only Will who might be struggling with his demons in the years to come. The other loser might be a jobless Will if Myers-Stratton blame him for a cancelled trial. An appropriate price to pay for someone who abused the very principles of the discipline on which he built his own success. Winners? I would also place me and Will in this category as well. Will because he has finally found that special person

*who will complete his life just as I had found my Luke. Am
I the only one who struggles to understand just why Celeste
has stayed with him? But maybe I have now seen a side of
the man I couldn't have imagined before we had met. Me as
a winner? Maybe because I have finally found the real Lydia,
who is perhaps not the headstrong, self-righteous stroppy
bitch she always thought she was. She is so much more than
that, even if I may say so myself.*

*

*One thing's for sure. No moral dilemmas were resolved in
those fraught few, life-changing days. Which should come
as no surprise to anyone, as scientists and clinicians have to
wrestle with such moral dilemmas and fine judgement calls
more often than they would like. The science is just not as good
as we would all like to think, nor as good as many believe. No
matter how many tests, computer models and clinical trials
are used to make sure our drugs are safe and effective, there
will surely always continue to be life-threatening side effects of
drugs that were not identified before they went to market. And
that is even without considering those maverick scientists out
there like Will who make up their own guidelines and rules.
Human physiology is just too complicated and genetically
diverse for us all to respond to a drug in the same way as
even our closest neighbour. There will always be losers. The
challenge for both scientists and clinicians is to ensure that
the winners far outweigh the losers, as to believe that there are
no risks will only lead to a world without medicines. Maybe
a strapline to one of Celeste's business presentations. A facile
moral dilemma that is unlikely to be resolved in our lifetime.*

VIII

I held tightly onto his hand. As I always did.

"Good morning, my love. Are you awake yet? Squeeze a bit harder. Ah, yes. You're in the room."

Louisa came up to me as she often did whenever she was on shift.

"Your man's been full of the joys of spring the last few days. Not sure what's got into him, and the doctors are genuinely encouraged that he is making progress again after that recent setback. Still a long way to go and of course you know that full well, but there's no couple more deserving of a full recovery than you two."

"Well, thank you, Louisa. That's very kind of you to say so."

I waited for her to walk away, smiling back at me as she left.

"Alone at last and have I got some big news for you today! But first of all, perhaps you can answer a question that has been bugging me for days. You must remember my face, surely, so squeeze my fingers extra hard if you think I've got a big chin."

IX

"I really have given this a great deal of thought, and I can't really come up with another sensible option. After all that has happened over these last few desperate weeks and my shock that you are still willing to even talk to me. Maybe even, I suppose, after all that has happened over the last few years. I think the time has now arrived to do what any decent man should have done long, long ago. Time for me to cross the water and come and live with you in Boston!"

He was surprised to see that she looked surprised. They were sitting next to each other in a hospital reception room waiting for Will to be called for his Huntington's disease blood test.

Celeste appeared flustered and struggled to find the words. "That is so thoughtful and so kind of you to offer. To pull up all your family and especially work networks that you have spent years nurturing to be right at the top of the Cambridge science tree."

"It's the very least I can do because it's the very least you deserve, Celeste."

"A very gracious offer but a gracious offer I'm afraid I will have to turn down. I just can't see it working."

Will looked visibly shocked. "So you just want for us to carry on living all these thousands of miles apart?"

"No. I don't think that's really a very sensible option either, is it, Will? I'm so sorry."

Will then said something he just couldn't believe he was actually saying. "That's it then. Looks like we've reached the end of the line, then. You and I."

"If that's want *you* really want, Will. Your call, of course. But I'd much prefer to come and live with you in Cambridge."

The waiting room in the Nuffield Hospital had never seen anything like it. All there that morning couldn't help but stare at that middle-aged couple holding onto one another as if there was no one else in the world.

*

Will and I? Perhaps we are not so very different after all.